OUT OF COMMISSION

The *Prometheus* and Tancred's *Nightstar* cut loose at almost the exact same time, scourging each other with hard-hitting projectiles and lethal spears of brilliant, gem-colored energy. On his rearview screen, Tancred Sandoval watched as the *Nightstar's* gauss slug smashed into the other 'Mech's body just below the cockpit, missing the killing-blow by half a meter.

Then, the *Prometheus* looked right into the rear camera, squaring off as it levered both arms forward and sprayed out twin ruby lances. One of the large lasers speared up, flooding the camera, and Tancred was slammed forward. The restraining harness dug into his shoulders, keeping him from any serious damage, and the rattled noble knew at once what had happened. As he rebounded back into the command couch, and stared into a shutdown panel and blackened screens, he faced the inevitable truth.

He was dead.

BATTLETECH®

PATRIOTS
AND TYRANTS

Loren L. Coleman

A ROC BOOK

ROC
Published by New American Library, a division of
Penguin Putnam Inc., 375 Hudson Street,
New York, New York 10014, U.S.A.
Penguin Books Ltd, 80 Strand,
London WC2R 0RL, England
Penguin Books Australia Ltd, 250 Camberwell Road,
Camberwell, Victoria 3124, Australia
Penguin Books Canada Ltd, 10 Alcorn Avenue,
Toronto, Ontario, Canada M4V 3B2
Penguin Books (N.Z.) Ltd, 182–190 Wairau Road,
Auckland 10, New Zealand

Penguin Books Ltd, Registered Offices:
Harmondsworth, Middlesex, England

First published by Roc, an imprint of New American Library,
a division of Penguin Putnam Inc.

First Printing, September 2001
10 9 8 7 6 5 4

Series Editor: Donna Ippolito
Designer: Ray Lundgren
Cover art by Fred Gambino
Mechanical Drawing: Duane Loose and the Fasa art department

 REGISTERED TRADEMARK—MARCA REGISTRADA

Printed in the United States of America

PUBLISHER'S NOTE
This is a work of fiction. Names, characters, places, and incidents either are
the product of the author's imagination or are used fictitiously, and any
resemblance to actual persons, living or dead, events, business establishments,
or locales is entirely coincidental.

This book can only be dedicated to the legion of BattleTech™ fans out there who have been so supportive of the universe in general and, in specific, of the passing of the torch.

Acknowledgments

I cannot say enough good things about Michael A. Stackpole, the man who brought to life so many wonderful characters and events in the BattleTech™ universe. I am sorry to see his departure from the BattleTech™ line. I am also very proud to take up the flag he carried. A good portion of *Patriots and Tyrants* is based on the final outline Mike wrote for FASA, and is used with his endorsement. I hope to share with him the success of this novel. Any mistakes are mine alone.

I would also like to thank Jordan Weisman, Ross Babcock, Mort Weisman, and Donna Ippolito, who have also been important supporters.

Other messages for those associated with FASA: Randall Bills (congratualtions on *Path of Glory*), Bryan Nystul (Goodbye, my friend), Sharon Turner-Mulvihill (Thank you), Christoffer Trossen (Welcome aboard), Annalise Raziq (Appreciations!), and Chris Hartford (Also, thank you).

More thanks for Don Maass, my agent, for bearing through the latest round of project shuffling.

Love to my family, Heather, Talon, Conner, and Alexia. Also to the cats Rumor, Ranger, and Chaos whom I firmly believe read this page when I wasn't looking.

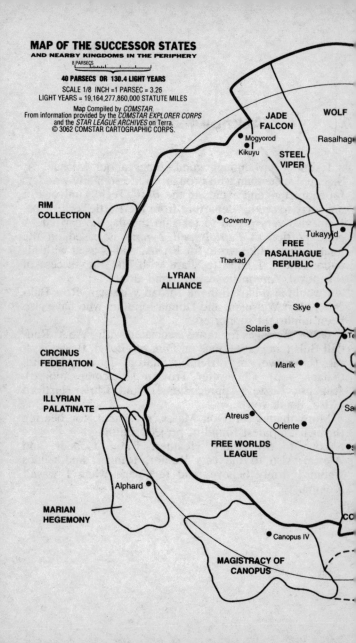

MAP OF THE SUCCESSOR STATES
AND NEARBY KINGDOMS IN THE PERIPHERY

8 PARSECS

40 PARSECS OR 130.4 LIGHT YEARS
SCALE 1/8 INCH =1 PARSEC = 3.26
LIGHT YEARS = 19,164,277,860,000 STATUTE MILES

Map Compiled by *COMSTAR*.
From information provided by the *COMSTAR EXPLORER CORPS*
and the *STAR LEAGUE ARCHIVES* on Terra.
© 3062 COMSTAR CARTOGRAPHIC CORPS.

JADE
FALCON

WOLF

Mogyorod

Kikuyu

Rasalhag

STEEL
VIPER

RIM
COLLECTION

Coventry

Tukayyid

FREE
RASALHAGUE
REPUBLIC

Tharkad

LYRAN
ALLIANCE

Skye

Solaris

Te

CIRCINUS
FEDERATION

Marik

ILLYRIAN
PALATINATE

Atreus

Sa

Oriente

FREE WORLDS
LEAGUE

Alphard

MARIAN
HEGEMONY

Canopus IV

CO

MAGISTRACY OF
CANOPUS

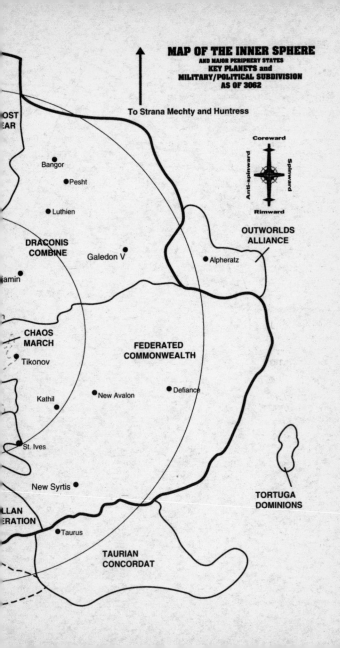

MAP OF THE INNER SPHERE
AND MAJOR PERIPHERY STATES
KEY PLANETS and
MILITARY/POLITICAL SUBDIVISION
AS OF 3062

To Strana Mechty and Huntress

Coreward

Anti-spinward

Spinward

Rimward

●OST
EAR

● Bangor

● Pesht

● Luthien

**DRACONIS
COMBINE**

Galedon V ●

**OUTWORLDS
ALLIANCE**

● Alpheratz

jamin

**CHAOS
MARCH**

● Tikonov

**FEDERATED
COMMONWEALTH**

● Kathil   ● New Avalon   ● Defiance

● St. Ives

● New Syrtis

**TORTUGA
DOMINIONS**

LLAN
ERATION

● Taurus

**TAURIAN
CONCORDAT**

Overture

1

ComStar Garrison District
Tukayyid
Free Rasalhague Republic
25 December 3061

Cheerful flames danced and snapped in the great fire-place, radiating warmth into the rooms Victor Steiner-Davion shared—unofficially—with Omi Kurita in the ComStar compound on Tukayyid. Stepping closer to the fire, he chucked a handful of crystals into the blaze, and the orange flames leapt up, tipped with purple and green and blue. He retreated quickly from the intense heat.

The fire was too hot for them to pull up chairs or to spread a thick rug on the hearth, but its warmth could be enjoyed from the divan they'd drawn up to the edge of the flagstones. Omi waited for him there, legs pulled up under her with a casual, sensual grace Victor admired.

She looked lovely, dressed tonight in a dark-green silk kimono that complemented the green and gray flannel shirt he'd chosen to honor the Christmas festivities. An obi of brilliant, shimmering gold accented her slender waist, and her raven hair was pulled back in the severe Kurita fashion. He liked the way a few tendrils had been left to curl softly around her face, an artful suggestion of casual disarray.

"Beautiful," Victor said, sitting down beside her on the low-built couch. The silk of her kimono whispered against his touch as he slipped one arm around her shoulders, and he breathed in the jasmine scent of her perfume.

Omi widened her eyes with exaggerated innocence. "Yes, the fire is very nice."

"I was speaking of the company," he said. "The fire pales by comparison."

That brought a smile. "You have the heart of a warrior, Victor, but never let it be said that you do not own the soul of a poet." She leaned back into his embrace with an ease that had grown in the nine months since Victor's return from the Clan homeworlds.

On the long journey back to the Inner Sphere, he could never have dreamed that fate would lead him to this moment or that he would find himself a man without a home. He'd believed that returning at the head of the victorious Star League army would bring peace to his realm. Instead, he found himself dethroned by his sister Katherine and forced to accept refuge in the Draconis Combine. In another strange turn of events, he'd recently been named Precentor Martial of ComStar.

Yet Victor probably would not have minded ending his days as a warrior after beating the Clans in their own homeworlds. He had already seen too many wars in his thirty-one years—interstellar wars over territory, ideology, vengeance, and sovereignty. He'd even seen the great Federated Commonwealth—a union created by the marriage of his parents—broken in two when Katherine seceded with the Lyran half a few years back.

He'd also lived to see at least one dream of his parents realized: the Star League reborn. After more than three hundred years of bitter warfare, the five Great Houses and other important nations of the Inner Sphere had put aside their differences, reuniting to meet the Clan threat.

So, for now, Victor could relax, but he knew he could never rest. Perhaps that was his karma; as Omi's people believed, a man's fate was a man's fate.

"Well," he said, "the poet in me is very happy you are here to share this day."

"As am I, my love." Omi looked up at him, her porcelain skin flushed in the warmth of the blaze. "Though perhaps we could have done without such a large fire. It is not so cold just now."

"It's tradition," Victor said quickly. "You, of all people, should know how important that is."

Though it was winter here on Tukayyid, the ComStar headquarters simply wasn't far enough north for snowfall or freezing temperatures. He enjoyed the lodge-style décor of his residence anyway.

"*Ah, so desu,* Victor. Is that so?" She smoothed an imaginary wrinkle from her kimono. "And this morning? That was also part of your . . . traditions?"

Victor had the good grace to blush furiously. "I wouldn't mind making it a Christmas tradition," he said, almost shyly. "And New Year's. Birthdays. National events. Tuesdays."

"Tuesdays?" Omi gave him a puzzled look. "What is so special about Tuesdays?"

"We'd make them special." Victor grinned as it became Omi's turn to blush. "And speaking of special times . . ." He reached behind him and drew out the small package from the spiced pine credenza set behind the divan. He presented it with a slight flourish. The slim box was carefully wrapped in red-and-gold-striped paper, and tied with gold ribbon that tumbled over the sides in spiraling curls.

Omi accepted it with both hands. "It's wonderful," she said, admiring the wrapping. "But I thought we were exchanging gifts after dinner. With the others."

Victor's sister Yvonne had traveled with them from Tharkad, where the Star League had recently convened, to Tukayyid, declining Katherine's pro forma invitation in favor of Christmas with her brother and Omi. Tancred Sandoval, the Baron of Robinson, had escorted her, detouring from the journey that would eventually take him home to the Draconis March. Also joining them was Anastasius Focht, who Victor had succeeded as Precentor Martial. A small gathering, but these were among the people Victor treasured most in his life.

"I wanted you to have this before. Go ahead," he said. "Open it."

The box had been wrapped in such a way that it could be undone without having to tear the paper. As its top lifted away easily, Omi's eyes widened as she saw what it contained.

"It was my mother's," Victor told her. She watched wordlessly as he lifted out a bracelet of exquisite diamonds and perfectly formed pearls, which he then fastened around her wrist. It was subtle in design, elegant rather than showy, just as Melissa Steiner-Davion herself had been. Just as Omi was. Melissa's loveliness had stayed with her to the end of her days, and Victor was sure Omi's would too.

"It's beautiful," Omi said, almost whispering. She ran one finger over the soft, velvet interior of the box. Necklace and earrings were included. She paused at the empty depression and glanced up for the briefest moment, but Victor knew she would never ask directly about the one item that was obviously absent from the box.

"The ring," Victor said. "She was wearing it that day."

No need to explain which day. One of the most beloved rulers to ever reign over either the Steiner or Davion realms, Melissa was a woman dedicated to her family and to bringing peace to the Inner Sphere. Yet, she had met her end in the most violent manner, killed by an assassin's bomb.

It had taken some doing to gather the evidence implicating his sister, but Victor now had everything but the smoking gun to prove that Katherine had been the mastermind behind her mother's assassination. His people were still working to uncover conclusive proof. When he had that . . .

The silence stretched out, broken only by the furious popping of burning wood. Finally, Omi asked, "Your sister—she sent this to you? Along with your personal belongings?"

He nodded. "Katherine thinks the loss of the ring mars the perfection of the set. I imagine she also hoped it would be a constant reminder to me of our mother's death. A twist of the knife in my heart."

Victor lifted Omi's hand to his lips and kissed it tenderly. "By giving it to you, I reclaim the set as a treasure. I think my mother would be happy that it is now with you."

"You honor us both, Victor." Omi's blue eyes glistened with tears. "You are a credit to your parents."

Victor knew that Omi understood the unspoken meaning of all this. The missing ring was more than a reminder of his mother's death—it was also the one thing Victor could never give Omi. They had come so far, but he was still the son of Hanse Davion and rightful Prince of the Federated Commonwealth—and Omi was still the daughter of the ruler of the Draconis Combine. Despite Victor's growing friendship with Theodore Kurita, centuries of fear and hatred between the two realms created an insuperable wall. Hard-line elements on either side of the border would never accept a formal union.

"I shall wear them this evening," Omi said. "I hope Yvonne approves."

"She will. I only wish Peter and Arthur were here as well. I will miss them." That was true, though Victor realized it was the lack of closeness that hurt most. Arthur had installed himself in the Draconis March, and Peter . . . all Omi would tell him was that Peter was safe and wished to remain in seclusion.

"Yet Baron Sandoval has joined us," Omi said gently. "And he represents the future of the people in your Draconis March."

The March was a geopolitical subdivision of the Federated Commonwealth, stretching along the border between what had been known as the Federated Suns and the Draconis Combine. Duke James Sandoval, Tancred's father, ruled the region in the name of the Steiner-Davions. The people of the March were violently opposed to any alliance with the Combine and numbered among the most outspoken critics of Victor's relationship with Omi.

"Things may change," she added softly.

"Yes, but not in our lifetimes," Victor said. "Perhaps in our children's time."

Omi quickly glanced down and away.

"Sorry," he said at once. "I meant for the next generation." Children were even more impossible for him and Omi than marriage.

Omi placed a hand on his cheek. "This is not a time for sorrow, Victor."

She stood up with a soft rustle of silk and the scent of jasmine and glided to the other side of the room. She knelt down and removed a small but gaily wrapped present from a wooden chest.

"It is only fair," she said, coming back to the divan and placing the box in Victor's hands. "I have something else for you, but that can wait until after the others have gone."

Victor hefted the box in his left hand. It was no more than a few centimeters to a side, but its size belied the solid weight of whatever it contained. He noted that the wrapping was exquisitely constructed from paper folds and fastened without the benefit of tape or ribbon. The soft red tissue was embossed with silver dragons that gleamed in the firelight. He carefully unfolded the paper to keep from tearing it.

"A rock?" Victor asked when he opened the box. He picked up the fist-sized stone and examined it with bemused interest.

Omi nodded. "A stone." Her eyes narrowed as if she wasn't sure whether he was teasing her or was sincerely baffled. Then, he could no longer hold back a grin.

"You!" she said with mock irritation. "You've spent

too much time with my brother Minoru not to know its significance. I found this on Tharkad and heard it calling your name. I thought it proper to commemorate your acceptance of bushido.''

Heard it calling his name? This time, it was Victor wondering if she was serious. "I feel silly, Omi, correcting you on your own customs. But isn't bushido a path, not a destination?''

"To commemorate your traveling the path,'' Omi said with the barest of sighs that said she was all too used to the tedious literalness of detail-oriented men. She turned slightly toward the sword rack standing on the credenza. "My father did well when he presented you with the swords of a warrior and named you samurai.''

Victor glanced back at the katana and wakazashi in their black-lacquered stand. He'd built the stand himself, his first attempt ever at woodworking. The supports weren't quite even, the edges not as smooth as he might have liked. And if one gave it more than a passing glance, it was easy to see where the lacquer had run in spots. He smiled. Were he to point out those flaws to Omi, she would tell him that imperfections were what defined a thing.

"Where will you plant it?'' she asked.

Victor held the stone with three fingers and studied its uneven, pockmarked surface. According to the tradition, he would need to give it a name and plant it in a garden.

Shot through with veins of reddish-blue quartz and stained a mottled green along one side, the stone certainly had character. Victor could imagine it wintering among nasturtiums in the shade of his well-cared-for roses, where only an infrequent shaft of sunlight would find it. But when it did, the quartz would catch fire and sparkle—a fleeting shout in an otherwise tranquil setting.

"In your palace on Luthien,'' he said absently. "In the garden I raised during my recovery. That is the proper place for it. Until then, it will have to be as homeless as I am. Maybe I can find a temporary place for it on the grounds here.''

Victor continued contemplating the rock. He had spent much time with Omi's brother Minoru Kurita, meditating on the infinity expressed in simple things such as rocks, flowers, a feather. Those lessons came back to him now. The streak of quartz was like a river cutting through gray foothills. The crystalline facets formed a path of glowing steps—or a trail of tears. Yes, the stone was speaking to him.

"I will fight no more, forever."

Omi, who had been silent during his reverie, glanced at him sidelong. "What did you say, love?"

Victor smiled a bit sadly and placed the Warrior's Path stone on the credenza. "An old saying, from the time before mankind left Terra. A vanquished leader's promise." He hugged her, thanking her for the gift. "My foolish hope."

"Hope is never foolish, Victor. Without hope where would we be, you and I?" She took his callused hands in her soft, slender ones. "When we met on Outreach so long ago, who could have dreamed we would ever be together? Our two nations? My father, your father . . ."

"Your brother," Victor reminded her, smiling at the memory of Omi's other sibling, the proud samurai Hohiro Kurita. "He was ready to take a swing at me that day. I still think he was the hardest person to convince, though your father certainly threw enough tests in our way."

He didn't add that his own father, Hanse Davion, would surely have tested the relationship just as vigorously had he lived to see it.

She nodded. "I think your rescuing Hohiro from the Clans and saving me from the assassins on Luthien went a long way toward easing their fears. You certainly made an impression on the people of the Combine."

Victor slipped one hand free of her grasp, rubbing unconsciously at the place on his chest where he had been pinned to the floor by an assassin's katana. "Made quite the impression on me, too."

Omi kept hold of his other hand. "My point, Victor,

is that things are changing. We are changing. All of us. Someday, we can hope that our people will understand."

"We don't want much, do we?" He kissed her hand, then looked up at her with a wistful smile. "Just a miracle."

Mischief sparkled in Omi's eyes as she began to unfasten her obi. "I feel silly, my love, instructing you on your own customs. But isn't Christmas the time of miracles?"

2

The Triad, Tharkad City
Tharkad
District of Donegal
Lyran Alliance
25 December 3061

Katrina Steiner-Davion wandered through a realm of glittering jewels, lush furs, stunning art, and exotic crafts. A music box she'd just wound chimed the tune of her favorite ballad in pure, crystalline notes, and the scent of flowers and spices wafted from the various perfumes she'd sampled. In one hand, she held a tall flute of champagne, from which she took the occasional sip.

The large, rectangular room was just one in the extensive library of the Royal Palace on Tharkad, this section dedicated to the history of the Lyran Alliance. Right now, it also housed the many gifts Katrina had received from her Lyran nobles. Presents covered the reading tables and floor-to-ceiling book shelves, or were piled in expensive drifts along the paneled walls. Even the hearth and mantle of the unlit fireplace had been recruited to hold gifts.

Katrina moved slowly among the treasures, already dressed for the winter ball that would begin later in the evening. The fine white brocade of her gown was shot with glittering silver threads, and she knew its slim line made her look even taller. One shoulder was bared, a somewhat daring statement for the Lyran Alliance, where the people still thought of her as their "virgin princess." The bodice of the gown, however, was cut modestly enough and set with gleaming seed pearls. Her golden blonde hair was left loose to curl gently around her face and shoulders. It was a new look for her, softer and sweeter. She would be the sensation of the night's festivities.

And that was as it should be. Katrina glanced into a full-length mirror that leaned against one wall, admiring herself. The mirror, another gift, was flawless and framed with golden teak from Novara. It would have been beautiful except that the wood was etched with silver gauntlets, the emblem of the Lyran Alliance. Tacky, Katrina decided, dismissing it and the world that had sent it.

She had left the unwrapping and arrangement of the gifts to servants and the Lyran Intelligence Corps. It had freed up her time and saved her from the danger that an assassin's "gift" might have been slipped in among the rest. A small tag was attached to each item so that Katrina would know whom to thank if she decided that a gift warranted a personal note.

Each beautiful item begged for attention. Most she would look at once, perhaps twice, and then never see again. But what could people expect? Between the Lyran Alliance and the Federated Commonwealth, she ruled nearly nine hundred worlds and billions of lives. Even signing a form letter of thanks to each noble in the Lyran state would require hours—days!—of effort. And nearly every Lyran world was represented in this room, from Barcelona to Solaris VII and from Lambrecht to Langhorne—a testament of her people's love and respect for their Archon-Princess. As for those few who had not presented her with a gift . . . Well, what easier way to identify the disaffected and disloyal?

Despite the widespread propaganda touting her strong leadership and popular support, Katrina harbored no illusions about her degree of control over her realm. She still held the Alliance firmly in her grasp, and she was loved and even idolized by many, though her detractors had lately managed to chip away at her popularity. She wasn't sure whether they were her brother's supporters or merely a vocal minority that took perverse pleasure in destroying that which was perfect.

As for the Federated Commonwealth . . .

Katrina frowned, an expression she tried never to indulge except in her most private moments. She did not like being away from New Avalon and the Federated Commonwealth just now. Many of its nobles were staunch Davionists who saw Victor as his father reborn—if in a much shorter package—while troublemakers in the Draconis Combine were openly calling for her younger brother Arthur to take the New Avalon throne. Others continued to propose Victor's return. It didn't matter that Victor had effectively renounced the throne and had settled on Tukayyid as ComStar's new Precentor Martial.

Victor.

Katrina felt a stab of contempt. Little Victor, unable to relinquish his military toys and now forced to live at the sufferance of ComStar. Tukayyid, in what was left of the Free Rasalhague Republic, suited him. Two ancient enemies lay to either side of it, and Clan-occupied territories were poised like a hammer over his head. He should never have been born first, she thought. He could lead, yes, but never rule. If their parents had only recognized that, she would never have been forced to take such drastic measures.

"You should have left well enough alone, Victor," she said aloud to the empty room. "Your constant meddling will cost you now."

It was Victor, in his capacity as Precentor Martial, who

had cast the deciding vote against her when the Star League Conference convened on Tharkad last month. Katrina had coveted the position of First Lord since the day the League reformed, but politics had kept her from it. This time, she had plotted carefully to finally win the election, only to be barred from it again. She was enraged that Victor was the one who had blocked her way, but she could be patient. Theodore Kurita's term would be up in three years, and then the position would finally be hers—or there would be hell to pay! In the meantime, her revenge was already in place. She would allow her brother to live, but he would be punished.

Taking a sip from her glass, Katrina continued to wander the room. A vial of perfume from Timbiqui caught her attention. She rubbed a tiny amount onto her wrists and then dabbed a drop behind each ear. Then a carved piece of New Capetown ivory drew her eye, but she forgot it a moment later. Next, a reproduction of the Antelli Bagruett painting *Winter on Coventry* caught her interest. Beautiful, of course, but a copy? That was a lackluster gift.

She made a mental note of the giver's name: Baroness Trembeau of Crimond, a world with known sympathies toward Victor. She would have to remind Crimond that Victor was not coming back. Perhaps it was time for the planet to suffer a shortage of luxury items that would turn the lower nobility against the ruling baroness.

Shipping delays occurred all the time; they were, in fact, Katrina's most useful strategy, one she employed freely. The lack of luxury items would teach the nobles a lesson, while food shortages and unemployment would turn the common people against the nobility. And, of course, the media, controlled by her agents, would lay the blame wherever she needed it to fall. Only when such measures failed did she resort to sending in troops. She had no doubt that, eventually, she would bring the Commonwealth to heel.

It was only a matter of time.

A stole of silver Drosendorf sable, feather-soft and

shimmering in the light, was worthy enough for a pause. She stroked it softly, her blue-polished nails sinking into the exquisite feel of the lush fur. She picked it up and checked its color against her gown. Jeriah Maltz, Duke of Drosendorf, was a strong supporter of Katrina and the return to Steiner traditions. It was for people like him that she had co-opted her famous grandmother's name. She would favor him tonight by wearing his gift for all to see, a sign to others who wanted to earn her favor.

The case of Glengarry Reserve did nothing for her, though Katrina made a note to send Grayson Carlysle a personal note regardless. His Gray Death Legion occupied a critical planet in one of her more rebellious districts. Also near the case of whiskey were a carved totem from Loric, a tiara from Landgrave Cavanaugh, who was still trying to catch her eye, a marble statue from a marquis on Venaria, and . . .

Katrina stopped and stared. When had Lady Hamilton developed such exquisite taste?

Katrina lifted up the gown, which was draped over the back of an antique chair. It was emerald green satin, with stars embroidered in a shower from the left breast to the right waist and down the side. The cut was revealing, one she could never wear in the Alliance, though it would work wonderfully at the reception planned for her return to New Avalon.

"I must find out who designs your wardrobe, Marguerite," she murmured. "Whoever she is, you don't deserve—"

The words caught in her throat as Katrina spied the spun-glass mycosia blossom, perched delicately atop a small pile of gifts. It caught and held the light in a prism of scintillating colors, sending a rainbow shimmering along the two broad, thin leaves that cupped the delicate flower. The mycosia had been her mother's favorite, the very bloom that was used to kill her. The assassin had formed pots from an explosive, planted them with mycosia, and delivered them to a charity reception where Melissa Steiner-Davion was to speak.

"Who—" Katrina said aloud. "Who dares send me such a gift?"

She reached out for the small tag fixed to the end of one leaf, careful not to touch the delicately crafted blossom. The lettering was tiny in order to fit on one side: Commander Emeritus. Baron von Arc-Royal. Grand Duke of the Arc-Royal Defense Cordon.

Morgan Kell.

Retired commander of the Kell Hound mercenary regiment and a cousin to the ruling Steiner line, Morgan Kell was possibly the single greatest thorn in Katrina's side, after Victor. Though reluctant to formally challenge his Archon, Morgan had taken the opportunity—during one of Katrina's rare moments of weakness—to carve a minor realm out from the Lyran state. He now held absolute control over a sixteen-world district in a kind of military dominion that ignored any directives from Tharkad. His publicly stated goal was protection of a sizeable portion of the border between the Lyran Alliance and the zone occupied by Clan Jade Falcon. Privately, he accused Katrina of assassinating her mother—and, by association, of being responsible for the death of his wife and the loss of his arm, secondary casualties of the assassin's efforts.

Katrina took up the blossom with great care. It was so delicate and airy that it felt almost weightless in her palm. Nestled in the center of its five delicate petals was a hologram of her mother. The face of Melissa Steiner-Davion looked out at her daughter with the same sweetness and love she had always bestowed on her children.

Katrina's hands shook with rage. "Stop it," she ordered herself in a whispery voice. "Stop it now." Slowly, she regained her composure.

"Impatient, Morgan?" she asked, still staring at the object. "Hoping to goad me into making a wrong move? I think not."

Morgan Kell and Victor might think they knew something, but they could prove nothing. There was no one out there who could hurt her. Using this gift as a threat was very petty, very unlike Morgan, but if he'd been reduced to gestures like this, Katrina was safe.

She brushed away the thought that Morgan Kell was not known for empty gestures, but she couldn't help wondering what he thought he knew.

She scarcely needed a new reason to revisit the problem of the Arc-Royal Defense Cordon, and she decided to do so immediately after the ball. Or even during. Whisper some poison in the right ear. Find a friendly landgrave within the ARDC perhaps? If she remembered correctly, the Cordon world of Atocongo was due for its annual influenza season. It would be a shame, and a drain on Morgan's resources, if medical shipments to the planet should be lost or delayed. Because of it, the virus would eventually spread through every one of his worlds.

She let the spun glass flower tumble from her hands onto the carpeted floor. She lifted the hem of her dress and brought one foot down hard, once, smashing the delicate object.

Yes, she decided, an outbreak of influenza would distract Morgan Kell. And before long, Victor would also have plenty to occupy his mind.

She smiled thinly, imagining the two of them at some future date: railing against the fates, knowing she had manipulated them both, punishing them so easily through what they cared about. Morgan, through his insignificant Defense Cordon. Victor, through a special torment even now in the making.

Katrina stared at the broken glass on the floor, knowing that somewhere out there among the stars the assassin responsible for their mother's death was even now seeking to deliver the same fate to Omi Kurita.

3

Granite Falls, Robinson
Draconis March
Federated Commonwealth
25 December 3061

Christmas dinner at the Sandoval castle proceeded with a stately air, with plenty of time for the many guests to enjoy each course and each other's company. The huge, burnished oak dining table was covered in fine damask and set with a feast worthy of the ancient Romans. Exotic fruits and a simple yet delectable selection of garden vegetables. Wild fowl stuffed with herbs and served over beds of seasoned rice. An interesting salad of pale greens and dried nuts with a whisper of raspberry vinaigrette. Platters of spiced ham and blackened fish. A special, light apéritif was served between courses to clear the palate, and a choice of fine wines was decanted with each main dish. A small army of accomplished servants attended the guests, making sure everything proceeded without a hitch.

Slender blue tapers and garlands of Robinson blue fir also graced the nine-meter-long table, where Arthur Steiner-Davion sat chatting amiably with those around him. He was three seats down from James Sandoval, master of Castle Sandoval, who presided at the head. The servants had just brought out a thick cheese soup, a specialty of the region that everyone pronounced the best they'd ever tasted. As always, husbands and wives sat cross-corner from one another to facilitate conversation.

James Sandoval, master of the Draconis March region, had made sure his fiefdom was well-represented tonight. Besides the twelve noble members of his immediate family, there were a marquessa, four counts, and two knighted barons. Talk ranged from the latest rumors of troop movements in the nearby Draconis Combine to speculations about high-level politics and what the new year might bring.

Arthur found it stimulating to mix with such powerful and interesting people. He also enjoyed the fact that a servant was just now refilling his glass with more of the excellent wine.

"Be careful, Arthur," James Sandoval said, pausing in his conversation with Daffyd Owens, Count Cartago. "You're smiling, and tomorrow the scandal-vids will be claiming that you've stopped worrying and learned to love the Draconis March."

Arthur laughed and returned the salute with his glass. He admired Baron Sandoval, who carried his sixty-seven years with the strength and grace of the former Mech-Warrior he was. He especially admired that the duke no more concealed the seriousness behind his jest than he did the fact that his iron gray hair was seriously balding.

Arthur gave a slight bow from his seat. "I *am* enjoying myself, sir," he said, imitating the duke's lighthearted formality. "And I thank you again for the invitation." In the last three years spent at the Robinson MechWarrior Academy, Arthur had come to feel at home among the big, close Sandoval family as well as among the people of the Draconis March.

He had come to better understand their plight, and had recently begun to publicly express his view that the needs of the March had been slighted, first by Victor's preoccupation with the Clans, and then by Katrina's preoccupation with the Star League.

The March bordered the Draconis Combine, enemy of the Federated Suns since time immemorial. Victor Davion, like his father before him, had allied his realm with the Combine's rulers in recent years in order to defeat the common Clan threat. Now, the Clan threat was no more and the Combine loomed as dangerously close as ever. Arthur's open sympathy toward the March and its people had made him popular among both nobility and commoners alike.

"You're welcome, my boy," the Duke said. "With my son Tancred visiting your family this Christmas, it is only fitting that I return the courtesy to another young man so far from home."

Arthur knew that James Sandoval meant no insult in speaking with such familiarity to a royal guest. Despite the fact that Arthur was a duke by birthright, he was only twenty-four and not vested with any real political power.

Not yet, at least.

He raised his glass high again. "To the good will and kindness of the Draconis March."

The toast echoed down the length of the table as everyone raised his or her glass, saluting Arthur and one another. He clinked glasses with both his dinner partners and allowed himself a healthy swallow of the spiced sirah.

"Better our courtesy than the treatment given Tancred and Yvonne," one of the Duke's cousins murmured with guarded bitterness. "Taken to Tukayyid to sit to table with a daughter of Kurita. It is an insult to the whole Draconis March." There were more than a few grunts of agreement.

Dorann Sandoval, the duke's niece, sat on Arthur's

right. She leaned close and nudged his shoulder with hers. "What do you say to that, Arthur?"

He knew that she, like her uncle a moment earlier, meant no disrespect. On Robinson, the Sandovals blended close-knit family life with courtly politics. Aunts, brothers, uncles, and cousins were often together, and the expression of divergent points of view was both encouraged and respected. The warm reception he'd enjoyed among the Duke's family made up for some of the loneliness of Arthur's childhood.

In many respects, the Sandovals offered him everything he'd missed while growing up. He was barely fifteen when his father died, and his mother had been obliged to take up the reins of the Federated Commonwealth. He'd also been separated from his brothers and sisters, thanks to his parents' decision to raise their children in various parts of the realm so that they would consider themselves Steiner-Davions of the new Federated Commonwealth and not simply Davions of the old Federated Suns.

Several conversations broke off as people near him waited for Arthur's reply.

"I'm sure my brother Victor meant no insult when he invited Yvonne and Tancred to join him on Tukayyid on the way home from the Star League Conference," he said. "If I know my brother, it's more likely that he didn't fully consider the implications." Arthur knew that once Victor's mind locked onto some single-minded track or other, he could easily overlook the importance of anything except what—to him—was of larger concern.

James Sandoval leaned in, his amber eyes afire. "Unfortunately, Duke Arthur, that failure has affected public opinion on several March worlds. Their call for Prince Victor to reclaim the throne or—no offense—for you to replace your sister Katrina, I find remarkably shortsighted. Why do we continue to ignore the threat of Kuritas?"

"No offense taken, Duke Sandoval," Arthur said. It was true that Victor supported non-aggression against the Combine. And though Arthur was flattered by the groundswell of March support for him to rule from the throne of New Avalon, he considered it well out of his reach. "Besides, I'm certain no March world would ever ignore the Combine."

"Unless they no longer perceive the Dragon as a threat," said Jessica Sandoval-Groell, James Sandoval's venerable sister.

Seated directly across from Arthur, she had remained quiet throughout the dinner, slow even to answer Arthur's earlier toast. He'd put it down to the dulled responses of age. But looking at her now, Arthur saw nothing dull in either her flint-gray eyes or her regal bearing. Was she implying that some worlds were ignoring a real threat or that there was no threat to be wary of? Though vague, it was the closest thing this evening to a dissenting opinion.

"Do you really think our military is so strong, Grandmother?" Dorann asked suddenly from Arthur's side, supplying a possible context for Jessica's comment. The elder woman stared calmly back without answering.

Dorann glanced down and then over at Arthur. "What do you think, Arthur?"

As a senior cadet in the Robinson Academy, Arthur felt qualified to field the question. "While I have no doubt we'd beat back the Combine if they invaded, they are by no means weak. They have rebuilt their military since the initial Clan invasion, and they showed remarkable strength in the Star League campaign to smash Clan Smoke Jaguar." He shook his head. "I would prefer not to face off with the Dragon just now. We're not as ready as we could be."

"The Dragon!" Marquessa Isabelle Rein laughed. "The mighty serpent. I think old Shiro Kurita must have had a confidence problem."

Laughter swept the room as the insult was passed along to the far end of the table, presided over by Duke Sandoval's second wife. Arthur caught even a few servants discreetly enjoying the ridicule. Next to him, Dorann

Sandoval blushed at the earthiness of the marquessa's humor, and he gave her arm a gentle squeeze. She was really quite charming, and the evening was young . . .

But Jessica wasn't laughing or blushing. She rode out the amusement with a smile, nodded once as if conceding a point, then stood. James Sandoval was on his feet in an instant, followed quickly by the rest of the Sandoval males, then by Arthur and the other guests.

"Retiring, Jess?" James asked as a servant moved quickly to draw back the countess's chair. "Dessert will soon be served. Please remain."

"Thank you, James, but I think not." She walked to the head of the table and placed her hands in his. "It's been a lovely evening, but I'm feeling a bit tired." Duke Sandoval kissed his sister on the cheek, then he and the other men sat down as she left the room.

In the meantime, the servants had begun to clear the soup bowls and glasses, replacing them with a dry apéritif served in crystal goblets so tiny that Arthur was afraid of snapping the stem of his.

"The fact remains," Sandoval said after a moment, picking up the thread of conversation, "that several worlds in the March have become too caught up in Fed-Com politics and have turned their eyes away from our true enemies. Daffyd, tell them what we were discussing earlier."

Count Cartago shifted his heavy chair to better face the rest of the table and wound up talking directly to Arthur. "That's right. I came over by way of Kentares, and Duke Eric Dresari couldn't stop talking about our duty to Victor. Kentares!"

Daffyd Owens shook his head in disbelief. "Is the Kentares Massacre forgotten? If any world has more cause to hate the Combine . . ." He trailed off.

Everyone seemed suddenly subdued by the allusion to the Kentares bloodbath. In a day of infamy that had not lost its horror even after nearly three hundred years, the Draconis Combine had butchered more than fifty-two million lives to avenge a fallen Coordinator.

The Duke slammed his hand down on the table. "That's exactly what I'm talking about. There's no reason to believe the Combine has changed."

He picked up his glass, saluted Arthur, and tossed it back with a practiced flick of his wrist. Arthur did the same, and the heady wine ran a fiery trail from his throat to his stomach.

"Well, Duke Kentares is saddled with a Lyran garrison force now," Sandoval continued. "Katrina sent them from the Alliance to bring him to heel. Eric Dresari has asked me to intervene, though of course I will not. Katrina, for all her faults, at least does not interfere with our efforts to protect ourselves from Kurita treachery. I've already got enough to worry about, what with the shipping problems that continue to plague our region." He shook his head in disbelief. "We've got people on Robinson going hungry, and Dresari wants to drag me into his dispute with the Archon-Princess."

This was news to Arthur. Lyran garrisons on Kentares? Food shortages on Robinson? He looked at the large wedge of steaming pie a servant had just set in front of him. The scent of apples and cinnamon was overpowering, making his mouth water, but it disturbed him to think that other people might be starving at this very moment. The warm cheer brought by his drink faded.

"I hadn't heard about this, Duke Sandoval," he said. "I trust it is not serious."

The Duke shrugged slightly. "We do have resources, Arthur," he said, glancing around the table. "The Marquessa, for example. She has several outlying worlds near the Periphery that produce an excess of foodstuffs, and her timely arrival with several cargo DropShips has allowed me to solve some of the shortages. For now."

He spread his hands. "We do what we can."

Arthur wadded up his linen napkin and tossed it onto his plate. "What can I do, sir?" He saw the Duke hesitate, reluctance obviously warring with an eagerness to help his people. "Truly, I'd like to help," Arthur said.

The duke sat back, seeming deep in thought. Light

chatter immediately resumed at the far end of the table, but not without furtive glances toward Arthur and Sandoval as everyone strained to follow the conversation.

"Maybe," the Duke finally admitted. "Maybe there is." He sat forward again. "There is a rally next month here on Robinson. Part of our Heritage Day celebration. I want to remind the people of the March that our enemies haven't retreated—that we must be more on guard than ever. If you, as a member of the ruling family, were to endorse the rally in some way . . ." He trailed off, waiting.

Arthur nodded quickly. "I will, and more. I'd be happy to say a few words at the rally if the commandant will allow it." Oratory was a gift Arthur had inherited from both his parents, though he rarely had the opportunity or the time to exercise it. "Perhaps I can even draw my sister's attention to the problems you're—we're—facing."

"My boy," James Sandoval said, obviously pleased, "I'm going to take you up on that. It may be just the thing we need."

He looked around, noticing the hush that had fallen over the table, and said, "Isn't this supposed to be a festive occasion? Eat. Enjoy." Then, in an undertone to Arthur, "Don't worry about the commandant. Major General Fortuna is my cousin as well as my ablest officer. She'll give her permission." He winked. "We'll work on your speech next week, you and I. I've some ideas—yes, quite a few ideas that might work."

There were nods and beaming faces directed at Arthur from all around the table. Dorann clapped lightly, hugged Arthur, and then, a bit embarrassed at her show of emotion, she retreated back to her dessert. But she found his hand beneath the table and took it tightly in her own.

Arthur had never felt so pleased with himself. He could finally do good things, important things, here in the Draconis March. Vowing to stay involved despite his Academy commitments, he returned to his dinner.

The pie was very good.

PART 1

Dissonance

4

Tancred Sandoval blinked away the sweat burning his eyes and blurring his vision as he tried to limp his *Nightstar* OmniMech around the side of a low knoll. A burnt-out leg actuator had the 'Mech swaying on its feet, cutting its top speed by twenty percent.

Alarms wailed, demanding attention. One threatened a heat-induced shutdown, brought on by heavy damage to the 'Mech's reactor shielding. Another warned of a targeting lock by the pursuing *Daishi*. The throttle was already full against its physical stop, and Tancred knew he'd never make it to cover. He had to buy himself some time.

He wrenched the control stick to the left, twisting the *Nightstar's* upper back toward the path of his retreat, and tracked his targeting cross hairs across the main viewscreen. The laser-illuminated reticle twitched and danced as the 'Mech's tactical screens half-flooded with static, and his sensors labored to maintain some semblance of a targeting lock as the *Daishi* swung into view. But it was the best he'd get, and he knew it.

Mashing down on his main trigger, Tancred fired a cross-body shot with his right-arm gauss rifle, followed by a cascade of burning energy from the particle cannon mounted in the *Nightstar's* right chest. There was no time even to check his own damage; he slapped at the shutdown override and prayed briefly for one more volley.

Though he'd caught the override in time to prevent the *Nightstar's* fusion engine from automatic shutdown, the power spike was bleeding more waste heat through the physical shielding. Heating units designed to simulate the searing temperatures of battle blasted a rush of hot air up his legs and the back of his neck, making the air so heavy he could hardly breathe. Light smoke wafted up from supposedly damaged sensors. The ozone scent of melted circuitry stung his nose and burned into his lungs. It was a new feature in the Com Guard simulator pods, and one Tancred could have done without.

Combat immersion, Victor Steiner-Davion had called it earlier, naming off half a dozen innovations, with more being planned every day. It was impressive—Tancred gave them that. He could hear the grinding noise of his 'Mech's left arm still trying to rotate in its fused shoulder joint, feel the erratic vibration from damage to his gyroscopic stabilizer, and hear the actual popping sound made when myomer muscles snapped under strain or damage. Only his mind reminded him that this was a simulated duel being fought between friends.

Simulation or not, the fight felt real. And Tancred hated to lose.

The *Nightstar,* squatting on its back-canted legs, wasn't the tallest BattleMech. At ninety-five tons, however, it was one of the heaviest, and packed a mean array of firepower. It was almost a match for Victor's Clan-built *Daishi*—but not quite. Victor had foregone two of his large pulse lasers, which would have kept the fight even at medium ranges.

"But I let him close," Tancred muttered, frustrated but keeping his voice low enough not to activate the mic. The *Daishi's* twelve-centimeter autocannon had sliced deeply into the *Nightstar's* right leg and torso with its depleted-uranium slugs. Now there was no getting away.

"Hey, Victor! You get any closer, the computers will start dinging you with splash damage. Or haven't you implemented that innovation yet?" Tancred would buy some time by keeping Victor talking. It wasn't his usual tactic, but perfectly fair if Victor fell for it.

His answer came in the form of a blistering attack as the *Daishi's* autocannon smashed hot metal into the *Nightstar's* already-ruined left arm. Then came a barrage of ruby laser lances, lacerating armor along Tancred's entire side. Energy bled into ruptured seams and through holes previously chewed into the 'Mech's titanium armor, which ran molten in several places. Other laserfire skimmed past his left leg's shielding to blister and cut through the armor over his right hip.

The *Nightstar* shook so violently under the barrage that Tancred could barely keep it standing. Then the right hip joint seized as molten metal pooled in the socket, binding up as it cooled. The huge machine stumbled forward, on the verge of tripping over its own useless limb. The receptors in Tancred's neurohelmet, which took direct readings from his own sense of balance, created a regenerative feedback loop that normally helped steady the massive gyroscope necessary to keep ninety-five tons of metal upright. It could only do so much, though, and right now, simply couldn't hold up under this kind of punishment.

Tancred knew he was caught in gravity's desperate grasp. Knew it, and instinctively fought against it as he arched backward in his seat, straining against the five-point restraint harness. He lowered the *Nightstar's* arms, using their weight as a counterbalance. He could also have planted the 'Mech's hobbled leg, anchoring himself in place to keep from relying on the damaged limb. That would have been the act of a cautious MechWarrior, but caution was not going to win this fight.

His balance temporarily maintained, he kept the *Nightstar* throttle-forward and angling for the same low hill he'd planned to use for protection. The injured leg came down hard, and the simulator pod jolted, making Tancred's teeth rattle. A sharp pain lanced the tip of his tongue, and he tasted blood. Damning the efficiency of ComStar's engineers, he swung the *Nightstar*'s right arm out wide for balance, and with one final stride, hobbled into the relative safety of the hill's lee.

"Last chance, Victor," he called, pivoting away from the *Daishi* and twisting his torso back to a full-front position. "I'll flip you for it."

He was not optimistic that his banter would distract his opponent, but he only needed seconds. Just long enough to turn his back, with its fresh armor, toward Victor's 'Mech. Long enough to wrench his right arm backward in the shoulder joint to fire directly into the *Nightstar*'s six. Long enough to jerk into the trigger—no time for eased shots.

But Victor wasn't fighting with the bravado Tancred was used to seeing him display. He'd changed since returning from the Clan homeworlds. Tancred should have known better than to assume Victor would be anything but a seasoned warrior.

The *Daishi* and Tancred's *Nightstar* cut loose at almost the same instant, scourging each other with hard-hitting projectiles and lethal spears of brilliant, gem-colored energy. Between washes of static, Tancred watched on his rear-view tactical screen as the *Nightstar*'s gauss slug smashed into the *Daishi*'s body just beneath its forward-thrust cockpit, missing the killing blow by half a meter. Armor flew off in a rain of shards and splinters. His medium laser poured its emerald beams into Victor's wounds, but scored no critical hits.

The *Daishi* was staring directly into the *Nightstar*'s rear camera, its blocky, wide-shouldered outline squaring off as it raised both arms and fired twin ruby lances. One of the large lasers flooded the camera with light, and the simulator pod slammed forward with all the force of a massive metal machine colliding with a wall at about twenty klicks per hour. The restraining harness that dug into Tancred's shoulders kept him from taking any serious damage, but he was shaken up and knew at once what had happened.

He rebounded back against his seat command, and all around him the instrument panel shut down and its screens went black. Only a single, dim red bulb lit the cockpit, telling him everything he needed to know.

He was dead.

Tancred shortened his stride as he and Victor walked down the hall of the training facility, falling into a natural rhythm with the younger man's stride even though he topped the Prince by a good twenty centimeters. Height wasn't the only obvious difference between them. Victor's sandy blond hair was a sharp contrast to the gleaming black of Tancred's, which was shaved except for the topknot that was a custom among Robinson nobility. He wore his braided into a tight queue. Victor had inherited his father's ruddy glow, but Tancred's family tended more toward pale skin—he didn't even tan well.

Any difference in age Tancred discounted. He was forty-two to Victor's thirty-one, which was close enough to make them contemporaries, just as their fathers, Prince Hanse Davion and Duke James Sandoval, had been of a generation. Those two had never really been friends, however. As ruler of the Draconis March, James Sandoval had often sought and failed to get Hanse Davion's ear. "Failing that, I'd have to kick him in the arse," the duke often said.

Similarly, Tancred had opposed Victor's early policies, especially regarding his stance of neutrality toward House Kurita. Unlike their fathers, however, the sons had developed a strong friendship. Of course, that hadn't kept Victor from blasting him right out of the simulated world.

Anastasius Focht was waiting for them in the review room, a private area where Com Guard officers went to analyze their simulated battles. Two large monitors were set into the gray-painted walls, and navy blue chairs were arranged around a circular table. The room had the same stark appearance of most ComStar facilities, one of the few things that had apparently not changed since Com-Star and Word of Blake had splintered into two organizations.

The other one was how serious the ComStar people seemed to be most of the time.

Focht waited while Tancred and Victor, dehydrated from their stints in the sauna of their cockpits, went to grab a couple of vitamin drinks. Then the three took seats at the table.

"I never should have gone for the hill," Tancred said to Victor. "I was so worried about my leg, and instead you popped me in the back of the head."

Victor smiled. "Actually, I thought that was a smart move on your part. You didn't have much front armor left, and your leg would have given way under a small laser. In a single move, you gave me a lot of fresh armor and no easy wounds to exploit. Except that I'd tagged your head earlier, so when the laser carved up into it . . ." He trailed off.

Tancred grinned. "Lights out. And for just a second there, I thought I'd taken you down first." He took a long pull from his vitamin drink, washing away the pasty taste of dehydration with another shock of cold orange.

Victor returned the smile. "You put up a strong fight, my friend. No reason to split hairs over who brought down whom first."

Focht had only listened up to this point. Though one of the ablest commanding generals the Inner Sphere had ever known and the former Precentor Martial of Com-Star, he seemed content to let the two warriors rehash the battle. But now he leaned forward, pinning Victor with a glare from his one good eye. "You didn't tell him?"

Victor smiled sheepishly. "I was getting to it," he said.

"Tell me what?" Tancred asked.

"Your last gauss slug punched through and crushed my gyro," Victor said. "My 'Mech went down, probably right after your screen went blank. You pulled the draw."

Tancred scowled at his friend. "And when was I going to learn this?"

Victor glanced quickly at Focht, then back at Tancred. "I figured you'd see it when you reviewed the battlerom footage."

Focht shook his head in mock severity. "What is the Inner Sphere coming to when the Precentor Martial of ComStar cannot be trusted?"

"I'd say that everything in ComStar must be proceeding according to its usual standard," Victor shot back with a sly grin.

They all knew that ComStar could hardly be held up as a shining example of forthrightness. As the self-proclaimed stewards of technology, its adepts had for centuries wrapped themselves in the trappings of mysticism while controlling the hyperpulse generator stations that made interstellar communications possible between the far-flung empires of the Inner Sphere. Some of their activities had not been quite so beneficent. Chief among those was the Com Guard, a secret army of more than seventy combined-arms regiments that the organization had brought to light some twenty or twenty-five years ago. Despite the fact that this army eventually mobilized to help stop the Clan invasion, the fact was tainted with the knowledge that ComStar had initially worked against the Inner Sphere and with the Clans.

Not even trying to deny the hit, Focht winked broadly, drawing a laugh from them both. Not everyone in Com-Star lacked a sense of humor, apparently.

Tancred took another sip from his drink, knowing he had to be thirsty when Vita-Orange actually tasted good. The stuff was great for fluid replacement, but it usually reminded him of diluted cough medicine.

"So, what's on your mind, Victor?" he asked.

"On my mind?"

Tancred nodded to Focht. "You didn't ask Anastasius here to supervise a routine sim battle. Isn't he supposed to be in seclusion, researching a book on the Inner Sphere?"

Focht nodded. "And I'm up to my eyeball in facts, figures, and finances right now, so I hope this is important. I'd also like to get this over with by sometime next year."

"All right," Victor said. "I need your counsel." He set his empty bottle on the table. "Did you hear about the speech Arthur made on Robinson last week?"

Both men nodded, and Tancred said, "I think my favorite part was 'Though some may claim to have the Dragon by the tail, its head remains free, and it is the Draconis March that will feel the sting of its bite.' He shook his head in amazement at the rhetoric. "Was I ever that bad?"

"Arthur may be a bit dramatic," Victor said diplomatically, "but it's the same message as always: the Combine is going to attack, and the March isn't ready."

"Well," said Focht, "in point of fact, it isn't."

"Not you too, Anastasius." Victor's face was a study in frustration. "You can't believe that Theodore Kurita is going to turn around and attack the Federated Commonwealth now that we've ended the Clan threat."

"Well, *I* don't," Tancred said. He rubbed the side of his face, gathering his thoughts. "I don't think my father does either, though I'm sure Victor will agree that it is the Sandovals' duty to maintain the March in a state of military preparedness. The last time we were caught off guard, it took the Kentares Massacre to charge us up enough that we could finally beat the Combine back. The Sandovals are weaned on that history."

"Not to mention that this is out of your jurisdiction now," Focht said to Victor. "ComStar should not involve itself in the internal politics of the various Inner Sphere states. So, unless Theodore Kurita plans to mobilize the Star League Defense Force . . ."

"That would go over well," Tancred said with a dry chuckle. "After the way Sun-Tzu Liao abused his position with those Star League 'peacekeepers' last year, I can just imagine my father's reaction to SLDF troops moving into the March."

Victor nodded. "I agree, but you aren't looking at it from quite the same angle as I am. What is Arthur trying to do?"

"Trying to find his place in life," Focht said. "And it's his call to make if he wants to take up the Draconis March as his personal crusade. I think he's wrong, but I really doubt he can do any real damage."

Tancred had to strain to hear as Victor asked quietly, "And how do you think my sister will react to his rabble-rousing?"

Focht mulled that over for a moment. "Politics was never my strong suit," he said slowly. "But I see what you're getting at. Katherine is a master at manipulating public opinion to suit her purposes. She'll let Arthur whip the Draconis March into a frenzy, and then she'll point them wherever she wants them to go."

Tancred had heard enough about Katherine from Yvonne and Victor to know that she was both manipulative and power-hungry. The way she had stolen the throne from Yvonne and, by extension, Victor, had required scheming and planning on a Machiavellian level. But he could also sense a kind of subtext in Victor's and Focht's comments.

"You think she's up to something?" he asked.

"I think she's finally losing her grip on the Commonwealth," Victor said. "She's been using delays in vital shipments to keep her worlds in line, but if recent troop movements are any indication, she's being forced to fall back on direct military action now. Kentares is under occupation and bucking the pressure. And last week, she moved the Davion Heavy Guards off New Avalon, supposedly to reinforce the garrison at the Galax shipyards."

Focht squinted, his mouth pressed into a hard line. "As I recall, the only regiments she's got on New Avalon are the ones whose loyalty to her is unquestioned."

"Almost. The First Davion Guards are still there, and I think they'd revolt before they'd ever let themselves get kicked off New Avalon."

Tancred thought this all very interesting, but he didn't get how it affected the Draconis March and his family. "I can't see her trying to do that on Robinson," he said. "My father has ultimate authority over most of the garrison regiments there."

Victor nodded. "That's true, but you've heard the public outcry for Arthur to replace my sister on the throne. If he stirs up enough trouble, even if it's aimed at the Combine, she might use the unrest as an excuse to move in and secure a potential rival."

"That's a dangerous game to be playing," Tancred said. It was a game hinging on a very big if—would Katherine actually use one of her own family as a cat's paw and then casually discard him?

"I still can't tell if you're looking for trouble, Victor, or trying to prevent it," he said. He drained the last of his Vita-Orange in one gulp and wrinkled his nose at the sickly, stale aftertaste.

"I want to make certain Arthur doesn't overreach himself," Victor said. "I'd like your help, Tancred. I'm asking you to go home to Robinson and try to talk to Arthur for me. See if you can't divert him toward more constructive—or at least less sensitive—positions."

"In other words, keep him from playing into Katherine's hands," Tancred said. "I'll do it. Yvonne and I can be outbound in the next few days."

"Actually," Victor interrupted, "I want Yvonne to return to Tharkad. The people need to see that Katherine isn't their only choice. She can also serve as a reminder that Katherine seized power from her, a direct contradiction to Katherine's usual claim of statesmanship."

Tancred nodded agreement, though without much enthusiasm. He and Yvonne had become close during the time he served as her advisor on New Avalon, and she'd become a welcome addition to his life. "Perhaps we can set up some kind of JumpShip command circuit to get me there faster."

JumpShips were the only means of travel between stars, tearing holes in the fabric of reality to leap up to thirty light-years at a time between star systems. They then required a week or more to recharge their jump drives via enormous sails that collected solar energy. Command circuits passed DropShips from one JumpShip to another in a relay. One starship would stop to recharge, passing its cargo or personnel on to a waiting JumpShip that would take it to the next leg of the journey. Command circuits were hard to establish, as the demands of shipping were always clamoring for more ships and different routes. However, rank did have its privileges.

"I'll see what can be arranged," Victor said. "ComStar is working with Theodore Kurita to keep a partial circuit set up between Tukayyid and Luthien. Maybe we can tap into that and rig up a link to Benjamin. That would put you, at worst, eight or nine jumps from Robinson, where you—"

At the mention of Luthien, Tancred sat up, rigid. "I'll go *around* the Combine, Victor," he said tersely. "Down through the Freedom Theater and across the Chaos March to home."

Victor looked surprised. "I thought we were past this foolishness."

"It's not me, Victor," Tancred said. That might not be completely true, but it was close enough. "You know as well as I do that I can't travel to the Draconis March riding Combine vessels. What do you think that would do to my credibility with the people of the March? And with Arthur?"

Victor blew out an exasperated sigh. "The other way will take weeks—maybe months."

"Tancred is right," Focht cautioned, placing a hand on the prince's arm. "He's fighting nearly a millennium of prejudice—not just his own, but his family's and his people's as well. You need to remember your own troubles in trying to get along with Hohiro Kurita—and you both had excellent reasons to work together." He paused. "Small steps, Victor. Small steps."

Tancred could tell by Victor's defeated look that he conceded the point. His own mind was already so focused on the trip home and how he would approach Arthur—and his father—that he almost missed Victor's next words. When they finally registered, Tancred felt the cold touch of the grave sweep over him for the second time this day.

"And if my sister doesn't allow us small steps?" Victor had asked. "What happens then?"

5

The sun was low in the sky, casting long shadows across the vast park surrounding the Palace of Serene Sanctuary. A group of palace gardeners laughed and chatted softly as they gathered their tools and equipment, finishing up for the day.

Tending the bonsai and flower gardens and keeping the flagstone paths swept until the black stone fairly gleamed, they worked tirelessly to keep the park grounds immaculate. The park boasted no showy fountains or lagoons or sunken ponds. Its only "waterway" was a stream of turquoise gravel that wound its way through the greenery to become "rapids" and then a waterfall of tiny pieces of obsidian carefully cemented together.

A light breeze carried the perfume of early-blooming roses toward the lone gardener who continued working while the others shouldered their bags and left. He raked his bonsai garden with a fine-tooth bamboo instrument, making elaborate patterns in the sand. Subtle waves rolled across the coarse grains, lapping against the minute rock wall that divided the bonsai garden from other areas of soil and colorful flowers. Larger, rougher waves broke against the base of several large stones, arranged inside the static ocean in apparent random order. The truth was that they had been placed most carefully in a way that would hold different meanings for each viewer.

To the gardener everyone knew as Randal Kasagi, they meant death—and life.

Today he had arranged the garden into an abstract image of Imperial City, the capital of Luthien and seat of power for the Draconis Combine. Though much of the planet was covered with the sprawling metropolises needed to house workers for Luthien's huge factory complexes, Imperial City might have been lifted from a thirteenth-century Terran tapestry depicting an ancient feudal city of Nippon. It seemed only fitting that he map it out in a zen garden.

The small island of sharp-edged stones, in whose center a proud bonsai spread well-manicured branches thick with green needles, was the Palace of Unity from which House Kurita ruled. Randal Kasagi could see the actual building from here. Though a good six or seven kilometers distant, the palace was tall enough to be visible from anywhere in the city. Constructed entirely of polished teak, it was as much a work of art as a building. From this distance, though, it was a dark tower, glaring down imperiously on the capital's lesser buildings.

The Palace of Serene Sanctuary, so close he could count the stones in its outer wall, was a smaller, though still grand edifice. Serving as the private residence of the Keeper of the House Honor and a place of quiet reflection, its sturdy stone and tile construction made it no less a fortress. Randal Kasagi had imaged it with a large piece of agate, touched with cultivated moss to represent its gardens. He had also teased a piece of bloodred sandstone into its eastern shadow, nearly burying it in a backwash of sand. That was an image of his own garden, a poor second to the palace's but still important.

Important to him, that is. Significant because of his presence. The palaces were there because one or the other of them would be the place Omi Kurita would die.

When he'd accepted the contract from Katrina Steiner-Davion, the assassin had not thought that getting to the Combine's lotus blossom would prove so difficult. Indeed, her residence on Tukayyid meant setting himself against ComStar, whose members were—without peer—the masters of information-gathering. The Com Guard had also turned the former farming planet into an armed camp, preparing themselves against any Clan treacheries.

Better to do it on her homeworld, he'd decided. Yet in his month on Luthien, he had been forced to narrow his options to one of the heavily secured palaces. The ruling Kurita family moved in its own circle, so far outside the normal run of society that predicting their moments of exposure was next to impossible.

Though this rigid stratification hindered him in some ways, it worked to his benefit in others. People rarely noticed anyone below their own rank, making his efforts at infiltration easier. It also cut down on the possibility of chance disaster by eliminating unknown players who might trip him up. Once the job was complete, he would have only local law enforcement to worry about.

Most amusing of all, though, was that even the assassin had his place in this society. He was ninja, the name given to the ancient shadow warriors of feudal Nippon who dealt in stealth and treachery and death. Perhaps, in that spirit, he should choose from among the more time-honored methods for Omi's death. Poisoned needle? A silent stab of the knife in the middle of the night? No, he decided finally. Getting caught up in the romance of the role would be both stupid and careless.

He would leave the romance to Victor, who would feel

the bite of tragedy again soon enough. He returned to his work.

The assassin felt the other's presence even before he heard the slap of thongs against the flagstone path. He bent forward and extended his rake, digging lightly into the sand as he eased into a long pull. The time-worn handle was smooth in his hand, and he concentrated on the feel, ignoring the approaching figure.

"*Hoi*, Randal-*san*. Shouldn't you be getting ready to go home now?" Cleo Larson, his supervisor, stood a respectful distance from the edge of his garden, admiring it without implying that she took any credit for its beauty. "The vehicle will be here soon, *wakarimasu-ka*? Do you understand?"

The assassin hauled the rake through to the end of his pull, slowly, without acknowledging her presence. Randal Kasagi, the gardener, would never have broken his concentration from the task at hand. Some small pieces of shell rasped between the bamboo tines as he completed his sweep. Then he reversed the head, using the broad back of the tool to smooth a beach along one wall of the garden. About where the spaceport should be. And the trio of round gray stones would make perfect DropShips, he decided. A drop of sweat rolled off his brow as he worked, splashing into the sand to ruin one cresting wave. He smiled at that, again because Randal Kasagi would have smiled.

"*Hai*," he finally answered. "*Wakarimasu*. But I am not finished."

The older woman nodded, her pale skin hanging off her face in folds. She wore work clothes, the knees of her trousers stained from tending the flower beds. Her only concession to the Combine's Japanese culture was the silk headband she used to tie back her silver-gray hair.

"It is never finished. *So desu-ne*? Isn't it so? And you have raked yourself into a corner."

He half-bowed in agreement with both observations. Not quite a corner, though. Actually, the assassin stood in a patch of sand from which he'd been able to reach most of his garden. He had raked carelessly around his own feet, disturbing the garden and placing himself in the midst of turmoil. And that too could be read in many different ways. His position also happened to correspond to the hostel where he was living, the better to give himself perspective on his map. After he killed Omi Kurita, his survival would depend on how well he knew the area.

"Your work is very fine, Randal-*san*. You learned this on Marshdale, yes?"

"Yes, Cleo-*san*. For a time, I was forced to tend a garden for one of the Smoke Jaguar scientists. A bio-engineer." He shook his head, flicking more sweat from his brow into the perfectly crested sand. "One day he planted a sprig of climbing violet in the center of the garden, because he had worked to develop a new strain and wanted to display it."

She shuddered. "How awful for you that he could not appreciate your work, Kasagi Randal-*san*."

The assassin shrugged, unassuming, as a gardener should be.

Of course, there was no Randal Kasagi. Not on Marshdale or on Luthien. He had falsified documents to give himself a partial history. That was the marvel of the Combine, that a man of menial labor was generally accepted at face value. The assassin had come as a gardener, and so he'd been put to work as a gardener. No one would bother with a reference check unless he moved into a more important position, such as part of the palace staff, but even then, the lack of documentation on Marshdale would not damn him. The world was only recently liberated from Smoke Jaguar occupation. Many records had been lost, and there were more than a few people seeking to escape the occupation's legacy by moving to other worlds.

The disguise was simple enough. Asian ancestry was by no means mandatory, though he'd chosen it anyway for aesthetic reasons. Time in a tanning bed with the proper skin agents had given him a jaundiced color. He had texturized his hair for a coarser look. A touch of collodion at the corner of each eye—the nitro-cellulose glue shrinking as it dried—produced epicanthic folds; more at the corner of his mouth gave him the tiniest scar. A childhood accident, he told those few who asked.

"The truck will be coming soon," Cleo reminded him again. "You should prepare."

"I will walk back. It is not far, and I am still not finished." He placed a hand at the small of his back and stretched to ease the pain familiar to most gardeners. Randal Kasagi also had a touch of early rheumatism in his back that aggravated the condition and gave him a slight limp by the end of the day.

Cleo bowed, honoring his dedication to the park, and, by extension, the Combine. With another appreciative glance at his work, she retreated.

The face of Omi Kurita lingered at the back of the assassin's mind as he continued to work, every move slow and deliberate. Another universally loved woman. And, once again, a gardener. He remembered the fatal bouquet he had delivered to Melissa Steiner-Davion. He would have laughed had Kasagi had any reason to do so, but he permitted himself only a smile as the breeze dropped a rose petal onto his meticulous work—a splash of blood in the pale, dry ocean.

But in the wrong area. It had fallen into what would be the craftsman district of Imperial City, and that wouldn't do at all. Rather than risk marring the petal's frail beauty with the rake, the assassin strode across his afternoon's work, destroying its harmony. He picked up the petal with careful fingers, and let it fall instead into the short, stabbing pine needles of the bonsai. Much better, he decided, turning his eyes toward the distant Palace of Unity.

Then he resumed his earlier position and slowly began to rake the sand smooth once more, striving for the perfection that Randal Kasagi would strive for, yet never reach.

Soon, he promised himself. Soon.

6

Katrina Steiner-Davion sat back in her wide-armed chair and looked around her office. Even ten years after her father's death, she could still feel his presence in this office that had once been his in the palace on New Avalon. So strong was the feeling that she was having difficulty concentrating on the briefing being given by her new intelligence officer.

She remembered Hanse Davion as a strong and capable man who smelled of starched uniforms and the occasional brandy, but who always had time to give her a big hug or a kiss on the forehead. His memory still lingered, just as the Davion legacy still permeated the Commonwealth, but one day she would be free of both. The day when she had finally eclipsed her parents' marks on history. The day the Star League became hers.

Richard Dehaver was midway through his report on the Capellan invasion of the St. Ives Compact when she finally forced her attention back to his words.

"The Black May attacks are escalating," he was saying, speaking of the chemical weapons the Capellans had unleashed in their war on the St. Ives Compact. "Reports put the death toll from nerve agent attacks at over seven thousand."

Katrina still found the man's flame-red hair and freckled nose incongruously boyish for someone who was the head of her Military Intelligence Investigations Office. But his eyes told the tale. Sunken and shrouded, their green was so dark as to look brackish. They were eyes that had seen too much.

She met his empty stare. "Have any nerve agent attacks been made against Commonwealth soil?"

"No."

"Then the numbers are of no importance. So long as the fighting distracts George Hasek and his worlds in the Capellan March, we shall let it run its course."

Katrina did not mention the private agreement she'd made with Sun-Tzu Liao to ignore his war against St. Ives so long as none of her holdings were threatened. That was an agreement known only to her own Lyran intelligence corps—but she knew she could rely on their loyalty. The Ministry of Intelligence Investigations and Operations had yet to earn her complete trust, though Dehaver was proving most accommodating thus far.

Dehaver shrugged and paused briefly. "Tormano Liao is dead."

Katrina blinked and sat up in her chair. Until now, that had been only rumor. "You have confirmed this?" she asked, and he nodded.

Katrina spent a few moments considering her feelings on the matter, then said, "That is unfortunate." It was the only eulogy her old advisor was likely to get.

Tormano had been an asset early in her reign, helping Katrina consolidate power and covering the few mistakes she had made. But he had resigned his post to run off

and get involved in the Capellan struggle for control of
St. Ives, likely with an eye toward a throne of his own.
Richard Dehaver, raised and trained right here on New
Avalon, could handle the job just as well.

He keyed for the next page in his noteputer; then he
set a data crystal on the polished wood surface of her
desk that she could feed into the built-in computer. Two
other crystals and a ream of hardcopy littered the desk-
top, available if she wanted to follow along with his presentation, but Katrina preferred to listen. And plan.

"The situation in the Draconis March did not change
much during your journey from Tharkad to New Avalon," he said. "Your brother Arthur has given two more
speeches since the Heritage Day festival. I've included
transcripts. He does not mention Victor, and he carefully
avoids accusing you of ignoring the interests of the Draconis March. Though he did credit your rule with removing the—his words—'myopic focus on the Clans.' "

Katrina laughed, the merriment at her brother's tactics
refreshing but short-lived.

"Arthur always fought to be independent, being both
ambitious and young," she said. "But I sense the duke's
hand in this as well. Fortunately, James Sandoval knows
better than to challenge me if he intends to maintain his
momentum against the Combine. It sounds like we
should ease some of the shipping troubles Robinson has
been experiencing of late."

She pushed some of the hardcopy aside. "What has
been Arthur's effect in the rest of the March?"

"In general, he's been very useful, giving an unknow-
ing boost to our underground operations. He stirs up
the people's emotions, and our recruiters channel those
emotions into activities designed to strengthen your support there. The People Unbound and Marchers Against
the Dragon have done phenomenally well . . ."

"But?" she prompted, hearing his slight hesitation.

"But we still have a problem on worlds where the
nobles and the people are diehard Davionists. Your ear-

lier efforts to remake yourself in the Steiner image may
have been too successful."

That was as close as Dehaver had ever come to criticiz-
ing Katrina. She felt her face get hot with anger, and the
skin at the corners of her eyes tightened. She didn't care
for his implication at all, but for now, she was more
interested in his information.

"Which are the trouble spots?" she asked.

"There are trouble spots on any given world," he said,
tapping the side of the computer to remind her that the
information was available in greater detail. "But we are
having particular problems on Kentares, where Duke
Dresari has apparently given up trying to get help from
James Sandoval and has appealed directly to Arthur for
support against you."

Her anger flared brighter at Eric Dresari's stupidity
and his blatant challenges. "That man needs a lesson in
manners," she said icily. "It is Lord Roland maintaining
my garrison there, yes? Get word to him that I expect the
interference to cease immediately, however he chooses to
handle it. Kentares is too touchy politically to allow the
Dresari family such a platform to oppose me."

And if that didn't work, then it would be time to drop
another regiment onto Kentares and divest Dresari of
his noble title. Katrina knew that the rest of the Commonwealth's nobles would oppose such a drastic step,
but if Dresari continued to oppose her, she would have
no choice. "And damned if I won't break Marcus Roland
as well. See that he knows that. Anything else?"

"Our underground efforts on Benet III are experiencing interference from a grass roots movement to declare
Arthur Prince of the Commonwealth. On Benedict, it
has moved beyond grassroots, with several minor nobles
championing him as a"—he checked his noteputer—"a
'conscientious leader who understands better the traditional affairs of House Davion.' Quite an endorsement."

Leaning forward, Katrina drummed her fingers slowly
against the wood of her massive desk, marking time
while she considered. Dehaver stood waiting silently.

On the count of twenty, she said, "Benedict is a mineral-poor world, as I recall."

He nodded without needing to check his notes, well-briefed, as always, on this kind of information. "Benedict's industry relies heavily on trade with Savonburg and Palmyra. It is actually part of Duke Savonburg's fief," he said.

"Good. So we start some new dissent on Benedict—small but very vocal, a movement agitating for increased independence from the world's trading partners as well as declaring strongly for Arthur. This will make them, and the Benedict nobles by association, seem ungrateful as well as subversive. Palmyra will restrict trade, and Duke Savonburg will ride herd on the nobles for me. Make sure that his private militia has increased access to military supplies if needed."

Dehaver nodded, rapidly entering the information in his noteputer. "And the name for the organization?" he asked.

Katrina thought for a moment. "Hands Off Benedict. And make certain its membership is limited to reactionaries. No deep thinkers." She pressed her hands together and leaned forward with her chin resting on the sharp tips of her blue-polished nails. "So, assuming Kentares and Benedict are neutralized, your final evaluation of Arthur is . . . ?"

"Very positive, and growing more useful every day."

"Try to keep it that way. Handle Arthur carefully, and never let him feel the bit. Just so long as he remains useful."

DeHaver's dark eyes narrowed. "And if he ultimately proves intractable, no longer useful?"

Katrina finally turned her attention to the hardcopy on her desk, fishing through it for a holograph of Arthur in his cadet's uniform. He stood proudly in front of the Academy on a bright, sunny afternoon, his brown hair slicked back impeccably and his blue eyes bright.

"Let's hope it does not come to that," she said. "A

spirited little brother is fine for getting people worked up, but to make them act . . ."

She set the holograph back on her desk, face down. "For that, nothing is better than a martyr."

Bueller, Robinson
Draconis March
Federated Commonwealth

The hoopla surrounding Tancred Sandoval's arrival on Robinson began when his DropShip touched down. It started with a rousing march tune blasted through a public address system powerful enough to drown out the fusion drive's dying roar, and did not end until well after Arthur Steiner-Davion's normal curfew. During all those hours of ceremony, both public and private, Arthur had seen Tancred welcomed home by the entirety of the First Rangers, elements of the Tenth Lyran Guards stationed on Robinson, and in a receiving line of nobles at the Ducal Hall that would have made the master of ceremonies for any grand ball on New Avalon green with envy.

Arthur met Tancred briefly and for the first time when he was introduced by Major General Fortuna, who was present as a representative of the Academy Training Battalion and who he was attending.

Tancred looked visibly worn out, but he threw off his fatigue and gave Arthur's hand a vigorous shake. "I look forward to speaking more with you later," he said, a comment that set off warning bells in Arthur's mind.

Later, it turned out, meant well past midnight. There seemed no end to the people Duke James Sandoval had paraded out to meet or renew acquaintance with his son and heir. Some of the females expressed real regret that Yvonne had not accompanied Tancred to Robinson. More, though, brightened at the lack of royal competition for a handsome man who was considered one of the Inner Sphere's most eligible bachelors.

Not that Tancred took advantage of his status, Arthur noted. He charmed several young women whose parents were apparently promoting them as potential brides, then turned to greet other guests, apparently without offending the young ladies.

Arthur's reverie was interrupted by James Sandoval, who wanted his opinion on staging a series of military operations between the Rangers and the Academy Training Battalion, who would act as Combine aggressors. He wanted to know how well Arthur thought the cadets would stand up to such a war exercise.

"We're green as Dobson moss," Arthur said candidly. "But the general has been working on special maneuvers that might help us fight a few steps above our true level, things like shock tactics and unconventional formations. I'm sure the whole unit would be eager and willing to do our part."

"Which will amount to dying in a particularly convincing manner," Tancred said, joining Arthur and the duke. "All the better to make the Rangers look good. Right, Father?"

Tancred had been circulating through the reception hall, trading toasts and looking dashing in his uniform of the Federated Commonwealth Armed Forces. Now, out of the public spotlight, his shoulders slumped and his eyes drooped just enough to show that his reserves were wearing thin. But if he didn't care for the marathon reception event, why had he put up with it for so long? Arthur wondered. Surely, he could have slipped out before now without giving offense.

James Sandoval looked apologetically at Arthur. "I doubt any military forces on Robinson require a staged victory to make them look good," he said. "Certainly, the Rangers do not. But it never hurts to stay focused and sharp through some extra training."

"And a little Drac-bashing will make certain that everyone remembers who to stay focused on," Tancred said with a weary smile.

The Duke shook his head sadly. "I've been wondering

lately if you remember who the real enemies of the Draconis March are, Tancred."

Arthur was fascinated by the exchange. It was obvious that father and son did not really get along, but they didn't display the rancor that usually attended such father-son rivalries. He compared it to memories of his own father. Hanse Davion had always gotten on well with Victor, and yet consistently butted heads with his headstrong son Peter. There had been affection between them, but it was more like the healthy respect one has for a worthy adversary. Arthur had been only fifteen when Hanse died, and his father had seemed to view him as still a child. It put into perspective Tancred's performance tonight: the younger Sandoval tending to the duties set by his father, no matter how he might feel about them.

It also added a new dimension to an exchange between them at the spaceport, which Arthur had witnessed off to one side. Greeted by the First Robinson Rangers in parade review, the duke had guided Tancred to a podium.

"Just a few brief words," his father had requested, that is, ordered. Holocams were busily recording the event for posterity as the Baron Robinson took the stand.

"My friends," he'd said, "it is good to be home again." Cheers and applause followed, forcing a pause. "I can't tell you how proud I am of all of you. That the First Robinson Rangers helped put an end to the Clan threat is something we can be proud of for the rest of our days. I can now say I've seen the best we have to offer, and it is not lacking. And I know you will remain on guard against all the enemies we may yet face—from without or within."

Tancred had stepped down to thunderous applause, giving his father a jaunty smile. "Brief enough?" he asked.

Duke Sandoval did not look particularly pleased. "We can edit it," he said.

Arthur realized now that Tancred's implication was that the most important enemy the Rangers would ever face was the Clans. That might very well be true, but it didn't make military preparedness in the March any less necessary.

"So, Tancred," he said, inserting himself into the conversation, "how is my sister?"

"I assume you are asking after Yvonne?" Tancred's tone was warmer than when he'd addressed his father. "She's fine, and she asked to be remembered to you, Arthur. She wanted to come, but other duties kept her from doing so."

"And Victor?" Arthur asked, knowing that the elder Sandoval would not inquire after his brother.

"Living in peace right now, and hoping to remain that way. It would be nice if we could give him that. I think he's earned it."

The pieces fell into place in Arthur's mind. Tancred visiting Victor on Tukayyid. The early return home, minus Yvonne.

"Victor sent you back here, didn't he?" Arthur asked abruptly.

James Sandoval's eyes darkened, and he turned to his son. "Did he?"

Tancred glanced at his father. "He asked me to take care of some matters for him while I was in the March, yes. Does that make my arrival any less welcome?"

"No," the duke said, and he embraced his son warmly, though his tone revealed a shade of doubt. "You've been away too long as it is." He signaled to a nearby server and chose glasses of wine for himself and for Tancred.

"Arthur?" he asked.

"I'll stick to cider," Arthur said. "The commandant was gracious in granting me an extension of curfew, but I don't want a foggy brain for classes tomorrow." He was glad now that he had kept a clear head, the better to observe Tancred Sandoval.

"Pity," the Duke sighed. "You're missing a rare treat. This is a late harvest riesling from Harrows Sun. Very rare." He sampled it with a connoisseur's appreciation. "Harrows Sun was once a March world, you realize, home to some of the best vineyards in the Inner Sphere. We lost it to the Combine in the Fourth Succession War. My agents continue to smuggle the wine out, and we rebottle it here on Robinson under the label of Freedom Sun wineries."

He smiled a touch sadly at his son. "It was the wine Tancred's mother and I used to toast our wedding."

Tancred put his glass back on the tray untouched. "You'll excuse me, Father, but I've an early day planned as well. Though I'd hoped we could meet over dinner tomorrow?"

"I'd be delighted, of course. And the family and a few other guests will gather for a banquet this weekend to celebrate your return." Duke Sandoval nodded at Arthur. "We would be honored if you would join us, too, Arthur."

Tancred had already begun his retreat, but he turned around before getting very far. "Arthur, I assume the Battle Academy still teaches fencing?"

"It does," Arthur said cautiously. "Captain Wingate's class."

"Perhaps you and I could meet for a match then. What do you say?"

"I'd say your reputation precedes you. I'm not in your league," Arthur demurred. Tancred Sandoval was a known master of epée. "Weren't you a member of the 3034 Olympic Fencing Team?"

"3038. Call it a training session, then. I'd like to see if Wingate's training is still what it used to be."

And if Arthur didn't agree to the match, Tancred would find another way to get him alone for the private talk Victor must have asked him to have.

"All right," he said. "I'd like to see how the Academy's all-time champion is holding up. Next week? Monday?" Tancred nodded and withdrew for the night.

By not resisting, Arthur knew he was making it easier for Tancred to complete his "mission." That was all right. Finding out what Victor was up to might be important. And if Tancred simply wanted to use the time to chat, Arthur could learn from that as well.

From now on, he would be watching Tancred Sandoval very closely.

=== 7 ===

First Circuit Compound
Valnya, Tukayyid
Free Rasalhague Republic
24 May 3062

Victor Steiner-Davion stood in the midst of the six crystal podiums arranged around the ComStar First Circuit chamber on Tukayyid. Each podium belonged to one of the Circuit members, and the floor was inlaid with the golden star crest of ComStar. Subdued lights illuminated the podiums, while a glaring spotlight picked out every detail of his simple Com Guard field uniform. The Primus's podium was elevated slightly above the others, and the radiant point of the inlaid star ran from Victor's feet directly to her position. The whole thing was simple yet dramatic, and according to Focht, an exact re-creation of the Hilton Head facility lost when ComStar lost Terra to Word of Blake.

With the Free Worlds League now allied with the Blakists, the podium usually occupied by Precentor

Atreus stood vacant at Victor's back. Also behind him was Precentor Rasalhague Gardner Riis, the least influential member of the First Circuit now that most of the old Rasalhague was under Ghost Bear control. Riis and Precentor Sian wore their hoods drawn over their heads, still protesting Victor's appointment as Precentor Martial of the Com Guard.

Primus Sharilar Mori, on the other hand, had thrown back the hood of her white cloak. "Greetings, Precentor Martial," she said formally. "Thank you for responding so promptly to our summons."

Mori had aged in the past ten years, which had carved deep lines around her eyes and grayed the hair at her temples. Only Huthrin Vandel, Precentor New Avalon, looked older. His age-blasted visage could more easily have been that of a centenarian than a man of seventy-two.

And with one foot in the grave, Victor thought uncharitably.

Though Vandel was careful to conceal any sign of favoritism, he covertly supported Katherine, aiding her by misdirecting communications and imposing news blackouts. If Victor ever acquired proof, it would be one more support kicked out from under his sister.

"That is your prerogative, Primus," he replied. Mori or a Circuit majority could overrule Victor in military matters, and he remained properly deferential to the chain of command. "I assume you wish an update on Com Guard readiness?"

"Precentor Martial, we trust you to inform the First Circuit of any problems or progress," said Gavin Dow, Precentor Tharkad, his silver hair glowing in the light. "Has there been either?"

As if he didn't already know, Victor thought.

The Lyran Alliance precentor was exceptional among the First Circuit in having come up through the ranks of Com Guard. It was rumored that he had also served in ROM, ComStar's feared intelligence arm. Though he was now comfortably middle-aged, the fire of a man twenty years younger still burned in his eyes. He and Huthrin Vandel were the two men considered to be rivals of the Primus.

"No," Victor said, "unless you would like to review the projections for upgrading BattleMech forces with the C3i computer."

"Actually I would," said Dow, and Victor was not surprised. "Thank you for the invitation. Shall we meet in one hour, before you begin arrangements for your journey?"

Journey? Victor looked at the Primus. "You are mobilizing the local Com Guard?"

"No," Mori said, obviously displeased that Dow had preempted her announcement. "But you did request permission to visit our Lyran Alliance garrison posts. Or had you forgotten?"

In fact, he had. One of Victor's new priorities was to fortify his position among the Com Guard divisions as quickly as possible. The Guard had already suffered a new wave of defections to Word of Blake over his appointment as Precentor Martial. Some of the remaining ones questioned his right to lead, and he knew that the ranks of the Guard also included Blakist sympathizers who operated as spies and potential traitors.

"That request was made but two days ago, Primus, and the priority was only level two. I did not expect an answer from Tharkad for another week."

Victor knew that was because Nondi Steiner, Katherine's regent and their aunt, would refer this decision—like most others—to Katherine, who was currently residing on New Avalon. His sister had made it abundantly clear that he was not to enter her Alliance without express permission.

"Communication times between Tukayyid, Tharkad, and New Avalon have been much improved of late," the Primus informed him. "You will soon receive a report for evaluation of the strategic implications. Suffice it to say that, for now, Katherine Steiner-Davion refused."

"She didn't just say no," Huthrin Vandel said with

gusto, relishing his role as the bearer of bad tidings, "but—"

"I get the idea, Precentor New Avalon." Victor stoically weathered the other man's angry glare. Vandel would have to do more than serve as Katherine's mouthpiece to get under his skin. "If Katherine refused the request, then where am I going?"

This time Gavin Dow waited for the Primus to nod permission before speaking up. "To the Alliance, Precentor Martial. In three days." He smiled, obviously satisfied with himself. "The Primus came to me for a solution, and it happens that General Nondi Steiner recently requested Com Guard troop shifts in the Lyran Alliance. I believe you were privy to that request?"

Dow turned to the other precentors without waiting for a reply. "Our contracts include clauses that allow local authorities to draft Com Guard troops for defense of a planet against outside aggressors. General Steiner asked that we shift more divisions closer to the Clan border, but not in the Arc-Royal Defense Cordon."

It was a request that would lighten the load on regular Lyran Alliance troop deployment, while putting pressure on Morgan Kell and his ARDC. Victor recognized the brilliant strategy as well as his aunt's awkward hand in arranging it. Two good reasons, as far as he was concerned, for him to refuse.

"We declined," he reminded Precentor Tharkad, his voice flat and final.

"I have reopened that issue on your behalf, Precentor Martial. After a brief discussion, Nondi Steiner and Katherine agreed to let a representative of my choice visit each Alliance-stationed division for purposes of training, evaluation, and possible reassignment. Would that adequately describe your proposed visits?"

"Close enough."

"Then you shall be my representative. Within the next twelve months, we must move at least twenty percent of our garrison posts closer to the Jade Falcon occupation zone—terms I'm sure you can interpret liberally to suit your own needs."

Victor did not miss the precentor's implication that he had interests outside ComStar business. However, the terms were a fair exchange for the time he would get with such important Com Guard units. He suppressed a sharp rejoinder, and said, "Katherine will not be happy that you arranged this, Precentor Tharkad."

"Asking her forgiveness will be easier than trying to win her permission, Precentor Martial."

Victor nodded and turned back to Sharilar Mori. "You were correct, Primus, to trust Precentor Dow with the details. He did yeoman work." He didn't have to look at Dow to know that he didn't appreciate Victor giving ultimate credit for his work to the Primus.

"And I now have much to prepare for. If you will excuse me?" he said.

Mori nodded a dismissal, thanking him with a slight smile for his support. He turned slightly to face Dow. "One hour, Precentor Tharkad, and then we will discuss the new battle computers?"

Dow nodded. "One hour." His voice was perfectly controlled.

"Precentor Martial?" Idora Toshakara, the Precentor Luthien, leaned forward over her crystalline podium, breaking one of her renowned silences. In her mid-forties and the youngest member of the First Circuit, she had replaced Mori as representative to the Combine in 3052. She brought in Asian dignity what Precentor Sian gave up with her constant pettiness. "May I also attend your review of the C3i upgrades?"

"My pleasure, Precentor Luthien," Victor said. The original C3 computer system had been developed by House Kurita, so it made sense to work with them on the improved networking system. It was only natural that Toshakara would be interested in the reports.

And he suddenly realized one other thing. With his departure imminent, Omi would probably return to Luthien. The fledgling Toshakara had enjoyed a boost among the First Circuit while ComStar was hosting Omi Kurita on Tukayyid. Dow was surely conscious of the change in the dynamic. And while Omi's departure wouldn't actually undermine Toshakara's position, it served to underscore Victor's own loss.

Three days, he realized. Three short days. Then he and Omi would be separated for as much as a year, maybe even longer.

Victor wondered now whether Gavin Dow's actions were a boon—or a curse.

8

Bueller, Robinson
Draconis March
Federated Commonwealth
26 May 3062

Tancred Sandoval leapt back as Arthur lunged, his epée singing straight for Tancred's heart. Clashing steel rang sharp and short as Tancred parried, feeling the strength of Arthur's blow through his own sword, and then spinning back in on the riposte. He extended into a long-reaching attack aimed as much at driving Arthur back down the fencing strip as it was at scoring. Arthur managed to pull his sword back in time to defend, and Tancred's blade glanced off Arthur's handguard. Then Arthur gambled, stood his ground, and immediately riposted with a high-line attack that pinked Tancred's shoulder.

"Touché!" Tancred called out.

Arthur dropped back into a defensive stance; he had been taught better than to relax his guard while on the fencing strip. He straightened and doffed his mask only as Tancred relaxed his own posture.

"Two touches apiece," Arthur called, unable to repress a smile. Tancred allowed him the instant of pride. Tancred had handicapped himself, but it was no small feat that Arthur had held his own against Robinson's fencing champion.

He and Arthur had commandeered the Battle Academy's fencing hall, staking out the center strip and acting as their own judges in a friendly match to five touches. Arthur was allowed full targeting for the epée, which was any upper-body touch. Tancred had restricted himself to foil rules, touches to the torso only. Their heavy jackets—Tancred's the white and gold of the Federated Commonwealth and Arthur's the red and blue of the Robinson Academy—absorbed the worst of the blows from the blunted-tip weapons. Around them, the bleachers stood empty, but the sound of the hard spring rain beating against the roof and the high-set windows was like the sound of continuous applause.

Lifting up his mask, Tancred wiped sweat from his upper lip. "I'd say Captain Wingate's teaching hasn't lost its edge. Your form is excellent, Arthur."

"Not holding up too bad yourself, for an . . . older man." Arthur's good-natured shot might have struck a nerve except for his easy grin and the fact that his heavy breathing somewhat ruined the effect.

"Did you keep in practice with my brother?" he asked, donning his mask again and returning to a starting position.

Tancred matched him, breathing the close air inside his mask slow and easy, knowing the risks of overexertion. He saluted with his signature slash, a cut right to left with his sword tip, then curling his blade over to slash past his right leg and then back up again. He dropped down into guard position and waited for Arthur to make the first move.

"Victor and I fence," he said, "but it's awkward. He uses saber rules. Slashing attacks."

Arthur moved first, then immediately fell back as Tancred whipped his sword in faster than expected. "You mean he prefers the katana," Arthur said, riposting. Even the muffling effect of the mask did not disguise his accusatory tone.

Falling back before the younger man's burst of energy, Tancred restricted himself to parries, trading precious meters for defensive position.

"Victor has worked hard to deserve the gift bestowed on him and Kai Allard-Liao by Coordinator Kurita," he said. "It's often called 'respect.' But if you're implying that Victor prefers the Combine to the Commonwealth, you're more misguided than I thought."

"You mean more than Victor thought."

The blunted tip of Arthur's foil slapped off Tancred's heavy, gold-embroidered glove, and he cursed himself for being distracted.

"Touché!" He doffed his mask again and cradled it in his free arm. "You do your brother and yourself a great disservice, Arthur, with those kinds of accusations. Victor is worried for you, not about you."

Not bothering to lift his mask, Arthur stomped back to his starting position. "Tell my brother I've learned to take care of myself. Just like the Draconis March has."

Leaning back into a defensive crouch, Tancred used his off arm for balance and easily knocked aside Arthur's first vicious lunge. "Well, both you and the March are waving red flags at Katherine. It's a wonder she hasn't charged in here with a Lyran regiment or three. Duke Kentares could tell you about that lesson." The steel of his sword rang, vibrating violently as he parried a second and third attack, and then riposted with a midline stab.

"Eric Dresari brought it on himself, agitating for rebellion against Katrina," Arthur said. "So long as the March doesn't threaten her, she doesn't threaten us."

"That's what Yvonne thought," Tancred retorted, "that she could trust Katherine so long as she did nothing to threaten the Lyran Alliance. Look where that got her." He didn't miss the fact that Arthur used his sister's adopted name, which was usually the sign of a supporter.

Arthur was retreating in the face of a series of feints and thrusts, trying to regain his advantage. He had to know that talking during the match hurt him more than it did Tancred. But he also had a young man's determination to be heard, and to be right.

"Yvonne invited Katrina to take over the throne on New Avalon," he grunted. "Point! Damn." Arthur slid the mask off his face, sucking in lungfuls of air while staring defiantly at Tancred.

Tancred would not give Arthur the satisfaction of seeing his own flushed face. He walked back to the starting line. " 'Invited,' " he scoffed. "That's certainly one version of events. Another is to say that Yvonne was manipulated."

He rested his weight on one leg, prepared to retreat. They saluted each other. Tancred watched for Arthur's giveaway, a slight telltale movement in his off arm as he tensed for an attack.

"Are you too blind to see that Yvonne is as much an outcast now as Victor?" he went on. "Was she invited back to New Avalon? Did Katherine allow her an actual voice at the Star League conference? She's living on Tharkad now, Arthur, with no voice in her homeland." He dropped his voice to a stinging whisper. "Don't you care how much Yvonne has been hurt?"

So sure that Tancred would fall back and be goaded into moving too soon, Arthur feinted and lunged and was neatly impaled as Tancred ducked low and riposted with a solid thrust to his breastbone.

"Point!" Arthur called, though it was hard to tell whether he was more furious with himself or his opponent. "Four-three, your advantage."

"My advantage," Tancred said.

He and Arthur lifted their masks and stared at each other. Tancred saw that, true Arthur's Davion blood, he obviously did not like to lose. That he didn't seem to consider Katrina a danger told Tancred that he had to find a way to wake him up.

"Have you even thought about what Katherine might do?" he asked as they saluted each other and settled into their en garde positions.

Fooled once into moving too fast and too confidently, Arthur began with a feint and thrust that nearly clipped Tancred's mask. Tancred parried and traded two steps for maneuvering room.

"Have you even thought about what the Draconis Combine might do?" Arthur retorted, trading parries and thrusts. Steel sang out in flurries of ringing tones as first one and then the other pressed the attack. "What if—just what if—the Dragon attacks? Are we ready? Peace is a wonderful thing, Tancred, but do we buy it at the cost of our defensive ability?"

Arthur's sword flashed out in wild, almost reckless strikes as he allowed his emotions to affect his concentration. "The Combine does not let peace stand in the way. Look how Theodore Kurita has reassigned his regiments now that the Smoke Jaguars are destroyed. Three new regiments posted along the Draconis March border. Three!"

Arthur lunged, but he overreached and threw himself too far forward. Tancred glanced Arthur's stroke aside, tripping him. Arthur stumbled to one knee, letting his sword-hand drop to the ground as he tried to catch himself. Tancred's epée sailed in with slow, easy grace, tapping Arthur on the chest just above his heart.

"Touché," Tancred said casually. "Match."

Arthur removed his mask and set it on the floor as he sat back on his heels. He wiped damp strands of hair off his brow with the back of his gloved hand. "The Draconis March will defend itself, Tancred. If you won't see to that, I will."

Tancred shook his head, wondering if anything he'd said had gotten through to Arthur. He wanted to believe it had. He stepped back, saluted with his signature slash, and removed his own mask.

"You know," he said, "it's quite remarkable. I see your lips moving, Arthur, but all I hear is my father's voice."

Saul Klinger peeled off his rain slicker and galoshes, then tossed them to the young man waiting to help him. The bóy bowed his head, keeping his eyes averted, then retreated to have the gear dried and ready for Saul's departure.

That left Saul alone with Kelly Phillips and Dan Grendle, his two co-conspirators. They were meeting today to decipher a message just arrived from their master, knowing it had to be something important. The rest of their Robinson-based cell would receive only a late report of this meeting. They had not been called in to protect Saul Klinger's position.

Someone that close to Arthur Steiner-Davion was a man to be protected in all ways.

Accepting a cup of hot tea from Dan Grendle, Saul warmed his rain-chilled hands around the sides of the mug and inhaled deep its orange-scented steam. He muttered a brief prayer of thanks, toasted his friend, and sipped carefully. The first taste scalded his tongue, obscuring any real flavor, but it warmed him as it burned down his throat.

"Blake's will," he said, "I needed that."

Phillips leaned in. "Is he the one?" he asked. "Is it time? Our master must be informed."

"Our master also advocates patience. If he has waited so many years, what is another minute to you?"

Saul tried another tentative sip and looked at Grendle over the steaming rim of his mug. "What about today's transmission?"

Demi-Precentor Grendle was the cell's active man inside the local ComStar HPG station. Thin to the point of emaciation, he displayed an inner calm that some said came from spending much time in their master's presence. Long, stringy red hair fell away from a receding hairline. Tangled and knotted, it was obviously of little concern to the humble man.

He drew a small noteputer from within his gray robes, and loaded in the verigraphed missive. It was one of many messages stolen from ComStar's files here on Robinson. First, because it contained a special wisdom. Second, because the message had obviously been altered, though the verigraph supposedly proved it could not have been, and that had to be kept well-hidden. The verigraph code demanded a DNA check before allowing access to any information. Such files were guaranteed to travel across ComStar or Word of Blake stations without any chance of forgery, alteration, or improper decoding.

Except that this one had not.

"I find I am wanting," Grendle read the altered portion, set into the encrypted text but not itself coded. "It is the past, seen in light of the present. Let the light cleanse us. The future will prepare for itself, and for us. That is final. That is my judgment."

All three men stood there for a moment, reflecting on those words. Of course, it was Phillips who finally asked, "And the key?"

"The first word is only one letter, which means it remains, but we look to the second for the key. That is four letters. So, we read every fourth word, starting again with the first. It then tells us, 'I am the light. Let us prepare for final judgment.' We were right. Our time approaches."

"But are we ready?" Phillips asked. "Is Arthur Steiner-Davion the one we seek? To be reborn of fire and darkness?"

Saul sighed, long and audibly. He had hoped for clearer guidance from today's message. "I don't know yet. I listen and watch—I know him as well as anyone— but I see no evidence yet, and I must be certain. What if we are wrong?"

Kelly Phillips flushed, his bald head crimson and his face tight with anger. Of the three, he was the most dangerous. Wanted by the Robinson police as well as by

ComStar's ROM agents, he still found time to participate in several of the local underground movements, including the building of People Unbound. A radical for hire.

"It must be him," he snapped. "Saul, you must look harder. Find the signs."

Always the peacemaker, Grendle steepled his hands calmly. "If they are there, Saul, we will find them. Haven't we been assured of that?"

Saul wished he felt as certain. He trusted their master, but even that great man admitted that his vision was second to another's. What if he, Saul Klinger, missed the sign? What if he failed?

"What if Arthur is the one, and others mistake their role?" he asked aloud. "So much might depend on him, if he is truly the next martyr."

"Then we will know what to do," Dan Grendle said, never doubting that all would work out in the end.

For once, Phillips was in agreement. "It can be arranged," he said. He worked the air in front of him with his big hands, as if clutching an invisible neck. "Find out, Saul. Tell us he is the one.

"And then, when the time is right and if we must, we shall kill young Arthur Steiner-Davion ourselves."

9

Here, A Place
Arc-Royal Defense Cordon
Lyran Alliance
13 July 3062

Trotting the last dozen meters down the enclosed gantry, eager to reach the main spaceport for the world of A Place, Victor Steiner-Davion caught up with his advance team and nearly pushed past them to grasp the outstretched left hand of Grand Duke Morgan Kell.

He was glad to see Morgan looking well. Morgan was a large man, tall and solidly built, and despite his seventy-six years, his dark hair and beard still showed only a few streaks of white. He carried himself proudly, and the only hint of infirmity was his empty, pinned-up right sleeve. Morgan rarely chose to wear the cybernetic replacement for the arm he'd lost to the bomb that had killed Victor's mother. Victor knew that Morgan's beard hid a few more scars, and that his heart carried the invisible wound of his wife's death as well. She had died in the same explosion that killed Melissa. Victor and Morgan shared the pain of that day, and they both knew who to blame for it.

"Good to see you, Morgan," Victor said. Morgan was a friend as well as a distant cousin, and Victor didn't want to simply launch into his darker reasons for requesting the meeting. "Thank you for making the trip."

Morgan's smile was a touch lopsided. "You *are* welcome on Arc-Royal, you know."

"By you, yes. But I have no Com Guard troops on Arc-Royal, and my 'invitation' allows me to visit only Com Guard garrison sites. A Place seemed like the best choice." Victor extended his arms, displaying his ComStar garb of powder-blue trousers and smock trimmed in red and gold, though he eschewed the hooded cloak. The insignia pinned to the uniform's high collar was bordered in gold to indicate his unique rank as Precentor Martial.

Morgan nodded. "It's wiser to choose your battles against your sister. Phelan will be sorry he missed you, though." Phelan Kell was Morgan's son and khan of the renegade faction of Clan Wolf. Morgan was helping Phelan's Wolves build a new home within the Arc-Royal Defense Cordon.

"You didn't bring him?"

"The First Kell Hound regiment is off Arc-Royal just now, and I didn't want to tempt Katherine any more than necessary. As I said, it is wiser to choose your battles."

Further conversation was interrupted by the approach of Tiaret, Victor's bodyguard. Her pale blue eyes seemed impossibly at odds with the dark skin that spoke of her Terran African ancestry, but that was not the first thing people noticed about her.

Tiaret was a Clan Elemental, a giant, muscular infantry warrior genetically bred to fight in powered armor. She towered over Morgan Kell by a good thirty centimeters and dwarfed Victor by another twenty-five. Her head was shaved except for a short queue braided with a red cord at the back of her head. Victor had captured and taken her as bondswoman during the campaign against Clan Smoke Jaguar. As was the way of the Clan that had produced her, she accepted her captor as her superior, despite the difference in their size and strength.

"The area is secure," she reported, her eyes always on the move, searching for any possible threat.

Victor smiled slightly. This concourse had been cleared in advance by Morgan's people. "If you knew Morgan Kell," he said, "you would never expect anything less."

He introduced them and was surprised when Tiaret enfolded Morgan's hand in both of her own and bowed in respect. Few people commanded that kind of reaction from her.

"What's this?" he asked. "I know you two haven't met."

Tiaret straightened. "Morgan Kell is not unknown as a warrior among the Smoke Jaguars," she said, further honoring Morgan by using his full name. "He and Jaime Wolf courageously defended the capital of the Draconis Combine against the Smoke Jaguars during the invasion."

"You honor me by remembering," Morgan said, having learned enough about Clan etiquette from his son to be properly decorous.

She smiled, flashing her large white teeth. Then she turned and began to lead the way down the main terminal hall, a woman of power and grace and pride. Morgan, Victor, and a phalanx of guards followed behind. The spaceport's air conditioning had the air rather chilly, but Victor warmed up as he walked.

"Are you staying long on A Place?" Morgan asked.

Victor briefly counted up the travel time left to him if he was to make his next destination as planned.

"Four days," he said. "Long enough to inspect the Com Guard's 312th Division and set up a new training regimen. I'll spend more time here on my way back." He exhaled, short and sharp. "I need to cultivate stronger relationships with my important officers. Word of Blake has too many knives at my throat right now. I don't want to lose any more good men to those fanatics."

Even more telling than the defections was the Word of Blake JumpShip that had dogged Victor's travels since leaving Tukayyid, an ominous shadow hovering just out of range.

"Where do you go next?"

"Pasig, where the Ninth Division is stationed. They're some of my best troops, but their loyalty is shaky. I'll spend a month there. Ultimately, I'll end up on Mogyorod with the 244th—the Prince's Men."

He smiled at the thought. "They're behind me, but they're green as new grass. They lost many experienced soldiers to the Blakists."

Victor cocked his head and looked curiously at Morgan. "I'm sure this is all very interesting, cousin, but why are we avoiding the subject of Katherine?"

Morgan smiled at Victor's directness. "You never were one for small talk," he said, smoothing his beard with his good hand. "I'm trying to make certain you're keeping your priorities straight."

Then he quickly held up his hand to fend off Victor's protests. "Now, don't take that as interference or insult. You said yourself that you have greater responsibilities now and that you're making this trip for reasons related to your position as Precentor Martial—not to your birthright as Victor Steiner-Davion."

Ahead, Victor could see the main terminal, where crowds of curious bystanders were being held back by security. Their combined voices sounded like a dull roar as he glanced around for the exit they would use to bypass the crowds. "Are you saying that I often gnaw off more than I can chew?"

"Your mouth has never been the problem. But you have been known to spread yourself so thin that DropShips could fly through the cracks."

Victor's cheeks warmed slightly at the rebuke, but he took no offense. It was true that he had a tendency to take on more than his share of responsibilities.

"Noted," he said. "So I tend to my Com Guard business and just ignore what my sister is doing?"

Morgan shook his head emphatically. He glanced at the nearby guards and pitched his voice lower. "Absolutely not. But you don't have the evidence you need to prove her involvement in Melissa's death, and she hasn't tripped over any skeletons. Yet."

Their security detail guided the pair toward a door marked STAFF ONLY. Tiaret ducked through the opening and then waited.

"Trust me," Morgan said. "I've been . . . watching."

Watching, Victor wanted to ask, or chipping away at the edges, hoping to find the inevitable crack in Katherine's armor? He knew better than to assume Morgan Finn Kell would be content to remain a mere spectator in the investigation.

"And so we wait?"

"We wait. We watch. We plan." Morgan's left hand balled into a tight fist. He stopped just short of the door and looked Victor in the eye. "And when the time is right, we act."

Victor nodded decisively. "Agreed. Katherine has made mistakes, and we're finding them. Soon we'll have enough to unmask that 'sterling character' of hers, though she may do the job herself, the way things are going. I'll fill you in on what's happening in the Draconis March and on Sun-Tzu Liao's damnable offensive against the Compact, which Katherine seems to be supporting."

Morgan nodded. "Good, but let's save that for tomorrow after your inspection. Tonight, you rest."

Victor smiled. It would be good to relax with Morgan and a few other friends among the Kell Hounds. "I'll try," he promised.

A flash of mischief showed in Morgan's brown eyes. "I think I've got a solution to that problem," he said, ushering Victor through the doors and past Tiaret's formidable presence.

Victor gasped as he walked into the next room, where

Omi Kurita stood waiting. Her eyes lit up with joy even as she bowed. *"Konnichi-wa,* Davion Victor-*san."*

"Omi!" Victor nearly shouted.

He stepped forward to take her hands, heedless of the others present. She wore silk pants and a short jacket, garments more appropriate for traveling than her usual kimonos or formal gowns.

"I thought you were on your way back to Luthien," he said.

She had left Tukayyid the week before his planned tour of the Lyran Alliance garrisons, bound for home. Victor had resigned himself to at least half a year without her, and he couldn't have been more elated to be proved wrong.

Omi drew him aside just enough for the illusion of privacy.

"I had a dream, Victor, on my way home. I dreamt that you had some need of me." She smiled sheepishly. "Perhaps I am foolish to attach so much importance to a dream, but then I received a message from my brother, Minoru. It said to remind you of your promise to visit Clan Nova Cat in your capacity as commanding general of the Star League Defense Force. The message had followed me down from Tukayyid, and that it arrived just then . . ."

She trailed off, knowing Victor would draw his own conclusions.

Victor refrained from any outward public display of emotion, but he let his happiness show in his eyes. "Theodore-*sama* isn't expecting you back on Luthien?"

"When I informed my father that I intended to visit the Alliance, he asked me to sample the current attitudes of Lyran worlds toward his election as the new First Lord of the Star League."

So like Theodore Kurita, Victor thought, to make arrangements for his daughter to continue her relationship with Victor while providing enough reason for her travels that conservative elements within the Combine could look the other way. What the Commonwealth called hypocrisy was considered saving face in the Combine's Asian culture.

"You were right, Morgan," Victor said, without taking his eyes off Omi. "You have found a perfect solution."

Omi nodded, her face carefully arranged in an unreadable mask. "Then perhaps we may find a solution to your earlier request."

"Earlier request?" Victor knew Omi was teasing him, but he wasn't sure about what. "I asked for something?"

"Isn't tomorrow a Tuesday?" she asked innocently.

Victor couldn't help an embarrassed glance at Morgan and Tiaret, despite the fact that they couldn't understand the allusion. He stepped back and managed an appropriately formal bow.

"You're right, Kurita Omi-*san*," he said with mock gravity. "Let us begin immediately to find that solution."

10

DropShip **Galedon Rose IV** *docked to JumpShip*
Aoi Shinju
Nadir Jump Point, Caldrea
Benjamin Military District
Draconis Combine
21 August 3062

Randal Kasagi died on the jump between the Luthien and Avon star systems.

He'd booked himself into a cramped cabin with two other men aboard a common-passenger DropShip, his berthmates as fictitious as his Kasagi persona. Then, he vanished by stepping into the refresher station, where he peeled away the colloidal at his eyefolds and from the corner of his mouth. After a close shave, he splashed cheap cologne liberally onto his burning cheeks and spilled some onto his T-shirt.

The assassin then changed into a wide-collared shirt and three gold chain-necklaces, an imitation Franklin-Rigel watch, and trousers a size too small in the waist.

After slicking his hair back, "Jerome Castro" emerged to hit the cramped ship's bars, where he failed miserably at picking up women.

At Avon's zenith jump point, it took only a few moments of code-slicing to doctor the records. Kasagi and Ario Nurel, his third persona, supposedly transferred to alternate passenger DropShips. The assassin, as Castro, transferred to a waiting JumpShip, which immediately tore through the fabric of time and space, taking him to the Braunton system. From there, he transferred to a second DropShip and a cabin with another fictional roommate who provided one more change of identity.

And so it went, every jump taking him another thirty light-years away from the capital of the Draconis Combine. Each abandoned persona left false trails, making him harder to trace, until he finally settled into his permanent traveling identity of Terrence Gloster, a minor corporate officer in the holovid entertainment industry. Gloster settled into second-class accommodations aboard the *Galedon Rose IV,* just like any other Lyran national returning to the Alliance.

His latest transfer took place far above the elliptic plane of Caldrea, this time to the JumpShip *Blue Pearl,* otherwise known as *Aoi Shinju.* Although the assassin was worth millions ever since he'd pulled off the assassination of Melissa Steiner-Davion, Gloster possessed only a small expense account that allowed no more than two drinks a night and the occasional movie. He decided to splurge, taking breakfast on the Tramp-class JumpShip's grav-deck restaurant. The meal cost him a week's entertainment budget.

Gravity was a welcome luxury during long space voyages, but it did not come cheap. He lingered over a light meal of reconstituted eggs and toast smeared with jellied quillar, a condiment popular in both halves of the Federated Commonwealth but considered a luxury here in the Draconis Combine. The light sitar music the restaurant insisted on playing in the background annoyed him, as it would annoy most Lyrans. He rented an electronic reader from the waitress and dialed for the latest Alliance newsfax, which he enjoyed while sipping hot, bitter coffee.

The assassin hated giving up half a year's worth of preparations, but he'd been forced to change course and seek out Omi Kurita elsewhere. He knew the risks of killing her on Luthien, but he'd been confident that his patience and planning and rehearsing would have resulted in a well-executed hit. Then, word came through his carefully arranged intelligence channels last month that Omi had turned back from Luthien toward the Lyran Alliance. She was on the world of Pasig now, soon to be traveling farther out along the border between the Alliance and Clan Jade Falcon. There was no word on when she would return, if ever.

His client had asked for quick results, and the assassin had never disappointed a client. Of course, that didn't count the time he'd been cheated out of half his fee and taken it out on his stingy patron.

There would be no problem like that here, he knew. Katrina Steiner had no lack of funds. He also knew that she would never try to cross him. Who knew what he would do, what he might say?

Biting into his toast and chewing slowly, Gloster savored the quillar's fruity taste as he scanned the headlines on his reader. He frowned for the benefit of anyone watching, though he really wanted to smile. Today's headlines confirmed the past several months of rumors and intel reports. Events in the Commonwealth and the Alliance were coming to a head, with reports of unrest and even violence on several worlds.

Perfect, he thought. Chaos was good for business. His business, anyway.

At least it usually was. An article about Solaris VII suggested that things might not be so rosy on the Game World. The news was several days old, but it detailed the complete breakdown of civil order when the planet's 'Mech jocks took to the streets in a BattleMech-scale brawl.

The battle had begun with a fight between the FedCom and Lyran champions, but now the entire city of Solaris was in the grip of the mob. The assassin had large investments on Solaris VII, one of the Inner Sphere's best places for hiding large sums of money. No doubt, the damage was costing him thousands—hundreds of thousands—of kroner. Then he read on to learn of the destruction of the Solaran Broadcasting Corporation facility, and right there, he wrote off his personal stock to the sum of a half-million kroner.

He shrugged mentally. It was never about having the money. Getting it was far more interesting.

In other news, he read of the rumblings of discontent on the important worlds of Kathil, Robinson, Kentares, Galax, and others. The Duke of Savonburg was being branded an iron-fisted dictator for the harsh measures he'd used to bring the world of Benedict to heel. And Nondi Steiner, general of the armies of the Lyran Alliance, had issued yet another statement that the Alliance Armed Forces was not—repeat not—responsible for the attack on Combine troops stationed in the Lyons Thumb.

That convinced the assassin that he might have a better chance of hitting Omi Kurita while she traveled within the Lyran Alliance. Though the Lyons Thumb planets technically belonged to the Lyrans, Theodore Kurita had occupied the area with peacekeeping forces back in '57, at the invitation of then-Prince Victor.

Earlier this month, Lyran troops—alleged Lyran troops, if you listened to denials by the Alliance military—had hit Combine positions on three of the Thumb's planets. Theodore, acting in his role as Coordinator rather than as First Lord of the Star League, yesterday had formally claimed the Lyons Thumb for the Combine. It was "for the region's safety and prosperity in the face of an increasingly unstable Federated Commonwealth," he was quoted as saying.

Commonwealth against Alliance. Alliance versus Draconis Combine. Calls for Victor to come home and replace his sister while Katrina worried about how to respond to Theodore's seizure of Lyran worlds. In this kind of spiraling chaos, an assassin could work with near impunity.

A warning alarm rang out three times in hard, blaring tones, distracting Gloster from his newsfax. The *Aoi Shinju* was about to make its jump from Caldrea, rending time and space to transport itself and a pair of docked DropShips into the Shirotori system.

He washed down one last bite of eggs with juice concentrate, set his fork down on his plate, and gripped the edge of the table. All around the small restaurant, other customers were also preparing themselves, while waiters and busboys found seats for safety.

Then it hit, like a punch into the soft tissue of his brain. The forward bulkhead of the restaurant seemed to stretch away into infinity as he sat motionless, frozen between ticks of the clock before being pulled after it in a mind-numbing rush. The next instant, the room snapped back into place, exactly as it had ever been— and yet not quite. Each person had, for the briefest moment, seen into the infinite, and for a few seconds they could not look at anything in the same way.

The assassin did not care for the feeling—that he'd been touched by something larger than himself. It sparked just the slightest feeling of paranoia, and made him want to look over his shoulder to see if he was being followed.

He didn't, though. Terrence Gloster was an old hand at corporate travel, and so the assassin allowed himself nothing more than straightening his tie and patting the side of his neck with a handkerchief. He calmly returned to perusing the morning news, knowing that he was now only one jump from the Free Rasalhague Republic.

And another thirty light-years closer to his target.

11

Bueller, Robinson
Draconis March
Federated Commonwealth
27 August 3062

While waiting for Arthur to arrive, Tancred Sandoval amused himself with some solo practice up and down the Battle Academy's fencing strip. As he lunged, shuffled, advanced and retreated, he soon broke a good sweat, which he also enjoyed thoroughly.

At the sound of the hall door banging open behind him, Tancred pulled himself to attention and slashed a salute to his imaginary opponent. Then he walked over to pick up a towel he'd left on the floor with his other things.

"You're late," he called out as he mopped the sweat from his face and his shaved scalp.

"No," said his father, which was not the voice he was expecting. "You are. The First Rangers are packing their kits for an extended training maneuver in the mountains. You're going with them."

Tancred spun around quickly. "I already have an appointment," he said, suspecting that he no longer did.

"Arthur has been summoned to the commandant's office for a performance review. He will be busy for some time, and then I expect there will be errands for him to run, including a meeting with Rand Weylan of Robinson Standard Battleworks."

Meaning that James Sandoval had arranged for General Mai Fortuna to intercept Arthur Steiner-Davion and use Academy business to waylay him. Tancred set his mask and sword on the floor and wrapped the soft towel around his neck, grasping each end in a hand.

"Very nice, Father. I'm certain Arthur appreciates your attention to his career."

James Sandoval crossed his arms over his chest. "Weylan plans to award new 6M *Enforcer III*s to Arthur's cadre lance at commencement next month—one for each of them. Mai will offer him an honorary commission with the First Robinson Rangers, which I think is a fine post for the young duke."

He glared at Tancred. "And what have you done for young Arthur, Tancred?"

"You mean, what haven't I done? I haven't filled his ears with poison about the Draconis Combine, for one thing. I've been trying to be his friend."

"You're trying to make him Victor's friend! Arthur may be Victor's brother, but that doesn't mean he has to kowtow to the ideas of that runt."

His father's blunt words and accusatory tone shattered the fragile peace father and son had maintained since Tancred's return to Robinson. They'd spent three months dancing around this issue, respecting each other's position despite their disagreement.

"Why not?" Tancred retorted. "You expect me to kowtow to *your* views, Father. The difference is that Victor is asking Arthur to make up his mind after considering all the facts. He's not trying to force his position on him."

"Is that what you think I've done?" James Sandoval

asked incredulously. "Forced my views on you and Arthur? Tancred, you understand our family's responsibilities in the Draconis March. My views should be your views. And if I've presented my case to Arthur, as a Duke of the Commonwealth and as a cadet in the armed forces under my aegis, then I call that duty."

In the back of his mind, Tancred understood, but he also believed it was wrong. "I call it manipulation," he said, instantly regretting the words.

"Manipulation?" His father seemed at a loss. He ran a hand over his bald pate and then down over what little hair he had left.

"Have I ever stood in your way or attempted to talk you out of following your own path? You left Robinson to attend the Sakura Academy rather than our own. Fine. You accepted a position with the Commonwealth's Interior Secretariat. Also fine, though I had hoped you would return and eventually take command of the Rangers. Then I stood by and watched as you were taken in by Victor, introduced to our enemies, and began to support a stance of disarmament."

"Nonaggression," Tancred corrected him.

"You think one does not lead to the other?" His father spoke in an angry tone, clipping off each word as if speaking to a child. "What is the foundation of any military victory?"

Tancred remembered building that pyramid as a child. It was one of the first lessons his father had taught him.

"Preparation," he said. "Followed by vigilance, anticipation, and finally direction."

The Duke nodded curtly. "Good. You haven't forgotten everything, then. And how many are undermined by a policy of nonaggression, Tancred? How many?" He barked out the last question as an order.

"All," Tancred said. His father's arguments were well-ordered, and Tancred had to struggle against thirty-odd years of training and indoctrination to refute them. He was sweating again, but resisted the urge to wipe at his face with the towel.

Damn it all, he thought. At some point, this had to end.

"Father," he began carefully, "what is the foundation of peace?"

"Peace! The lad talks about peace!" James Sandoval stared up into the vaulted ceiling of the practice room as though expecting some kind of divine assistance. "Peace," he said finally, "will be decided by the Archon-Princess. Not by me and certainly not by a man working for ComStar. Has Theodore Kurita declared a peace? Are his borders open? Are his militaries standing down?"

He paused, then delivered the final blow. "Is peace what the Dragon was thinking about when he claimed the Lyons Thumb for his own?"

Tancred knew all about Theodore annexing the Thumb and apparently ordering additional regiments into the area to secure it. A report had come to him directly from Victor, so Tancred saw little reason to doubt it. He knew his father couldn't miss the implications of these developments. Theodore had, in effect, moved a number of Combine units that were friendly to Victor's cause close by, should the exiled prince need them. It also drew public attention away from Victor, though it certainly wasn't helping Tancred's case.

"The Lyrans attacked Combine garrisons first," Tancred shot back. "And the way you and Arthur are inciting the people of the March, who can blame Kurita for feeling threatened? Not that I think Theodore will ever back off from the border or give up the Thumb now that he has it. Were I the Coordinator, I'd be thinking about reinforcing my line against the Commonwealth with another half-dozen regiments."

"If you were the Coordinator?" James Sandoval sputtered for a moment, so shocked he could hardly utter the words. His high forehead flushed. "You'd send another six regiments against our border, would you?"

"At least."

The Duke of Robinson took a moment to compose

himself, but the effort obviously cost him dearly. "I've never questioned your loyalty before, Tancred, but now I'm demanding it. Your weekly fencing matches with Arthur are finished. You are to stay away from him. You will avoid public appearances, except at my request. And you will join the Rangers immediately for a very long training exercise."

Tancred managed to maintain a semblance of calm by again patting his face with one end of the towel around his neck. "I'll take that under advisement."

"Damn you, Tancred! You and your Aunt Jessica. I don't care what your personal views are. I am the March Lord, and you will not undermine either my authority or my obligations."

Tancred had never seen his father in such a fiery rage. He knew he'd scored only cheap points today. The genie was out now, and putting it away again was not going to be easy.

"I have no desire to undermine your efforts, Father, and I do respect your position as March Lord," Tancred said, speaking the truth. "But I have to question your methods. You once told me that a man should accept advice but always make up his own mind. That's what I've done." He drew in a steady breath. "And the more you push, the more I'm convinced that I'm right and you're wrong."

"No one likes to be pushed," his father allowed, "especially a Sandoval. But you've no right to push back in my March—in my home, Tancred! You want me to back off? All right. Marry Yvonne Davion."

The words caught Tancred totally unprepared, and he was momentarily stunned into silence. "Marry Yvonne . . ."

James Sandoval relaxed slightly, clasping his hands behind his back in a semblance of military rest. "That's right. Marry Yvonne. Let the both of you abandon your ties to Victor and let me invest you as my deputy minister of the Draconis March."

Tancred allowed his anger to bleed away, trying to

adjust to his father's sudden change in attitude and tactics. "What would that solve?"

"Maybe nothing. Or perhaps everything. But I'll give you this. Prove to me that your position comes from your own reasoning and not Victor Davion's influence, and I'll support your choice of ambassador for a diplomatic mission to Luthien. I'll even let you go, provided Victor will not be present."

He paused and regarded his son calmly. "Public support, Tancred. Isn't that what you want? A brake on the anti-Combine movement?"

So there it was, all wrapped up with a pretty ribbon and dropped into Tancred's lap. Except that the strings tied around the package also bound him tightly to the Draconis March, separating him from those he supported beyond its borders.

It also placed limits on his father, no mean advantage. Should he accept? Would Yvonne? He and she had carefully avoided rushing into a more intimate relationship, despite how close they'd become. They wanted to see what, if anything, would develop naturally.

Tancred knew what Victor would say. Victor would agree to the terms, forfeiting their friendship and his relations with his sister in order to bring stability to his torn nation. But this wasn't Victor's call.

"No," he said quietly.

James Sandoval shook his head, frustration warring with disbelief for control of his proud features. "You stubborn pup." Coming from his father, the diminutive wasn't quite insulting, despite Tancred's age.

"You want it all, don't you? Well, life doesn't work that way, Tancred. Everyone has to make choices sometime. Or do you honestly believe you'll get a better offer?"

His father's arrogance fanned the coals of Tancred's anger, but somehow he found the will to control himself. "I'm surprised you would settle for me bedding Yvonne while Katherine is yet unwed. Why not broker a marriage with her?"

"I would," the duke said quickly, "if I thought she'd have you."

Tancred shook his head in disgust and gathered up his mask and sword. As he moved to circle around his father toward the door, James Sandoval reached out to touch his arm. "I'm just trying to do what's best for the Draconis March," he said quietly.

"What's best for everyone isn't war. But that's where you're heading."

Tancred sidestepped out of his father's grasp. "And I'm not going to follow you there. I won't denounce you—I would never do anything to hurt the family or the March. I hope you know that. But I'll be watching.

"And if you want a fight, I'll give you one myself."

12

Wylden Plateau
Mogyorod, Mellisia Theater
Lyran Alliance
11 October 3062

Victor overrode the *Daishi*'s automatic shutdown and sat back to allow the 'Mech's heat buildup to dissipate. Its computer was still operating under the simulation protocols, but the 'Mech's alarms were silenced, and cautionary lights began to wink out. A strange silence settled in, and his breath rasped harshly in the tight confines of his neurohelmet now that the sounds of battle had ceased.

He shivered and dialed down the coolant flow to his vest. Like most MechWarriors, he wore only shorts, boots, and cooling vest in the cockpit, which could become like a furnace during combat. But now that the temperature was finally dropping, the sweat still covering his body sent a chill through him.

Eight warriors dead, Victor tallied—simulated dead,

and most of them tank crew. Thirteen more out of play with crippled BattleMechs. Victor had nine functioning 'Mechs left to his assault force, and considering the odds, he was lucky to have them.

The Com Guard's 244th Division had split unequally, giving Victor one regular Level III battalion against two green commands, supported by armor auxiliaries only for this exercise. He had left a string of BattleMech corpses and gutted armored vehicles across Mogyorod's Wylden Plateau, taking down two enemy forces for every one of his. A good day's work.

"Do you concede, Demi Shakov?"

His opposite number today was Demi-Precentor Rudolf Shakov, commander of the Sticks and Stones battalion. He was a promising officer, and one of the few Com Guard military commanders Victor had met who possessed a sense of humor.

"I still have a functioning leg actuator, sir." Shakov's voice came over the battlefield comm system without the faintest trace of distortion, as befitted a member of the caretakers of interstellar communication. "Limp over here, and I'll kick you right in the ammo bin."

"Thank you, Rudolf, but I'd rather practice my long-range sniping. Gamma team, locate the Demi's *Exterminator*."

Through his ferroglass shield, Victor watched three of the 'Mechs under his command begin to lumber forward.

"All right, sir, you win. I would prostrate myself at your feet, if I weren't there already."

Victor laughed, loud enough for the voice-activated mic to pick it up and let everyone know their Precentor Martial was not all work. Normally, he would have ordered the controllers to release his men first so they could form up and accept the dignified surrender of the opposing force.

Today, as a way of showing his satisfaction with both sides, he did it differently. "Base, this is the Precentor Martial," he said. "Simulated fire exercise is finished. Please release all 'Mechs. Repeat, all."

It took only a moment for the computers to download the security codes that released everyone from simulated damage. Around the plateau, the giant machines that had been frozen walked again. A few that had fallen over after losing power picked themselves up with the kind of majestic grace only possible for hundreds of tons of animated metal.

"So where did I go wrong, Martial?"

Victor had taken to shortening the longer Com Guard ranks, including his own. He hoped that it would make him seem more accessible to his men.

"We'll hold a briefing back at base, Demi Shakov," he said for the benefit of all those listening in on open frequencies.

Then Victor opened his personal channel to Shakov, wanting to give the man a heads-up. "Mostly, Rudolf, it was a lot of little choices that added up over time," he said. "You had too many laser-equipped machines, which put you at a disadvantage during the pitched battles as heat wore you down. You missed a good defensive spot about an hour ago that would have hurt me desperately. And you were a bit too eager to take me on personally. Nothing done today that another few months of training can't fix, though."

"Will the Prince's Men have your company that long?" Shakov asked. "You'll winter over with us?"

Winter over. Another of the long-outdated military terms that had survived the centuries since mankind first began spreading outward from Terra.

"I'm not too concerned about snowstorms," Victor said. "Aren't the next few months Mogyorod's summer?" Besides, a DropShip couldn't be grounded by snow in any case.

"Stranger things have happened," Shakov assured him. "I once thought it would be a cold day in hell before ComStar gave up Terra."

"We haven't given up Terra," Victor corrected. "Word of Blake has been lucky that ComStar has put other priorities ahead of them. But it's a short list. One day soon, Rudolf, the Com Guard will be called on to reclaim the birthworld of the Inner Sphere."

"My Prince," Demi-Precentor Shakov said, resurrecting Victor's lost title, "that will be a fine day indeed."

Victor's satisfaction with the day lasted only moments after his arrival back at the estate he shared with Omi Kurita. It had been loaned to them by Countess Rudmillia Drake, whose summer home it was.

Though walled, its open grounds had presented a number of security concerns. Every door and window of the three-story mansion was already tied into a top-flight security system, which Victor's people made even better with access to ComStar's premium technology.

It was only its proximity to the spaceport and to the main garrison post for the Prince's Men that persuaded Victor to accept the loan of the estate despite any complications it might pose. The countess assured Victor that Mogyorod was too remote for Katherine—not Katrina— to inflict any kind of lasting punishment for her courtesy.

Approaching the door, he first noticed an unnatural tension in the acolytes standing guard at the main gates. Nothing alarming in itself, but it was a promise of unsettling news afoot. The servants also appeared more attentive than usual. Dayhon Sur, the estate's headman, intercepted Victor before he could make any inquiries.

"The drawing room, sir," the headman said.

Dayhon preceded Victor, leading him under the grand stairs to a carpeted short gallery rather than going by way of the tiled foyer.

Victor heard the sound of women's voices ahead. It was Omi and one other who he thought might be crying. When he and Dayhon reached the drawing room, the headman placed one hand against the half-open door, briefly preventing Victor from entering.

"I will bring refreshments at once, sir," he said just a touch too loudly, giving those in the room advance notice of Victor's arrival.

Victor nodded. Dayhon knew his role perfectly, and

he had likely saved both Victor and the two women some awkward moments.

The two women stood as he entered the room. For once, Omi Kurita was not the first person to catch his eye, and he nearly collided with an end table as he recognized the room's other occupant.

"Isis?"

"Victor," Isis Marik said with a hesitant smile. Her voice was a near-whisper. "Thank you for having me here."

Isis Marik, daughter of Captain-General Thomas Marik of the Free Worlds League, had been expected, though not for another month. Omi had warned Victor of Isis's plans to visit now that Sun-Tzu had abruptly broken their engagement and left the young woman without a home. Victor had no idea why Sun-Tzu had behaved so cruelly or what trouble between Isis and the Captain-General kept her from returning to the Free Worlds League.

It wasn't her early arrival that surprised him, though, but her emotional state. She was obviously trying to hold back tears, but her eyes were already red and puffy from crying.

The look in Omi's eyes warned him not to make any immediate comment, so he circled around the edge of a long sofa and gestured them back to their seats. He sat down next to Omi, with Isis on the other side of her.

"You're early," he said, at a loss for the right words.

Isis nodded. "Many of my personal effects won't catch up until next month," she said in a small voice. "I used a shuttle wherever I could and caught the occasional outbound fast transport, which let me bypass the delays at a few ports of call."

But why was she here at all? Victor wondered, his gaze turning idly to the large bulletproof window that offered a view of the estate grounds. Why not return to Atreus in the Free Worlds League? Everyone knew that Isis's betrothal to Sun-Tzu had been a political match, and the marriage had been postponed many times.

"Your effects?" he asked, still trying to be polite.

"I'm traveling with the contents of an entire estate, I'm afraid. Whatever followed me off Sian is strung out behind me over several hundred light-years. There was no time for an organized—or dignified—retreat."

Omi patted Isis's shoulder reassuringly, her warm manner compensating for Victor's stiff bearing. "Isis came here directly by way of the Commonwealth and Rasalhague," she told him.

"You didn't visit the Free Worlds League first?" Victor asked, not sure what to make of that.

Isis shook her head. "The Capellan Confederation had become my home, Victor." She cast her eyes down as if ashamed. "Or at least I thought so. I've lived within its borders for the past five years. And even before then, I enjoyed visiting there to see my fiancé. I thought I knew it—I thought I knew *him*."

She was not the first person to fall into that trap. "Isis, you'd know I was lying if I offered you my condolences," he said. He knew he should feel more compassion for the bereft young woman, but had trouble imagining that she was actually upset over a breakup with Sun-Tzu Liao. He thought she should rejoice, like someone who's just learned a tumor was operable.

"I don't expect you to understand my life, Victor. Not when I don't either. But I still appreciate the sentiment." She sighed heavily. "I just didn't think it could all come crashing down in the mere blink of an eye."

Victor remembered how his own life had fallen apart when he returned from Clan space to find that Katrina had usurped the throne. At least it was Yvonne, his little sister, who'd been the one to break it to him.

"Sun-Tzu can be cruel," he said.

"I knew that. But sometimes he listened to what I had to say. And I truly thought he cared for me as I . . ."

"As you did for him?" Omi said. "Perhaps he did. Or he did as much as he was able. But his failure does not lessen your feelings, and it should not call your own judgment into question."

Victor watched as Omi's soothing presence calmed the distraught Isis Marik. He caught himself shaking his head, amazed that Sun-Tzu, with his treacherous nature, could ever have earned this woman's love. Of course, that was thirty-two years of prejudice talking. When it came down to it, he actually knew so little about Sun-Tzu Liao that he often had a tendency to dismiss him. It was a habit that had already cost Victor once.

Yet, knowing Sun-Tzu on more intimate terms had apparently not cushioned Isis's fall.

"Should we let your father know you have arrived safely?" he asked.

Isis gave a short, sharp laugh, on the verge of tears again. "What does my father care for my safety? Or anything about me, now that he has his new family and a new son to follow him?"

She paused and drew in a shaky breath. "I'm sorry. I just feel like I've lost everything. I didn't know where to go, and I've been imagining Kali Liao's assassins hiding in every shadow. Thugees under the bed."

She hiccuped a hysterical laugh at her own foolishness and looked at Omi. "You were so kind to me at the Star League conference, you and Dr. Lear. Your offer, to visit any time . . . it just seemed the only option left. Especially when I know that my father truly does not want me back."

"Of course," Omi said kindly. "He may surprise you, eventually. Fathers usually do. But you were certainly right to avoid that situation for now."

For a moment, caught up in Isis's pain and Omi's obvious concern, Victor considered breaking the news to Isis that the current Captain-General was, in fact, not her father. It had been almost five years since Victor had learned the truth. The Thomas Marik sitting on the League throne was an impostor, resurrected by ComStar after the real Thomas disappeared and was presumed dead.

Unfortunately, the ComStar records of how the switch was performed had been lost during the recent schism—

if they had ever existed. But Victor still had the DNA tests. It was one of the few secrets he kept entirely to himself. Not even Omi knew. If the fake Thomas Marik were not such a fine ruler, a man needed by the Inner Sphere as well as the League, Victor would have denounced him years before.

And however much pain Isis was in, this was not a decision to be made lightly. Instead, Victor found himself sincerely offering the hospitality of his home.

"Such as it is," he said. "We'll be here for another few months, perhaps into February, and then it's the long swing back through the Alliance and to Tukayyid."

"You will remain with us for as long as you desire," Omi promised.

Isis hugged Omi with a nearly desperate intensity. "Thank you, Omi. Kurita Omi-*san*," she added quietly, "I thank you."

Isis stood and walked over to hug Victor and Omi together. "Thank you, my friends. My only friends."

"*Do itashimashite,*" Omi said, laughing. "You are welcome, Isis."

Victor glanced at Omi over Isis's head. Her eyes thanked him wordlessly, and she awarded him a smile of approval for the way he had helped Isis feel more at home. Victor tipped a wink to her.

He turned back to Isis and patted her hand in a gesture of comfort. "Don't worry, Isis," he said. "Everything will be all right."

It would be perfect.

The assassin had temporarily commandeered the estate's utility building as a command post, reaching it via the sewers of a maintenance tunnel within the estate walls. Security was much stronger at the door than on the tunnel entrance, which looked like nothing more than a common manhole cover. So long as he didn't try to leave yet and there was no problem with the plumbing or the mansion's electrical service, there was little to worry about.

Most secure areas had at least one flaw. It all depended on how far you needed to penetrate. Today, on a simple reconnaissance, that wasn't much. He was just here to set up a laser-augmented listening device, pinging the invisible beam off the large drawing-room window, turning it into a huge microphone as the glass rattled ever so slightly from voices inside the room. Variations in the laser were then easily translated back into sounds, recorded on a hidden receiver while playing over the headphones he wore.

The addition of Isis Marik to the household was unexpected, and he would have to factor it into his plans. Still, the assassin knew that Isis's arrival would provide more opportunities than difficulties. It inserted a new variable into the usually structured lives of Victor Steiner-Davion and Omi Kurita—a modicum of chaos within which the assassin could work.

Omi Kurita would go to certain lengths to make Isis feel at home, for example, if the girl was really so distraught. Favorite foods. Household items. Maybe a type of flower . . .

No. No flowers this time, even if given the chance. Victor's people were good, and they would not let the assassin slip through with that kind of trick again. It would also alert Victor that he was nearby, if his security forces tumbled to the assassin's preparation.

The assassin hadn't forgotten that the only time he'd been captured was by Victor. If he were captured again, Victor would certainly not make the same mistake of leaving his mother's killer alive long enough to escape.

Isis would develop her own routine, one that might provide him access to the mansion. And unless Victor specifically requested additional security, the personal bodyguards attending him and Omi would now be spread among three royals instead of two. By that little fact alone, the assassin's opposition was reduced by nearly twenty percent.

Sewers, servants, suppliers—there were always ways inside.

And back out again.

13

Shoving the BattleMech's throttle to its limit, Arthur Steiner-Davion ran his new *Enforcer III* forward at a dangerous eighty-seven kilometers per hour. Each pounding step jarred the cockpit of the fifty-ton 'Mech, and the diamond-cut tread of its feet barely kept their grip on the street's ferrocrete surface.

Three-story barracks, home to the infantry trainees at Robinson's Battle Academy, pinned him in tight. One uncontrolled skid and Arthur would smash the *Enforcer* straight into the side of a building. He shoved that danger into the back of his mind as he continued forward, eager for the fight.

Today was no simulation.

House Kurita was actually attacking Robinson!

By arriving at a system pirate point—a perilous maneuver that allowed a JumpShip captain to bring his ship closer to a planet than if he used one of the two standard jump points—the Kurita force had managed to land unopposed. Coming out of nowhere, the attack had caught the planetary defenses totally off guard. Arthur was still not sure why the Dracs were doing this; there'd been no new hostilities between the Combine and the FedCom. But now wasn't the time to wonder about that; now was the time to act.

Reports on the attack had been short and conflicting, ranging from one battalion to three regiments of 'Mechs and more DropShips sighted. In Bueller, at the Academy, cadet MechWarriors had mounted whatever training machines they could—first come, first to fight.

A pair of *Chameleon*s, some older *JagerMech*s, even an antiquated *Mackie* with a single working PPC were lumbering around. Arthur was fortunate that his new *Enforcer III* had arrived and was coded for his access only. He wouldn't be left behind. And as his threat-detection systems flashed in warning, he took a firm grip on the controls and pushed everything but the looming battle from his mind.

The *Enforcer*'s computers could not quite get a lock on the firefight ahead. Two 'Mechs, maybe three. No—two! The computer finally managed a lock, and their identification was painted onto Arthur's heads up display. One was the gold triangle of a friendly 'Mech from the Robinson Rangers, tagged as a 9J *Nightstar*. The other, a bright, flashing red, was ID'd as an old CRK-5003 *Crockett*.

Firing his leg-mounted jump jets, Arthur channeled plasma from his fusion engine into the thrusters' reaction chambers. The *Enforcer* leapt skyward on fiery trails, crouching in midflight to present a smaller airborne target. At the apogee of his jump, the *Enforcer*'s computer tagged several more 'Mechs fighting a few streets over on the Academy grinder. Serving as a parade ground and staging area, the grinder was a large, ferrocrete slab of paved ground, a half-kilometer wide and nearly twice as long.

Arthur dropped in on its far side to pin the *Crockett* between himself and the *Nightstar*. The *Enforcer*'s alarms shrilled as the *Crockett* twisted to fire its weapons on both him and the *Nightstar*.

The *Crockett* was painted a flat black, showing no emblem but House Kurita's stylized dragon coiling against a red disk. What the 'Mech lacked in decoration it made up in offensive capability. Its paired large and small lasers, twin short-range missile packs, and medium-class autocannon quickly dealt out plenty of damage.

The *Enforcer III* was no soft touch either. It was among the newest redesigns of old Federated Commonwealth favorites, mounting an extended-range large laser and an ultra-class eighty-millimeter autocannon. Against that weapons package and the assault-class *Nightstar*'s twin gauss rifles and a particle cannon, the *Crockett* never truly stood a chance.

With his weapons hot and his targeting cross hairs already burning the deep gold of a solid lock, Arthur rode out the slight tremor as one of the *Crockett*'s lasers scored a deep, molten welt into his left side. Its six short-range missiles peppered the armor over both the *Enforcer*'s legs and its left arm, but did no serious damage. Arthur eased into his own salvo, toggling for full weapons and giving his new 'Mech its first real operational test.

Its large and small lasers speared scarlet light directly into the *Crockett*'s turret-bodied chest, melting off armor in molten streams. His autocannon drilled depleted-uranium slugs across the right shoulder, walking a line of destruction into the side of the *Crockett*'s head as armor flew off in fragments and splinters. Not quite enough to bore through and savage the cockpit, but certainly enough to shake up the Drac MechWarrior.

What Arthur started, the *Nightstar* finished. Manmade lightning crackled from its particle projection cannon, scouring armor off the *Crockett*'s right arm and clearing the way for twin gauss hits in its right flank. The large nickel-ferrous slugs caved in the 'Mech's entire right side, buckling armor and boring deep into the skeleton. At least one slug impacted over the missile bin, crushing fuel cells and rupturing the explosive payloads of several missiles.

Whether it was a stray spark or the incredible pressure on the impacted payload, something set off a chain reaction, and the ammunition exploded in hellish fury. A second but no less violent eruption followed as the conflagration also lit off the *Crockett*'s autocannon ammunition. The force of the detonations pounded through the 'Mech's internals, rupturing joints as fiery claws ripped at seams and welds. One arm flew off, propelled by the explosion straight through the wall of a nearby building. Then the fusion reactor collapsed, releasing its plasma in a raging inferno that ate through the rest of the 'Mech before erupting outward in an uncontrolled fireball.

The final explosion rocked both surviving 'Mechs back several steps. A dark cloud lifted over the remains of the *Crockett*. Arthur watched it roil skyward, breathing shallowly for the few seconds it took his heat sinks to shunt aside his engine's heat buildup. A cool fighter, the *Enforcer*. Arthur licked a hint of sweat from his upper lip and decided that he liked this machine.

"Are you going to stand there all day?" he heard someone say over the commline. "There's a battle going on."

Tancred!

Arthur turned his *Enforcer* around toward the *Nightstar,* which was already heading for the grinder's eastern exit. The traditional red-and-black camouflage pattern, exactly like the *Enforcer*'s, would not disguise the *Nightstar* in any terrain, but it wasn't meant to.

Arthur throttled up to a walk and only now noticed that the force of the *Crockett*'s explosion had ruptured two of his heat sinks. He wrote them off as nonessential. The *Enforcer III* had heat-dissipation ability to spare.

"Don't hold that sluggard machine back on my account," Arthur said. He could almost double the *Nightstar*'s best speed.

"Said the rabbit to the turtle. Come off my right, Arthur, and don't stray too far."

Arthur bridled. True, he was still a cadet for another seven days, and Tancred, who held the permanent post of colonel within the Robinson Rangers, commanded here. But Arthur thought he deserved more respect than blind orders.

"I don't need your protection, Tancred."

Working his foot pedals, Arthur veered off, preparing to use his jump jets to sail over the intervening buildings and hit the grinder with weapons blazing.

"Maybe I need yours, Arthur. That *Crockett* scored two lucky hits and blistered my right side. I'd like you to guard my flank. Together we'll deal out a lot more damage to the Dracs than either of us could alone."

Arthur throttled up, almost running past the *Nightstar* before he cut back. "All right," he said. "I'm in." He positioned himself off Tancred's side. The humanoid *Enforcer* stood almost at a height with the powerful but squat *Nightstar*.

"When I jumped, I saw some hard fighting on the grinder," he said. "I'll take right lead as we go in. Try to keep up, okay?"

"Sounds good," Tancred replied. "Keep to a walk, and you'll have a hard time shaking me."

Besides serving as the Academy's parade grounds and staging area, the grinder was also the place where the entire Academy would be called to fall out for morning exercises and the occasional ten-kilometer run.

Today it was hosting a far more grueling exercise. A lance of black-painted Combine 'Mechs held the ground. They had pinned a Ranger *Watchman* against the reviewing stands and were savaging it with concentrated fire. A *Blackjack*, painted the blue and red colors of the Battle Academy, already lay in ruin at one edge of the blackened hardtop. It was missing both arms, a leg, and much of its torso.

"Give that Ranger some help," Tancred ordered the instant their HUDs painted the picture for them. He fired one gauss rifle and his energy cannon, targeting the assault-class 11-A *Cyclops* first.

Arthur targeted the *Whitworth,* a smaller 'Mech and the enemy lance's only missile-support 'Mech. He was betting that the *Kintaro* would remain fixed on the *Watchman,* though the old 9R *Panther* presented a wild card.

A lance of scarlet energy from his large laser punched the *Whitworth* square in the back, getting its attention but failing to hit any critical equipment. The enemy 'Mech rounded on him, swinging first at the *Enforcer*'s shoulder and then at the hip. Arthur toggled in his autocannon, shrugging off flight after flight of the *Whitworth*'s long-range missiles as he returned fire with a mixture of energy lances and high-velocity metal.

Arthur kept track of Tancred and stayed close enough to help cover the *Nightstar*'s damaged side. He began to run a switchback pattern in an attempt to keep the Kurita forces guessing and hold them in place, while the *Nightstar* paced him at just under sixty kilometers per hour.

The *Cyclops* ignored them, finishing off the *Watchman* while the other three 'Mechs advanced to mix it up on the hardtop grinder.

The Kurita *Panther,* truly a signature design for the Combine, fired its long-reaching PPC, which lashed out repeatedly against Tancred's assault 'Mech. Armor sloughed away, but Tancred ignored the damage and instead spent two of his precious gauss slugs to smash gaping wounds into the *Whitworth.*

Arthur grinned savagely and sent a long burst from his ultra-class autocannon, pounding through one of those rents and digging into the ammunition bin that fed the *Whitworth*'s long-range launchers. Like the *Crockett,* the *Whitworth* suddenly ceased to exist in any recognizable form when a full ton of missiles ripped through the support 'Mech.

With the *Cyclops* finally turning to face the new danger, Arthur worked over the *Panther*. He all but ignored the *Kintaro*, which closed in at better than eighty klicks per hour to bring its shorter-range lasers and missiles into play.

At the last moment, Arthur called out, "Jog left!" and triggered his jump jets for a short hop sideways, displacing himself from the charging attack. A glance at his HUD showed that Tancred had managed a quick turn to cover Arthur's flank, putting himself in the way of the *Kintaro*.

The *Kintaro* pilot tried to swing back in at Arthur, not wanting to face off with Tancred's ninety-five-ton assault machine. He made a high-speed pivot on one foot, splitting the difference between Arthur and Tancred.

Attempting to fire his lasers and missiles and then pivot again, the enemy MechWarrior overreached his ability. A second of inattentiveness, a small hesitation in reflexes; that's all it took. The *Kintaro*'s metal-shod foot skidded on the black ferrocrete, hyperextending the hip joint. Stumbling gracelessly, the fifty-five-ton 'Mech fell to its knees and then came down hard on its wide-flanged left hip. It slid along another hundred meters of the grinder, sending up sparks and tearing into the previously smooth surface.

Twisting at his torso, Arthur pinned the fallen 'Mech with a blistering salvo of lasers and autocannon, and almost welcomed the heat surge that followed. Tancred added to the Kurita warrior's misfortune, saving his gauss slugs but flaying off almost a full ton of armor with his PPC and medium lasers. Then, he lifted one cloven metal foot and smashed it down into the *Kintaro*'s bulbous head, turning the cockpit into a tangled ruin of metal and flesh.

"Not too sporting," Arthur said.

"Wrong career or wrong world," Tancred shot back. "Take your pick. Now let's—Arthur!"

The warning was a second too late. The *Cyclops* had already delivered a gut-punch with its gauss rifle and the *Panther* a cerulean stream of energies from its PPC. With a violent shudder that wrenched one control stick from Arthur's hand, the *Enforcer III* doubled over and went down in a sprawling slide.

Arthur's body was thrown against his restraining harness, then his head snapped back against his seat. Only the bulky protection of his neurohelmet saved him from more than strained neck muscles.

Arthur relished the pain. It told him he was still alive. He glanced at the information his warning lights were giving him, and then began to maneuver himself back to standing.

"Nicked the gyro, but I'll live," he called to Tancred.

He swallowed, tasted blood, and noticed that his tongue was throbbing. Arthur shut off the pain and levered the *Enforcer* back to its feet, telling himself he wasn't about to bleed to death from a bitten tongue. It wasn't until he was up again that he realized Tancred hadn't responded.

Tancred Sandoval, it seemed, had gone to war.

Though the *Cyclops* and the *Panther* outweighed his *Nightstar* by thirty tons, the match was close to dead even. The two Combine 'Mechs were both older designs, lacking the true offensive power of newer assault 'Mechs.

Arthur watched the *Nightstar* wade into the best the two BattleMechs could hurl at it. Tancred went after the lighter *Panther* first, firing with one gauss rifle and then the other, the nickel-ferrous slugs a silvery blur. Next came his pulse lasers, while his particle cannon lashed out with brilliant energies.

The *Panther* reeled back under the furious onslaught, keeping to its feet through sheer determination as the pilot fought for his life. Fire belched from a rent in the 'Mech's torso cavity as the shielding on its fusion engine failed.

Tancred never let up, even after losing one of his gauss rifles when an arm dropped away. He punched a new gauss slug through the *Panther*'s lower torso, the deformed projectile crushing the gyroscope housing before exiting through the rear armor onto the grinder. The *Panther* collapsed like a puppet suddenly unstrung.

The *Cyclops* backed off, trying to put distance between itself and the rampaging assault 'Mech. If the *Nightstar* could withstand the best both Combine BattleMechs had been able to throw at it, the *Cyclops* didn't have a chance one on one. With a better movement curve, it might avoid that kind of point-blank slugging match.

But Arthur wasn't out of the fight yet. He ran the *Enforcer* across the grinder at his top speed to corral the *Cyclops* against the fortified wall of a barracks building. His front armor was more memory than metal, but damned if Tancred would be left to stand up to the Drac by himself.

The *Cyclops* swung around, turning a blind side to Tancred while its torso-mounted gauss rifle fired on the *Enforcer*. Arthur sidestepped just out of reach, then poured a long salvo of eighty-millimeter slugs into the *Cyclops*'s flank while his large laser burned an angry weal along the assault machine's leg.

On the other side, Tancred devoted two gauss slugs to shattering the last of the armor protecting the *Cyclops*'s chest. Orange flames licked out, doused only for a moment by the grayish-green eruption of a damaged heat sink.

Then Arthur's laser stabbed again into the rent, spearing through the engine. Golden fire blossomed but was quickly extinguished as dampening fields dropped into place, shutting down the engine but saving the 'Mech from a fiery death.

The MechWarrior wasn't so fortunate. A few moments later, Tancred's final gauss shot angled up into the *Cyclops*'s head, punching through the ferroglass shield and straight through the bowl-shaped armor dome that usually protected the MechWarrior. Tancred couldn't have planned a better shot even if he'd lined up against a shut-down target.

The *Cyclops* shook the ground when it fell, with a tremor Arthur felt even inside his shielded cockpit. His neck ached and his tongue hurt like hell, but he couldn't keep from grinning. He shifted position and saw that Tancred's *Nightstar* didn't look so bad, considering all it had come through. Then he saw something else.

"I thought you said the *Crockett* opened up your right side," he said in disbelief. "You said you needed my help."

Tancred sounded tired, but not remorseful. "I said *maybe* I needed your help. And that we'd do more damage together than alone. You're going to complain?"

Arthur looked back over the grinder. Four 'Mechs lay in ruins—a full Kurita lance. Plus the *Crockett*. And Arthur could claim the killing blow on two of them, plus assists on all but the *Panther*.

"No," he said, his grin returning full force. "Not today."

=== 14 ===

Avalon City, New Avalon
Crucis March
Federated Commonwealth
3 November 3062

The console screen was still awash with salt-and-pepper static, and its speakers blared a test-pattern series of tones that set Katrina's teeth on edge. She tapped the floor of the palace communications center with one impatient foot, glaring at the ComStar demi-precentor and his excuses for the delay in getting the HPG link up and running.

Katrina did not like to be kept waiting. She was the most powerful person in the whole Inner Sphere, wasn't she? If anything, others should be kept waiting for *her*. Her time was precious, and there weren't enough hours in the day to do all that was necessary to run her two Inner Sphere empires.

Unfortunately, waiting for this real-time hyperpulse link to be established was necessary. Katrina calmed her irritation and distracted herself by glancing around the near-deserted communications center. It looked more like a war room, with monstrous video screens dominating the walls and rows of computer stations ready to handle any number of incoming data streams. How often had it actually served as a supplemental war room under her father—or her brother?

Too often, she thought. War was a risky tool of state requiring that you stake your success or failure on the skills of others. Katrina preferred to maintain personal control whenever possible. On the rare occasions when it wasn't, she made sure to keep a hand in to tip the scales in her direction at crucial moments.

The static was finally replaced by a test image of a brilliant, two-pointed star set against a blue field: the ComStar logo.

"The final link has been established, Highness," the demi-precentor said. He bowed, his hooded cloak hanging loose on his spare frame. "I will wait outside."

As if that guaranteed any real privacy, Katrina thought. She was sure ComStar would provide her brother with a report of everything said if they could. Well, it wouldn't be easy. Richard Dehaver had assured her that this new cryptographic system would work. He'd better be right.

"It will work," Dehaver said, as if reading her mind. "My people personally carried the various crypto keys to Tharkad and several other important worlds. Once you activate the encoding, what passes between HPG stations is indecipherable."

And it was even more than that. This new system would make possible real-time transmissions between New Avalon and Tharkad, the two capital worlds of the Commonwealth and the Lyran Alliance, and thus allow her to rule both realms from one palace.

There was so much to keep track of, so many problems to handle. The riots on Solaris VII had flared up again, requiring a firmer hand to keep the pro-Davion populace in line. And Dehaver's agents were reporting new pockets of discontent in the Isle of Skye, as well as vocal condemnation of her leadership among members of the Lyran nobility.

Lyran! The same nobles she'd always relied upon as her primary supporters. They'd be singing a different tune if she were back in Tharkad, and now this new HPG system would put her there any time she wished. Katrina had invested billions in ComStar over the past couple of years to finance this "command circuit" of HPG stations linking her two capitals.

Most worlds had only a single HPG station, whose equipment could instantly transmit data to another such station as much as fifty light-years away. Then, the dish at the receiving station had to be swung away and pointed toward the next station, and thus was the message relayed from world to world. Relatively cost-effective, but inefficient.

To remedy that, Katrina had placed *two* HPG stations on every world between Tharkad and New Avalon. One station could receive data and transfer it to the other station via conventional transmission, then the data would be rebroadcast with a delay of mere microseconds, crossing hundreds of light-years in the blink of an eye.

That was an oversimplification, of course, but it was as much as Katrina needed to understand. Victor probably knew more about the technical aspects of such things these days. She pursed her lips, blowing a kiss to her poor brother playing with his war toys out on lonely Mogyorod.

She smiled at the thought. Victor would soon have other problems to distract him. How close was the assassin to Omi Kurita? A month? A week? A day?

The console screen finally transferred over to live video, and Katrina waited to see the face of Nondi Steiner. Instead, the screen displayed the visage of a strong-featured man.

He gave a slow bow of the head across the star-spanning connection. "Archon-Princess Steiner," he said, diplomatically omitting the last half of her surname and identifying her more strongly with the Lyrans.

"Precentor Tharkad," Katrina said coolly, hiding her surprise.

Gavin Dow, the First Circuit member who represented ComStar's interests in the Alliance, had recently been after Katrina to extend ComStar's contract to run the Lyran HPG stations. Today, he wore a professional business suit rather than the usual ComStar trappings.

"I didn't realize you were on Tharkad," she said. The First Circuit had recently set up its new command center on Tukayyid, protected by her brother's forces.

"I am attending to ComStar business in your Alliance, Archon. However, should you ever wish to reach me on Tukayyid, you can always do so with your new command circuit of HPGs."

Katrina felt a rush of anger. ComStar had linked Tukayyid into the new network? She knew that any world within fifty light-years of the circuit could do so easily, but Tukayyid would require several relay stations, and Dehaver hadn't reported any new ones being constructed. That was valuable information to simply hand over to her, which meant Dow wanted something.

"And does your business include interrupting a high-priority transmission?" she asked.

"No, Highness." His eyes narrowed at her abrupt manner. "It seemed a fortunate coincidence, and I thought perhaps we could talk."

"About what, Precentor Tharkad?"

"Before Theodore Kurita took over the Lyons Thumb, the ComStar resources on those worlds were under my administration, and I am still concerned for their safety. Especially now that the Coordinator has pulled certain regiments back from the region."

"Why would he do that?" she asked.

"You have read reports of the Alshain Avengers and their attack on Clan Ghost Bear, I trust."

She had. Three weeks before, the Combine's four Avenger regiments had gone rogue to attack their old homeworld of Alshain, now under Ghost Bear dominion. At the same time, other renegade forces had assaulted the worlds of Robinson, Doneval, and Markab in the Draconis March. The outcome of all the attacks had been disastrous, according to Dehaver's reports, the Avengers destroyed to the last warrior. But Theodore had yet to formally apologize or even make any private offers of restitution.

"Two days ago," Dow said, his deep voice stately and measured, "Clan Ghost Bear retaliated by launching a major counterattack against the Combine. The news reports will filter through your agents any day now. What they may not include, however, is the information that Theodore Kurita has pulled back the Ghost regiments in case the Bears are the vanguard of a renewed invasion."

"Which is all very fascinating," Katrina said dryly. "But I have an adequate intelligence staff, as you pointed out. Thank you for your concern, Precentor."

Dow frowned in irritation. "There may come a time, Highness, when you will value my support more highly. We have frequent business dealings, after all. It makes much more sense to stay on friendly terms."

"Then next time you should request an audience through proper channels," Katrina said coldly. She stabbed down on the terminal interrupt, rupturing the connection and, in effect, releasing all the HPG stations in her command circuit to return to their regular duties.

Richard Dehaver waved the two on-duty technicians out of the room, and they were barely out the door before Katrina rounded on him. "Why haven't I heard of this? When can I retake control of the Lyons Thumb?"

"Even with the détente your brother has forged with the Combine, news travels slowly out of their state," Dehaver said. "Why did you cut off Dow? You never heard his price for the intelligence."

Katrina waved away his concern. "Does it matter now that we have it? Besides, I know what he wanted. Territory. He hinted as much. The more worlds a senior Precentor administers, the greater weight his arguments carry in the First Circuit."

"I remind you, Highness, that your brother Victor controls no real territory anymore. Yet he still poses the greatest danger to your rule."

"Point taken," Katrina admitted. "As for Gavin Dow,

I'm sure we'll hear from him again. Though next time he'll be more cautious. Now back to my question, Richard. When can I retake the Thumb?"

The man's dark eyes stared back at her implacably. "You can't."

"You heard Dow. The Lyons Thumb is not secure. If we—"

"That entire region is unsecured, Highness," Dehaver said, showing questionable judgment in interrupting Katrina. "Robert Kelswa-Steiner is gaining more support in Skye to the point that it is becoming difficult to keep it out of news reports to other worlds. Between him and the need to shift more troops to Solaris VII, you have no nearby military forces available. And it will take military forces, which you've always been reluctant to commit. Theodore's worlds in the Thumb may be vulnerable, but they're not completely unprotected."

As much as she disliked Dehaver turning her earlier thoughts back on her, Katrina couldn't argue the point. Her rule was built more on political maneuvering than military command, and more military decisions had already been forced on her than she was comfortable with.

"So I let the Thumb go? Just like that? Eight of my worlds?"

"Theodore Kurita is there, Highness. You are not. And in exchange for those eight worlds, you can concentrate on Kathil and Kentares and Galax, among a dozen others. And you can throw more support behind Duke Sandoval on Robinson. If he rattles his sabers loud enough, Theodore may have to give you back the Thumb as a concession for the unsanctioned attacks made against you there."

The idea appealed to Katrina, especially as it lent itself more to political subterfuge, a game at which she excelled. She wet her lips slowly, thinking hard. "My brother Arthur certainly has been a help there, drawing followers like a lodestone draws filings. What has he done since the attack?"

Dehaver smiled without humor. "You mean since

being hailed as the 'savior of Robinson'? He graduated, with top honors, and accepted a post with the Rangers. I believe he is planning to speak at an anti-Combine rally next month. We have the People Unbound movement there ready to whip up the crowd."

"Strength of the mob." Katrina frowned, realizing again how much power she had granted Arthur to play with. "And Arthur's current value?"

"I hesitate to say that he has reached the pinnacle of his popularity. Your brothers—with the exception of Peter, whom we still cannot find—have an uncharted ability to muster power." Dehaver paused, considering. "Still, Arthur has about reached the point where his fame is still useful to us."

Katrina nodded. "And his communications have become a bit distant of late. He is forgetting to whom he is accountable. Perhaps it's time to remind him."

"Maybe it's time to think about immortalizing him," Dehaver said flatly. "If Victor and Arthur ever joined forces against you—"

"They won't," Katrina promised, anger coloring her voice at the thought of such an alliance. "I will never allow that to happen."

She nodded toward the door. "Bring that demi-precentor back in, and let's start putting the circuit back together. Perhaps Nondi has something positive to report." Of course, she didn't really believe that, and she could see that she'd failed to convince Dehaver that her brothers would ever join forces against her.

"They won't, Richard," she said again, letting her voice take on a softer tone. "You worry about Arthur. Take precautions as you see fit, but keep me informed. Nothing happens without my approval."

He nodded curtly. "And Victor?"

Katrina's smile was predatory, her white teeth flashing dangerously. "Leave Victor to me," she said. "He'll have other things on his mind soon enough."

= 15 =

Deschuttes, Mogyorod
Melissia Theater
Lyran Alliance
8 November 3062

The assassin's best opportunity came with the arrival of Isis Marik's personal effects.

Averaging one large shipment every week, DropShips had been delivering a seemingly endless stream of crates, pallets, and bundled packages. Clothing. Sculptures for the grounds and the home. Settings of rare china. A holovid collection that would make an entertainment mogul jealous. Two vehicles. The furnishings and sundry possessions that had filled her palatial estates on Atreus, and later Sian, were now straggling into Mogyorod like some kind of old-style baggage train strung out across several hundred light-years.

Seeing the list of cargo for the first time, the man known to his co-workers as Dan Cheurre—"Shay-Hurr," he told everyone twice, slowly, listening to make certain he got it right himself—had been momentarily stunned. Who in their right mind would cart several tons of such items from world to world? There were even a dozen houseplants, which had somehow survived the long trek without natural sunlight. Why not just replace them when you move? he wondered.

Except that Isis couldn't replace these things, the assassin realized. Most of her possessions were of Free Worlds League origin—things she'd grown up with, things she was used to. Like the soft velvet of her heavy Atrean tapestries or the spicy scent of the Irian lilac. These were things hard to acquire in the best of times. Other items from the Capellan culture in which she'd lived for the past five years were even more irreplaceable because of trade restrictions against the Confederation.

Most of her possessions were placed in storage as they arrived in Deschuttes, warehoused against the day—soon to come—when Isis departed. A large portion of every shipment, though, was taken to the Drake estates just outside the city, providing her with various items she might want or need: a van one week, two trucks the next.

And for all the moving, sorting, carting, and carrying to be done, there was Helping Hands, Professional Movers & Storage.

Dan Cheurre was slow. Not retarded so that someone would have to keep track of and worry about him—just slow. But he was a hard worker who never had to be told twice what to do and who worked steadily and methodically until the job was done. He was the kind of man labor-intensive companies loved to hire to satisfy Lyran preferential hiring laws: a man who never complained about the heavy work, the hours, or his six-month raise. He was often underfoot but never really noticed. After five weeks in the role, the assassin thought he was in the best shape of his life. His muscles had protested at first, but now a hot shower followed by a hot meal was usually enough to renew his strength.

And the work had paid unexpected dividends. Three times now he'd been in the Drake mansion, and he'd been able to create a map for himself by pacing out the hallways and rooms in measured steps. The security force was used to him, and if he took a wrong turn now and then, a servant simply corrected him and promptly forgot about it. And when Dan Cheurre crossed paths with Isis Marik one day, she looked right through him with the usual indifference of nobility for their inferiors. He'd even encountered Omi twice. She glided past with seemingly effortless grace, that slender neck so very fragile and vulnerable to a quick strike with a knife or a hard chop to the trachea.

The assassin had also experimented with slipping new items into shipments. They were all inspected, of course, but no one questioned the heavy-chained clock or the large, half-filled wardrobe. He now had a hiding place, half a disassembled pistol, two stabbing implements, and a garrote secreted within the mansion.

Tonight he chose the garrote.

The well-oiled door on the wardrobe eased open silently at five minutes to midnight, and he uncoiled from his cramped quarters with slow, easy motions that relieved the stiffness in his muscles. Anticipating that the room would be dark, he'd taught himself to move around in it blindfolded. Three steps forward, two side steps to avoid the heavy, carved chest, then forward again. Reach out at waist height, find the doorknob with a brush of his fingertips, and then slip out into the upstairs hall.

The mansion was usually silent at this hour, save for the ever-present sentries covering the main doors. Helping Hands had arrived with two truckloads this afternoon—not an uncommon occurrence—and the assassin knew that each driver would assume Dan had grabbed a ride home with the other. He'd dragged out the unloading so long that the sentry watch had rotated in the middle of the job. And that was how the fact that he disappeared inside the mansion went unnoticed, just as he'd planned.

The clock he'd smuggled in during an earlier shipment had been set on the wall in a small upstairs library. The

door was always open. The assassin crept past the hall-
way security cam, ignoring it as best he could. He headed
for the clock, which was on the far wall.

A small counterweight swung on a thin, flexible wire
behind one of the heavy chains depending from the or-
nate clock. The other end was attached to a ring hung
on a simple hook. He reached up and released it from
the clock. A small tapping sound as the ballast bumped
the wall set off a string of silent curses from the assassin
as he quickly grabbed the counterweight. The metal cylinder felt deadly cold in his hands. He slipped the weight
through the ring. Now it was only a matter of throwing
the loop around Omi Kurita's pale neck and giving a
hard yank. It would be over in seconds.

He knew from previous trips down the hall leading to
the main suites that the floor had soft areas that
squeaked and groaned. They were hardly noticeable in
the day but sounded like gunshots in the still of night.
He squeezed himself into an alcove, half-hidden by one
of Isis's sculptures, and counted down the long seconds
to midnight.

At the first muted chime of the large clock at the foot
of the stairs, the assassin began to move down the hall
with quick, even strides. He had twenty-five seconds from
the first ringing note to the last mournful gong. He
passed Isis's suite at three seconds, and then two empty
rooms at five. Seven, eight, nine, ten—he paused outside
the room Omi Kurita shared with Victor Davion to calm
himself with a slow series of deep breaths. Victor was on
an extended training maneuver, or simply working late,
leaving Omi alone.

Fifteen seconds, and the eighth chime.

The assassin eased the door open with a single, fluid
motion, entering and closing it behind him just as
quickly. Omi lay sleeping serenely on the wide bed, one
arm thrown across the empty space where Victor normally lay. The assassin thought the pristine white duvet
most appropriate—white was the color of mourning in

the Combine. Three strides took him to the side of the bed.

With the fourth step, he lifted one leg and planted his knee firmly on Omi's midsection, driving the air from her lungs.

Standard reaction: the victim sat bolt upright in bed, trying to draw breath to cry out. The scream died before it was born as the assassin dropped the cable around Omi's throat, took hold of the cylinder, and pulled. The wire dug into her soft throat, choking off all sound. One hard yank, and the garrote sliced so deeply that only Omi's spine prevented her decapitation.

As simple as that.

It was over.

The assassin turned his back on the thing lying on the bed and walked away. There was only one thought left to him now.

Review.

The assassin pulled rom-disks from his fifteen cameras and carried them to the far side of the small, empty warehouse that served as his makeshift studio. His feet traced a duplicate mockup of the Drake mansion's second story, with furniture and other obstructions marked with tape on the floor. The set had only one real wall—the one where the clock hung—and three doors held in place by skeleton frames. There was a copy of the wardrobe, and the bed held a life-size doll. It was enough to give him a feel for how he would move about, for the timing of his strike

When he reached the final wall, he stepped through it like a ghost, leaving his simulated run against Omi Kurita behind him.

He would spend the next hours studying every angle of the cameras, looking for the slightest misstep. Refining. Perfecting. Always with an eye toward a clean kill. He still didn't like his entrance, which depended on the drivers forgetting about him, but if they were running late and the trucks departed at different times, it was a statistical uncertainty he could live with.

The noise made while recovering his garrote had been unforgivable. That would need work. There was also the problem of Victor's necessary absence on a day when two trucks delivered more of Isis's personal effects. The assassin considered routing a series of false messages to Tharkad and back, using any number of dummy companies and mail drops, in order to delay Victor with falsified ComStar business or unconfirmed rumors of an atrocity on New Avalon, perhaps. It might be enough to hold him up, waiting for confirmation.

The assassin decided he would need at least another month of practice runs. Dan Cheurre needed the time to really establish himself with the security people. Then he would set up the delaying tactic and wait for the perfect day.

It would have to be early 3063, he thought.

Victor would get one final Christmas with his beloved. Then Omi Kurita would be dead.

16

In the offices lent to him in the Robinson House of Lords, Arthur Steiner-Davion labored over the note cards he'd spread out over a mammoth desk. The cards were like rafts on a red mahogany ocean, shuffled, arranged, and rearranged on the currents of Arthur's moods. A word changed here. A line struck out there. And the speech he would give before an anti-Combine rally next week was slowly taking form.

He paused and straightened up to ease the kink in his back, flexing his cramped writing hand. A sip of ice water washed away the plastic taste from his habit of chewing on the end of his pen while thinking. The other old habit was preferring pen and paper to even the simplest of word processors. Arthur had discovered long ago that writing out his thoughts in longhand often led to better, more stirring prose.

James Sandoval thought Arthur quaint to work up his own speeches rather than rely on a political writer—or, more precisely, the Duke's own political writer. Still, the Duke of Robinson himself had a knack for a clever turn of phrase, and Arthur had borrowed from many of his speeches of the past year.

Not this time. Arthur didn't want the Duke's ideas to influence his thoughts. Tancred had been right all those months ago on the fencing strip. Arthur had begun to speak with James Sandoval's words—not intentionally, and maybe not even by the Duke's design. Sandoval was simply a forceful man with adamant views, many of which—most of which—Arthur shared. But the idea of being manipulated had shaken Arthur.

No one was going to use him, he vowed. Not even the Duke.

Tancred also seemed to be trying to manipulate Arthur, but toward Victor's ends. Each Sandoval thought he was right and that Arthur's influence would help his cause. It wasn't malice, Arthur knew. More like motivated self-interest.

A light, hurried knock, and the door to Arthur's office swung open to admit his chief security agent. A compact man, calm and composed at all times, Saul Klinger would never have impressed Arthur as the dangerous type. But his references were impeccable, and he had seen Saul throw men twice his size across a tumbling mat in judo practice.

"You asked to be reminded an hour before your meeting with Duke Sandoval," Klinger said.

"Thank you, Saul. Which means I have thirty minutes, right?"

"The Duke is usually early, yes," Klinger said, shutting the door behind him. "That seems to be his way, at least where you are concerned."

Tancred, on the other hand, was simply punctual, even erring on the side of allowing Arthur more time with his thoughts. "So different, father and son," Arthur mused aloud.

He recalled the short battle of last month when the Combine had sent a battalion of suicide-samurai to attack Robinson. So few warriors had caused so much trouble that Arthur and Tancred had at first believed a full-scale assault was in progress. Regardless, they had cleaned house admirably. And then, afterward, all the holozines and news stations wanting interviews and taking pictures had given him an excellent platform for his message about staying prepared. He had reveled in the afterglow of battle, whereas Tancred had merely endured it with grim stoicism.

Until they'd found themselves alone, anyway.

"What are you doing, Arthur?" Tancred had asked even as the last camera flashes still danced purple spots before his eyes. "Do you want a war?"

Arthur bridled. "The Dracs attacked us, Tancred. Or don't you remember?"

"And they'll do so again if you keep this up." Tancred softened his tone, which took some, but not all, of the sting out of his words. "Your knee-jerk reactions, passed off as policy because of who you are, are just the thing to encourage brainless devotion to the old prejudices. On both sides."

That wasn't quite fair. Accurate, perhaps, but unfair nonetheless.

"Strange words coming from a man who put down three samurai," Arthur said. "Out there on the grinder—"

"Out there on the grinder I was fighting for my life, and yours too. But when the battle's over, it's time to look at the political implications."

"Did my brother teach you that?"

"No," Tancred said, "my father did. But I don't believe he's capable of doing so anymore. He looks, and he sees only the Dragon."

Before he could say more, Tancred was interrupted by the arrival of James Sandoval and a new cadre of reporters and holovid cameramen. Tancred gazed evenly, but intently, at Arthur. "What do you see, Arthur?"

Later, when Arthur gave the duke a tactful explanation for Tancred's departure, the duke simply shook his head. "Tancred gives too much credit to the collective memory of common citizens. By next week, they will have forgotten everything we say here, unless we shake them hard. Preparation will always be the key to defense. I'm glad you realize that, Arthur. You're a credit to your parents. There's another rally next month. Why not give a talk on your experience today? Let people know how things really are."

And Arthur's idea of how things really were was coming into better focus every day. " 'A little rebellion now and then is a good thing,' " he said aloud in his borrowed office. " 'God forbid that we should ever be twenty years without such.' "

"Sir?" the security man asked.

"Sorry, Saul. An old saying by a rebel-turned-states-man. Pre-Exodus. Much of the context has been lost to time. I used to think it meant that nobles had a duty to test boundaries and to take a stronger hand in matters that concern them." That was Duke Sandoval's view, certainly.

"Now I wonder if it means that power is meant to be placed in the hands of the citizens—as a way to remind the nobility of their larger responsibilities." That seemed to be Tancred's view.

"I suppose it could be read either way."

"That's the trouble with words, Saul. They aren't al-ways reliable. They can be twisted around and reborn to serve a new cause . . . Saul, what is it?"

Saul appeared momentarily stunned, his skin ashen but eyes full of a sudden intensity. "I'm sorry, sir. Twisted around and . . ."

"Reborn." Except that Arthur's words wouldn't be. He refused to allow it, promising himself that he would re-read each sentence for unintentional nuances.

" 'The tree of liberty must be refreshed from time to time with the blood of patriots and tyrants,' " he said, completing the third leg of the earlier quotation.

That was what had happened last month. And were

they really due for more? That was the question Arthur had to answer for himself, and then keep his decision from both Tancred and Duke Sandoval. No one could know what Arthur was thinking. What he would do.

That way, he thought, there was nothing anyone could do to stop him.

Kelly Phillips recovered Saul's note from one of their standard drops. This one, a safety-deposit box at a local bank, had been refitted with an incendiary sleeve and a special lock modeled after the verigraph. If the DNA of the opener did not match one of three people, the sleeve would incinerate the letter.

"How can we do anything else but teach the Combine a lesson?" the message read. "All know it is going to happen. The question is when, not if. Whatever you do, don't forget to tell him about our plans to join the army. Your brother-in-arms, S."

Short and simple, and the hidden text extracted from the message even simpler. Ignore the first sentence because it is a question, and change the key with every sentence thereafter. The code was therefore three-four-eight, as indicated by the first word of each new sentence.

Saul had done good work. They now had a direction. Phillips nodded, smiled, and let the secret missive cheer him as he read it through again.

"It is him."

Deschuttes, Mogyorod
Melissia Theater
Lyran Alliance

"Give it to us straight, Jerry," Victor said, even before his friend was all the way through the door of the Wylden Garrison Post. "What's the worst news off Kathil?"

He and his advisors had gathered in the post's main briefing room, whose dark wooden paneling and dark tapestry chairs were oppressive. Definitely not the usual ComStar décor, and despite Victor's royal upbringing, still a bit too stuffy for his tastes. He was beginning to miss Tukayyid, with its modern facilities and the vast intelligence resources at his disposal there. Mogyorod was not a place from which he could easily track the growing tensions threatening to erupt into violence across the Federated Commonwealth.

Victor had asked Precentor Raymond Irelon and Demi Rudolf Shakov of the 244th Division to sit in on his meeting with Jerrard Cranston—Irelon for his years of experience, and Shakov for his soothing manner. He was beginning to feel the absence of his other friends and advisors. These two would do, but who he really wanted was Kai Allard-Liao or Morgan Kell, or Anastasius Focht or Tancred Sandoval. Hell, he'd even take Phelan Kell and all his swaggering right now, though Victor already knew what Phelan's advice would be. It apparently came with being adopted into the Clans. Act. Intervene. Attack.

Jerry deposited a stack of papers and several data crystals onto the table. He scratched his blond beard and pondered for a moment. "The worst?"

That he had to think about it did not leave Victor feeling reassured.

"Well, the Eighth RCT took Yare Industries' geothermal plant away from the Second NAIS Cadre. It wasn't much of a fight."

Victor thumped his fist against the table. "So it's spreading."

He looked at Irelon and Shakov. "You've read the reports? The Eighth Federated Commonwealth RCT has been butting heads with the Kathil militia over which of them will garrison that world." A very important world, actually. The Yare shipyards were one of the few facilities in the Inner Sphere able to produce the JumpShips that made possible interstellar travel.

"Marshal George Hasek ordered the Eighth to turn responsibility for planetary defense over to the militia.

The Eighth's General Weintraub refused, citing his orders from Katherine—illegal orders, since they did not pass through the regular chain of command. About two weeks ago, the Eighth RCT attacked the militia. Now the local NAIS training cadre has also been drawn into the fighting."

Precentor Irelon held up one finger. "Don't misunderstand me, Victor. What you command, the Prince's Men will do. But how does this concern ComStar?"

" 'All that is required for evil to triumph is that good men do nothing,' " Victor said with feeling. "And don't give me that noninterference line. ComStar has been meddling secretly in Inner Sphere politics since centuries before either of us was born."

"Before the schism, before Anastasius Focht secularized us, I believe that was true." Irelon watched him with cloaked brown eyes. "So, do you plan to revive that tradition?"

"If I have to," Victor said. "Only if I have to."

Demi-Precentor Shakov smiled wryly. He had a narrow face but large, expressive eyes, features at home with great humor or great seriousness. "Well, now that we all know what we are, what can we do about Kathil? I didn't realize we had troops there."

"You don't," Jerrard Cranston confirmed. "But the Eridani Light Horse has fallen back to Kittery to lick the wounds they took in the Capellan war with St. Ives. As Commanding General of the Star League Defense Force, Victor could route them to Kathil."

Victor shook his head. "After Sun-Tzu Liao's treacherous use of Star League 'peacekeepers' and Theodore's annexation of the Lyons Thumb, Katherine's media machine would crucify me if I tried it." It was a mistake he might have made just last year, but he was learning. Above all else, he did not want to make matters worse. If he couldn't guarantee putting a stop to the fighting, it was better to let it burn out on its own. If it would.

As though reading his mind, Jerry Cranston tapped the stack of reports. "Thorin, Benet III, Nanking,

Brockway . . . they're all looking shaky. And that's being conservative. If Katherine orders stricter measures to suppress the unrest, we'll see open revolt on a half-dozen worlds, maybe more." He paused, blue eyes cautioning Victor. "And there's a new problem. Kentares."

"Kentares?" Irelon asked, astounded. "Was the Combine so stupid as to stage one of their raids there?"

"Not the Combine. Katherine. News has been blacked out, including the HPG stations, but ROM agents finally got the word out. Katherine has occupied the entire planet. The local commander, Lord Roland, either on his own initiative or Katherine's order, has apparently murdered the entire Dresari ruling line." Jerry lowered his gaze. "Eric's dead, Victor. I'm sorry."

The news rocked Victor back in his seat. Duke Eric Dresari had been one of his father's great friends and a supporter of Victor even in the times when he'd made obvious and damaging mistakes.

Irelon was shaking his head in disbelief. "Is it possible that Katherine could be so stupid, or so bloodthirsty?"

"Believe it," Jerry said, his voice sharp. "I've confirmed it through our best intelligence source on New Avalon. Underestimating Katherine is like toying with a viper. It's pretty and captivating, but you'll still be just as dead when it bites you."

It had been some time since Victor had heard such bitterness in his friend's voice. Not many people knew that Jerrard Cranston was really Galen Cox, who had believed himself in love with Katherine until he learned the truth about her with shocking abruptness. Katherine not only helped plan her mother's death, she also knew of a plot to murder Galen and said nothing, the better to protect herself.

Galen Cox "died" in an explosion, and Jerrard Cranston was born. Appointed head of the Star League's Intelligence Command, Cranston now traveled with Victor and fed anything noteworthy to his friend.

"Jerry's right," Victor said. "Katherine's capable of this, though I'm sure Lord Roland will take the fall. But if she approved or even knew about Dresari's murder, it's a dangerous step forward in her determination to hold power. The question is, what can be done about it?''

His three advisors made several suggestions, all of which were eventually rejected, either because they endangered the peace or brought Victor into direct confrontation with his sister.

"I won't accept this, gentlemen," he said finally. "As much as I want to avoid it, I'm being cast as my sister's opposition. I'm her enemy, yes, but I won't—I can't—break the peace. I want other options."

"Maybe there are none," Demi Shakov said simply. "You said it yourself, Highness. Your sister is taking her control of the Commonwealth and the Alliance to radical extremes. Unless you're prepared to meet her on those terms, or with military force, I can't see any salvation for you or us."

Victor frowned. "I'm not looking for salvation, Rudolf. And I won't break the peace first."

" 'All that is required for evil to triumph is that good men do nothing,' " Shakov reminded him with a predatory gleam in his green eyes.

"Shakov!" Precentor Irelon stood, shocked at his subordinate's manners. "Highness! Victor, I apologize—"

Victor waved him silent, staring at Shakov as if seeing him for the first time. Shakov held his gaze, surprising Victor with his depth of resolve.

"I won't lower myself to her level unless that is the last—and I mean final!—option remaining," Victor said.

"You are a most stubborn man, Victor Davion." Shakov shook his head, but still did not break eye contact. "When was the last time someone told you no and made it stick?"

It was Victor who looked away first. Glancing at Jerry, he rubbed at his jaw, feeling the memory of a long-forgotten ache. "I think it was 3049, actually. And it came wrapped up in a right cross."

"3050," Cranston corrected him, keeping a straight face to protect Victor's dignity. "But I wouldn't recommend trying it, Demi Shakov. Victor has taken a few more lessons in hand-to-hand combat since then."

Victor cracked a smile then, which quickly blossomed into a laugh that broke the tension. "All right, Rudolf. No asking the impossible, right? So, if we can't end-run Katherine yet, we have to wait for our moment. And I need to return to Tukayyid, soon. Jerry, how are the JumpShip circuits?"

"Not great, Victor," Jerry answered immediately, "unless you want to slog it home a week per jump. I don't have a command circuit planned until after the new year, and even then, it would only get you as far as A Place."

"You can hitch a ride on Word of Blake's *Divine Will*," Shakov said, referring to the Blakist vessel that had shadowed Victor to Mogyorod and that still remained at the system's nadir jump point. "I hear they'll take any ComStar personnel for a ride."

That brought a laugh from all of them, even Precentor Irelon.

"Thanks, Rudolf," Victor said. "All right, I'm here for the holidays, and then it's a slow boat back to Tukayyid. Jerry, see what you can do to keep a lid on things until next summer."

If Jerry Cranston thought the request unreasonable, he didn't show it. He stood up and nodded. "No promises, Victor, but I'll see what I can do."

"Just don't hand me any big surprises."

═══ 17 ═══

Bueller, Robinson
Draconis March
Federated Commonwealth
5 December 3062

Arthur Steiner-Davion stood in front of a podium emblazoned with the Sandoval crest in the Aeromark Media Station. His note cards safely tucked away after one final review, he stood tall in his AFFC uniform, with its cape and epaulets. Duke Sandoval had reluctantly given permission for officers of the Draconis March to return to the dress uniform of the old Federated Suns, probably thinking it better to compromise on the little things that didn't really matter. Today, Arthur had chosen to appear in Federated Commonwealth dress rather than slap his sister in the face.

His rank device proclaimed him hauptmann, a captain of the Federated Commonwealth, though birthright assured him the battalion-command rank of kommandant. The better to earn his command, Arthur had argued

Duke Sandoval into awarding him the lesser rank. Hauptmann was as low as James Sandoval was prepared to concede.

But those were military concerns. Today was for politics, and a new direction in politics at that. Arthur took a sip of lukewarm water from the glass handed him by one of his security agents, mentally reviewed his speech again, and then nodded his readiness.

The Aeromark Media Station had gladly turned over their main facility in exchange for rebroadcast rights to Arthur's speech. The security team had swept the entire building, clearing out all six floors of station personnel, two insurance firms, an accounting firm, and a double handful of small-business offices. The station's chief producer and his best technician remained on hand, one for the political advantage and the other in case of technical problems. There was also a film crew, brought in at the last minute, using station equipment. Arthur would appear on the magnavision screen at the city of Bueller's local sports stadium, where today's rally was taking place. His speech would boom out over the public address system to tens of thousands of loyal March citizens.

Of course, Arthur would have preferred to appear in person, but Saul Klinger, as chief of Arthur's security, had vetoed that idea, and the Sandovals agreed. Everyone seemed extra edgy lately, but Arthur knew that the last few anti-Combine rallies had gotten out of hand. The resulting riots were blamed on the People Unbound and a few other radical groups—the same people Arthur was supposed to incite again today. Well, he would, though perhaps not in the way anyone expected.

The station producer signaled the thirty-second warning, and Arthur pulled away the tissue tucked into the neck of his high-peaked collar. It was intended to protect his uniform from the stage makeup one of the crew had insisted on applying to his face. He wadded it up and handed it to a security man, who retreated off camera. Arthur gripped one side of the podium in each hand,

and caught the flash of his Battle Academy class ring in the studio's strong lights.

"Here we go," he said to himself as the caution light flashed green. Then it burned steadily, and Arthur was live to forty thousand people. He could not voice his final thought—not with the holocam and microphones taking live feed—but it was there.

I'm sorry, Victor.

Tancred Sandoval stood next to his father in the Sandoval stadium box, where they had invited other family members and friends among the nobility to join them for Arthur's speech. Even through the protective ferroglass shield, he could feel the energy of the thousands of people below like an electrical charge dancing over the small hairs at the back of his neck.

He had never seen the stadium filled to such capacity. Overfilled, in fact, with people illegally choking the aisles and another several thousand crowded onto the field, restrained by bright yellow ropes and far too few security guards. With the escalating violence of these anti-Combine rallies, it was a tinderbox just waiting for a spark.

Waiting for Arthur Steiner-Davion.

Neither Tancred nor James Sandoval would be speaking today. Tancred had refused to support the rally with anything but the minimum requirement of his presence, and Duke Robinson wanted the day to belong to Arthur. A few relatives would make brief appearances later, though Tancred was worried about their safety. General Mai Fortuna already stood on the field, easily identifiable in her razor-creased uniform boasting forty-three years of decorations. But she was a hero of Robinson. Tancred doubted she had much to fear from these people.

To great fanfare, Arthur's image suddenly filled the huge magnavision screen that towered over the crowd of forty thousand-odd people at the west end of the stadium. The background roar of conversation died away into an eerie silence, though whether the crowd was cowed or captivated, it was impossible to say.

The young man's blue eyes gleamed with inner strength, reminding Tancred of the fearless Hanse Davion. But his proud, almost sad smile—that was Melissa, Arthur's mother.

Tancred was sure that the thousands in attendance were probably making the same comparisons, consciously or otherwise. Arthur had the best of both worlds in his visage.

"History teaches," he began slowly, "that within the blackest times there always remain the guiding lights of hopes and dreams for the future, while even the most resplendent moments cast long shadows that again threaten darkness. Such events, for ill or good, must concern mankind. For in reaching a pinnacle of history, those moments when great events are afoot and compel even the greatest of leaders to act far and above their normal station, the path is no less severe on the person, the proletariat, the Commonwealth."

Tancred caught himself nodding agreement, but checked himself, wanting to concentrate instead on the ideas behind the stirring words. Whatever he'd expected from Arthur's opening remarks, it was nothing like these sentiments. Arthur's earlier speeches had begun in the middle of the action, the better to capture his listeners' emotions and draw them into agreement. Here, he seemed to be laying the groundwork for something different. Something bigger.

"In keeping with such times," Arthur continued, "great sacrifices are demanded at every level, as well as a selfless willingness to meet any sacrifice. But coupled with history's demands is the inevitable and unalienable right to freedom of expression. The right to give voice to our fears and concerns, our needs and desires, becomes all the more essential. For no leader can presume to impose any one view over that of the multitude."

Tancred noted his father's tight-lipped grimace and the way he continually checked his watch. And with good reason. Arthur had promised a forty-minute address, and now, barely a minute into the presentation, neither Sandoval had any idea where the young man was going with it.

But wherever it was, Arthur would carry the crowd with him. Tancred was beginning to get the feeling that neither he nor his father—not to mention Victor or Katherine—would thank Arthur for today's address. He could see it coming: Arthur was cutting himself loose of any tethers to establish his own voice—his own path. Tancred would congratulate him later, in private. Because these were important words—immortal words. You could not kill such a message.

Only the messenger.

The first muffled report almost escaped notice—a hollow, thumping sound like that of a distant accident. The magnavision cut to gray static and then went black. Most survivors of this day would remember that transmission loss as their first warning of the bedlam to come—a warning that arrived far too late.

A fireball erupted over the northwest corner of the stadium as an explosion tore up through ferrocrete and steel to blast the stands and bury several hundred spectators under tons of debris. Other explosions followed, rocking the long eastern and western stretches, and that was all Tancred saw.

The reinforced floor of the box bucked wildly, throwing Tancred, his father, and their guests across the room. Tancred hit the floor in a roll to absorb the impact, smacked his head sharply against the wall, and fought back a wave of darkness. He took his consciousness in both hands, dragging himself back from the edge of the abyss, and the room around him came into focus.

James Sandoval sat against the ferroglass shield, holding an obviously broken arm and staring dazedly at the tumult of bodies, chairs, and fallen plaster. A huge crack had fractured the shield, but the transparent wall did not seem in any danger of toppling, so Tancred checked on other guests and family first. No one was seriously hurt—not in the box, anyway.

The view out over the stadium told a different story. Plumes of smoke and dust rolled lazily skyward, marking the sites of fires and shattered areas of the stands. Those people on the field had been fortunate to be out in the open, but they were quickly bringing down misfortune on themselves as they stampeded for the debris-choked exits, trampling each other to escape, though the immediate danger seemed to have passed. James Sandoval got shakily to his feet and joined Tancred in gazing down on the scene of death and destruction.

There was no mistaking the hard glint in his eyes. "Kurita," he said, spitting out the word.

Tancred then remembered that first, distant explosion and the loss of transmission to the large stadium screen.

He turned to race for the door.

Arthur!

=== 18 ===

Katrina sipped her morning tea as she finished reading the report handed to her over breakfast. *Delicious*, was her first thought. The news was the best she'd had in a long time.

Her eggs were cold and her wheat toast soggy when she finally set the hardcopy aside. The cinnamon-spiced tea, at least, was still warm.

She set the hardcopy on the small table that had been set up on the balcony of her suite in Davion Palace, and smiled. Life was good. Spread out at her feet was Avalon City, seat of the throne that had been her father's and her mother's and now hers. It had been Victor's, too, but he'd never deserved it. He would never understand the realities of holding so much power.

Richard Dehaver, who'd delivered the report, stood nearby holding up the wall with his narrow shoulders, waiting to be acknowledged. Katrina continued to ignore him as she watched the city stir to life, the distant sounds of traffic just beginning to compete with a steady drizzle that made an entrancing pattering against the balcony awning. It was springtime on New Avalon's southern hemisphere, the seasons a few months off the Terran-standard year. It would be deep into winter now on Tharkad, the ground iced over and snow piled into deep drifts.

And on Mogyorod? *Merry Christmas, dear brother. I hope you can return your present for Arthur.*

"Your thoughts, Richard?" she finally said.

"I recommend that you withdraw into seclusion for a few days and let the media do most of the work. If you must make a public statement, it should be very brief and very emotional."

Katrina nodded. Her thoughts exactly. "I want Arthur's final words saturating the holocasts and radio networks on every world in the Commonwealth," she said calmly, as if ordering up another cup of the spiced tea. "Follow it up with any footage or reports coming off Robinson. The people will be outraged, and in a crisis, they look to strong leaders."

She thought the timing of this was truly exquisite; it would solve so many problems. "This will also serve to distract attention from our efforts to consolidate power on the rebellious worlds. Send messages out at once to each of them."

"Video?" Dehaver asked.

"No. I'm far too distraught to appear in person at the moment. Prepare written missives to Kathil, Kentares, Benet, and any others. Keep it short and vague." She thought for a moment. "Along the lines of 'Due to tragic family matters, I am authorizing our representatives to take on broader local powers, and I expect to see all pressing business brought to a speedy conclusion.' Have that prepared for my signature by this afternoon."

He nodded. "It will be done."

"And I want my brother's body brought back to New Avalon immediately. We will lay him out in state and I can grieve—very publicly. I suppose it's too much to ask for an open casket?"

Dehaver's grimace was eloquent. "We've barely found enough to fill a small bucket, Highness. I believe we have a hand and maybe part of an ear." He shrugged. "We hope to uncover more under the debris."

Katrina could have done without the specifics. She had refused to read the coroner's report on her mother, and certainly had no desire to remember her poor brother any other way but as the healthy, vibrant young man he was—had been.

Dehaver took a step toward the door. "Will that be all, Highness?"

Katrina nodded a dismissal, but stopped him before he could get through the balcony door. "One thing, Richard. I did tell you that nothing goes forward without my express orders."

"You did, Archon," he replied stiffly. "And since I would never act without direct authorization, you can be assured that no one in my organization was responsible."

She nodded again, satisfied with the way matters had turned out. She also appreciated the protection such distance from them gave her. Dehaver would act as he saw fit, she thought as he left her. He had always been worried about Arthur, and, truth to tell, Katrina would have authorized the operation had he proposed it.

Worlds in rebellion and the heavy-handed tactics needed to keep them in the fold were yesterday's worry. All anyone would remember now were the first words of Arthur's impassioned address, which had lauded the importance of the struggles and the will of the people.

And the other thing they'd remember was that Arthur Steiner-Davion was dead.

Deschuttes, Mogyorod
Melissia Theater
Lyran Alliance

Victor sat down heavily, nearly missing the sofa as he staggered to keep from landing on the drawing room floor. His legs felt like lead weights. The wound that had never healed, the one that had cut so deep the day he learned of his mother's death, was ripped open by another irreparable loss.

His brother was dead.

Omi was at his side in an instant, enfolding Victor's hands in her own, sharing his pain. Her calm presence reminded him of how Minoru, her brother, so often spoke of death as a natural part of life, but that did nothing to fill the void that yawned within him.

Standing nearby, Jerrard Cranston turned off the holovid screen and its final image of the devastation in the Robinson sports stadium. He waited respectfully for Victor to compose himself. His blue eyes were hard with anger, while Tiaret averted her gaze, ashamed for Victor's sudden weakness.

Oddly enough, it was her reaction that gave him strength. To a Clan warrior like Tiaret, death was not only accepted, but embraced as a way of gaining immortality through the Clan eugenics program. Tiaret would judge Arthur on how he had met his death, on whether he'd run away or died fighting to his last breath. Well, the recent raid on Robinson had proved Arthur no coward, and in his own way, the young man had gone down swinging.

Victor wished he knew where Arthur had been heading with that speech. He had intended to be shocked and appalled at his brother's words, send him a message stating his extreme displeasure, and then privately share Arthur's triumph the next time they met in person.

None of that would happen now. And Victor knew who was to blame.

"Katherine," he said, forcing himself to take a deep, steadying breath. "Katherine is responsible for this."

"We do not know that, Victor," Omi said gently. "Certainly, there are other forces nearer your brother with even more reason to favor such drastic measures."

"That's true," Jerry said, though his tone belied his words. "Duke Sandoval has placed the whole Draconis

March under martial law and is mobilizing for a reprisal, claiming that House Kurita is responsible.

"My apologies, Omi," he said, softening his voice, "but you can imagine how Sandoval and the rest of his March would skew this. Tancred is there, and he will know that your father would never sanction such an attack, but there are other forces also at work inside the Combine these days as well. The October raid on Robinson proved that."

"*Hai*," Omi said. "There are conservative elements on both sides of the border that want nothing more than to shatter the peace between our nations. But to do so now, while the Combine is at war with the Ghost Bears, is madness. At least on the part of the Combine."

Victor looked up sharply. Was Omi suggesting that James Sandoval might have had something to do with Arthur's death? Fanatical the man might be, but Victor couldn't believe he would conspire against one of Hanse Davion's heirs. Not directly, in any case.

"Katherine," he said quickly. "It has to be her. But I need proof, Jerry. I need to know."

"It doesn't matter," Jerry said, but he had that same angry look in his eye.

Victor shot to his feet in fury. "It does matter. Arthur was my brother!"

"Galen is dead Victor," the other man said with solemn flatness. "Your sister didn't set the bomb that killed him, but she killed him just the same. Now Arthur is dead, and I wouldn't be surprised if she had him murdered, too." The anger in his eyes changed to pain. "What matters now is that more are going to die. A lot more, if we don't stop her."

"How bad?" Victor asked, his voice tight.

"Bad enough. There are four worlds in open rebellion as we speak, counting Kentares. I can name five more that will explode when news of Arthur's death hits, and another dozen that could go either way. Your sister sent out orders to all garrison commanders this morning, giving them more authority to deal with local disturbances. The wording is vague, but no one will mistake her meaning."

"Martial law," Victor said, forcing himself to pay attention to all this talk of politics despite the ache in his heart. "She's turning to the military to solve her problems, using Arthur's death as a distraction. And she'll stand by while Sandoval starts his own private war with the Combine as payback for Theodore annexing the Lyons Thumb."

It all fell into place. All except the timing. Victor looked sharply at Jerry Cranston. "How did you get the news about Katherine's orders so quickly?"

Jerry raised his eyebrows. "Doubting me, Victor? Quintus Allard-Liao was on New Avalon when your sister moved in to the palace, and he went underground immediately. With the war against St. Ives and her other political troubles, she hasn't bothered to ferret him out. He copied the message batch compiled by Dehaver and delivered it to one of my agents."

"No," Victor said, calculating how long it should have taken for a message to reach Mogyorod. "I mean, how did it get here so fast? You said news of Arthur's death arrived only an hour ago."

"Ah, that. Wish I could take credit, but you know that HPG circuit of Katherine's?"

Victor nodded.

"Well, ComStar still administers most of those installations, and your Primus worked up a new procedure. Large chains of those doubled stations routinely swing through a command-circuit alignment every eight hours for burst-transmissions. The intel on Katherine's orders caught up with the news concerning Arthur at the station on Coventry, landing in my lap in one package."

Arthur . . . Victor winced at the fresh reminder of his brother's death. Would he ever know for sure who gave the order? Once he was finished with Katherine, he wouldn't rest until he found out. "I asked you to give me until next summer," he reminded his friend.

Jerry shook his head, looking defeated for the first

time this night. "I'm sorry, Victor, but it can't be done. The Commonwealth is heading into all-out war, and we're also on the cusp of one with House Kurita. This is going forward with or without you. I say it should be with."

Victor looked at Omi, who had withdrawn slightly at the news of preparation for attacks against her homeland. She gazed back at him, her blue eyes showing that she trusted him to act in all their best interests.

"With," she said.

Of course, Tiaret would vote for battle, but Victor wanted to hear her say it anyway. He turned to her with the unspoken question.

In her subordinate position, Tiaret usually declined to offer advice on command matters. She was loyal to Victor, but she still lived by her Clan upbringing and training.

Victor stared at her, pitting his will against hers. She hesitated but met his gaze and held it. "With," she said finally.

It was for Victor to cast the final and ultimately decisive vote, making it unanimous. He looked around at each of their faces.

"With," he said, and it was the most heartbreaking word he had ever uttered.

=== 19 ===

Deschuttes, Mogyorod
Melissia Theater
Lyran Alliance
8 December 3062

How strange the uniform felt. It was one Victor knew well from the history of his people, but had never worn until now. The green cotton jacket was heavily starched and razor-creased, the collar and cuffs trimmed in the gold brocade of a command officer. Matching stirrup-trousers. Roweless spurs on his boots, a Davion tradition signifying his position as a MechWarrior. And instead of the full cape, standard since 3042, he wore a half-chest breastplate of golden bronze in a sunburst pattern around his left shoulder.

It was the full military dress of the Armed Forces of the Federated Suns. A uniform last worn—officially—during the rule of his father and before the creation of the Armed Forces of the Federated Commonwealth.

"Not quite the uniform I'm used to," Victor admitted.

Lyran-raised and a graduate of one of the most prestigious Lyran military academies, he felt displaced wearing this uniform. Conspicuously absent were almost every decoration, award, or ribbon to which he was entitled. Only the rank badge of field marshal and the original crest of the Federated Suns graced the uniform.

"A necessity," Jerry Cranston argued again for the benefit of Countess Drake and Demi-Precentor Shakov, who were also present in the broadcast studio. "A revolution needs a legitimate identity, and Katherine is too well entrenched in the Alliance for you to raise a Lyran standard."

Victor looked at Omi, who stepped forward and gently drew him aside. The men gave way as she claimed Victor.

"You must do this," she said in a low voice. "Your people need you."

He nodded, knowing how much courage it took for her to say the words. "It seems we are always having these conversations, Omi-*san*. How often have we been separated by the needs of our people? Outreach. Tharkad. Luthien. So many times." The list of worlds where he and Omi had said goodbye, in person or through vids, just now seemed endless.

Omi smiled at him, her eyes calm as a clear blue sky. "And how often has our reunion been all the more joyful? I will be waiting, Victor. Always. Tonight, I will be waiting at the estate."

"You're not staying?" He had assumed she would wait in the wings while he recorded his statement. His people had commandeered the local broadcasting station for the fateful announcement. Everyone was here. Almost.

"Isis is alone at the mansion," Omi reminded him. "And when you finish here, you will be locked away for most of the night with your advisors."

"I'll be back before midnight," he promised. She was right, but it was still difficult to let her go.

"That would be good, Victor-*san*. We have some matters to discuss, you and I. Important matters. Personal. Perhaps . . ." Omi hugged herself. "Victor, I would never intrude on the memory of your brother, but perhaps I know something that can ease the pain." She smiled then, a mysterious smile. "Though I do not promise not to complicate your life immensely."

Was Omi suggesting that they take their union to a new level—one they had always considered unattainable? If so, it was a hope that would give him courage to live through this evening, and a thousand more after.

"We will talk and talk and talk," he said.

Omi made a half-bow, then turned to go.

Victor caught her arm. "Take Tiaret with you," he urged. He nodded toward the big Elemental, who stood off to one side, always alert for any threat.

Tiaret frowned, obviously about to protest, but Victor spoke first. "Please see Omi home safely and catch up with me at the garrison post. I'd appreciate it."

Tiaret nodded reluctantly, took position in defense of Omi Kurita, and escorted her from the room. Next to Omi's dainty presence, Tiaret's huge, muscular form looked more threatening than ever.

"Was that your idea?" Victor asked Jerry once Omi and Tiaret had left through the far door.

Jerry Cranston had the grace to shift uncomfortably under Victor's hawk-like gaze. "I thought it would be easier on you both. In case you didn't notice, Omi is not terribly at ease with the Federated Suns uniform. You've never played up your Davion heritage quite so much before."

Victor nodded. Jerry was right. "Let's get this done, then."

The simple stage had already been set. A low podium to better display the uniform and to give Victor's one hundred-sixty centimeters an extra stretch. On the wall behind it hung the Federated Suns flag, its colors edged in the black of mourning.

Victor waited as the producer counted down from three to one. He gripped the podium with both hands and stared directly into the holovid camera.

"Good citizens of the Federated Commonwealth," he

began. "I could wish many things for us. That the great union of two nations which my parents forged would not have foundered. That I would never have found it necessary to leave you while fighting to end the Clan invasion." He paused for the briefest of heartbeats. "That my sister, Katherine, could have quelled her hunger for power, no matter the price.

"But wishing will not make it so. Such dreams have already died."

He drew a deep breath and let it out slowly. "And any hope I might have had for peace between the two realms I once led died with my brother Arthur, who was killed two days ago in a vicious terrorist attack." The words brought a wave of pain, but Victor held on to his stiff, formal bearing. A show of strength would carry more military minds than an outburst of emotion. Katherine courted the masses. Victor did not have that luxury yet.

"Arthur was a soldier, a good man, and he was learning to become a leader of men, women, and worlds. For that, someone decided that he had to die. Arthur's death convinces me that my duty to protect the Commonwealth can no longer be denied. The troubles on Solaris were a harbinger of what has come, and Arthur's violent death underscores the fighting already taking place on worlds such as Kathil, Robinson, and Kentares.

"His death will not be in vain. No longer will an unfit and unjust ruler sit on the thrones of the Federated Suns and Lyran Alliance, one who has seen fit to bring violence against her own family, betraying the memory of our father, our mother, and the trust of the people of both realms. There is blood on Katherine's hands, and no amount of propaganda will wash them clean."

There it was—the gauntlet thrown down with a vengeance. Victor would never rest until he found conclusive proof of his sister's involvement in the deaths of both Arthur and their mother. In the meantime, as his dear sister had taught him, accusations carried as much weight as proof in the heat of the moment.

"None of us wishes to see more conflict, but we can no longer ignore the problems plaguing us. Now we must live with the results, however painful, as we acknowledge the irreconcilable differences that continue to divide my sister from me. It is no longer possible for me to stand back in the interests of peace. The time has come, my people, where no other choice remains."

He paused, drawing himself up proudly, making himself as tall as any man needed to be.

"None," he said, "but war."

Victor knew that a mere holovid would not be enough to convince his people. They would need some time to reflect on his words. He did not doubt that eventually they would be won to his cause, and that there were already many who knew in their hearts that Katherine's rule must end.

"This mandate has been pressed upon me by Katherine's tyrannical actions, and by the sacrifices of patriots already fighting on the worlds of Kathil, Benet, Kentares, Demeter, Bromhead, and others yet unreported. We will resist with any and all means at our disposal the efforts to subjugate and enslave our freedoms. We fight with the truth on our side, and we simply ask that everyone listen and judge accordingly.

"In the end, I know we shall be victorious, re-establishing a trustworthy and accountable government among our people, worlds, and nations."

The producer, caught up in Victor's words, almost forgot to order the cameras off.

"And you're clear," the man finally said, rendering an impromptu Lyran military salute.

"You did it," Jerry said, the first to reach Victor's side. "You gave enough to make people sit up and take notice and start asking questions. And the only one who can really be hurt by questions is Katherine."

"It's a start," Victor said. "We'll need constant public statements, and it will be all the harder to work our way through the whole of the Alliance. Send it out, Jerry.

And put out the call to all troops as well. Start bringing them in."

"It's being done right now," Jerry promised. "On worlds where Katherine has seized or cordoned off Com-Star facilities, my agents will personally deliver the vids. We're ready, Victor."

"Oh, we're ready for anything," Victor said quietly, for the ears of his chief advisor alone. "Anything but whatever we haven't thought of."

The sentry, making a quick pass along the darkened hall and not thinking twice about the open library door, never saw his killer. An arm speared out with a chop to his trachea. The sentry barely had time to choke out a gasp before the arm snaked around his throat, clamping down on any sound. Yanked backward by his unseen assailant, the sentry clawed uselessly at his holstered pistol. There was the sharp crack of upper vertebrae breaking, and he went limp.

His role as Dan Cheurre abandoned, the assassin lowered the inert form to the carpeted floor, then began to make his way down the upstairs hall, stalking his final prey. A Mauser & Gray flechette pistol rested comfortably in one hand, and his dark eyes swept the shadows. The sentry had been unexpected, and he must be alert for any other surprises.

He shifted his weight evenly from one footstep to the next, his passage silent as a snake on the thick carpet. Any time the floor settled under his weight, the assassin froze in place. The mansion was so quiet that he easily detected the tiny noises coming from the end of the hall.

He knew it was Omi Kurita, in her room, preparing for the night. The pattern did not vary, so he continued forward. Past Isis Marik's suite, then an office door standing open, and now only three rooms away from his victim. The sound of his own shallow breathing seemed impossibly loud.

He hadn't expected the light left burning in Victor's office, and it threw a bright swath into the hall. That required one more adjustment to his carefully rehearsed plans. A quick check assured him that the office was empty, and he continued on toward Omi's room, switching out the light behind him. It was unusual for him to make changes to the environment of a hit, but he preferred the dark over the negligible risk that someone would see him.

The only true risk he'd taken tonight was in forging documents and arranging to get more of Isis's belongings out of storage in Deschuttes for delivery to the mansion. It couldn't be helped. The death of Arthur Steiner-Davion had forced him to move up the timing attack; he had no doubt that Victor and Omi would now quit Mogyorod sooner than anticipated.

That didn't worry him. He had two choices—postpone his plans and hit Omi Kurita wherever she next took up residence or pull it off earlier.

Confident in his planning, the assassin had decided to move.

The floor creaked again, forcing another pause. He knew just the briefest moment of pique that he'd been unable to wait for midnight and the cover of the chiming clock. But he couldn't be sure whether Victor would stay away all night, and he wanted to be long gone before Victor could pick up his scent.

There was no change in the small noises coming from Omi's room. His instincts told him he was close enough, and he took the last five strides quickly. With his needler in one hand, he used the other hand to shove the heavy door open.

Standing there was Victor's bodyguard, the dark-skinned Elemental, and the assassin's nerves screamed danger.

Omi sat at the vanity, frozen in the act of brushing out her hair. Half-hidden as she was behind the Elemental's muscular bulk, the assassin's shot was chancy at best. And Tiaret always went armed with a large gyrojet pistol riding leather beneath her left arm. She was fast, too, though not fast enough to beat a trained professional with his weapon already drawn. The assassin squeezed the trigger twice.

Needlers were a particularly nasty weapon that fired hundreds of tiny, needle-like flechettes shaved from an ammo block of polymer. With a ratcheting scrape, the first flurry of razored darts caught the Elemental in her side, shredding skin and muscle. The second burst took her in the chest just as she freed her recoilless slug-thrower from its holster. The impact failed to knock her back. It did throw off her aim, and the gyrojet's discharge roared out as it sent an explosive-tipped bullet into the wall twenty-five centimeters from the assassin's head. Tiaret tried to drive forward, but crumpled to the floor with her first step. A burnt-plastic stench hung heavy in the air.

With his plan for a quiet escape all lost to the vagaries of chance, the assassin had a clear view of Omi Kurita. She was holding a thin stiletto with a bloodletter groove, but it wasn't anything that could deflect a needler. He shifted aim, ready to finish the contract, but a flash of motion out of the corner of his right eye warned him to duck away, fast.

Too late. Agony lanced though him as Isis Marik plunged a short-handled knife into his chest with a scream and a wild, overhand stab. The assassin yelled in surprise and pain, nearly dropping the needler as his arm went numb. He managed to hang on to the weapon, whipping it back with a flailing sidearm blow that smashed into Isis's face. He felt her cheekbone give, and she fell heavily at his feet.

He booted her away with a vicious kick, hardly able to believe that she'd managed to hurt him. The blood running down the knife that still protruded from his chest made for a convincing argument.

The deafening discharge of Tiaret's gyrojet again went off, the bullet catching the assassin in the side, cracking a rib before it skipped off into the wall behind him. The impact spun him around into that same brocad-covered wall. Flipping back around, he saw the Elemental propping herself up on one thick arm, her gyrojet unsteady but pointed in his general direction. He half-fell, half-stumbled through the doorway and up the hall as the gyrojet roared again and blew a fist-size chunk out of the wall where he'd just been standing.

This wasn't—couldn't be—happening. That thought stayed with him as he stumbled back to the stairway. He killed the two security agents rushing up the stairs with lethal sprays from his needler. Their deaths were so easy. How had everything else gone wrong? It was far different from the time Victor Davion's people had caught him by baiting a trap. Tonight he'd been the hunter, not the hunted. He had been in control. There had been no mistakes—he never made mistakes.

The assassin wheezed, coughed, and tasted blood.

Exiting the mansion by a side door, he drew on his last reserves and trotted out to the utility building. By moonlight, he checked his wounds. Bad. The bullet had torn a large piece from his side, which was bleeding freely, and Isis's knife had taken him in the upper lung.

He pulled it free. A letter opener! His skin crawled, and he shivered. Brought down by a slip of a girl armed with a letter opener. He heaved the knife out over the lawn and nearly fainted from the exertion, but held on to his intent. Run! Escape!

A half-dozen weak kicks staved in the door to the utility building. He stole a flash from one cupboard and then escaped into the sewer systems that had given him access to the estate earlier in the evening. They would track him this far, but there were endless klicks of tunnels and pipe with multiple hiding places he'd set up well beforehand. He splashed through ankle-deep water and muck and then tripped over his own feet, sprawling forward. He slowly crawled back onto his hands and knees, wheezing for breath.

He would escape, or he would die down here. Alone.

That thought chilled him more than anything. He couldn't die! He was the one who held the lives of others in his hands, giving or taking them by his own actions.

By his whims. By the contracts he took. He had never failed—would never fail.

The idea gave him strength born of desperation, and the assassin stumbled back to his feet, plodding onward. But it didn't last. With every step, his legs felt heavier and his breath came in ragged gasps. His wounds burned, distracting him as he tried to remember the escape paths he'd planned. His vision narrowed to the hazy beam being thrown by his flash. This wasn't happening.

It was the last thought in his mind as the darkness crept in, threatening to sweep him away to unconsciousness and death.

It wasn't happening!

20

Deschuttes, Mogyorod
Melissia Theater
Lyran Alliance
12 December 3062

Isis Marik swam through stifling night. The dark wrapped around her with a liquid warmth, pouring into her ears and pressing heavy fingers against her eyes. It weighed on her arms and legs with numbing force. Only the uneven rhythm of her own heartbeat kept her company: four or five irregular beats, one slow, rasping breath, and repeat.

Her memory came in fits and starts, like holo stills flashed out in a dark and empty theater. Being left alone in the mansion. Sitting in a darkened office, unable to sleep. The creaking steps of some faceless bogeyman. Gunshots! Loud, roaring reports, and the smell of burnt plastic. She remembered a warm jet of blood trickling over her hand. Then pain, and the void.

Isis pushed back at the enveloping blackness, fighting

it, reaching for a coherent thought. Not me! That realization came first. The assassin hadn't been sent for her, as she'd feared. As she'd expected.

Four more beats, and another scraping shift. Footsteps, not her heartbeat. Someone pacing. She recognized the sound now. Remembered too many lonely vigils of her own: waiting for her father's infrequent messages, for Sun-Tzu's decisions, for rescue, and for something so commonplace as hoping her fiancé would actually arrive for dinner. Always waiting. And then always sent away.

She tried to force her eyes open, but for some reason, her right eye stubbornly remained closed. Some vague notion in the back of her mind teased her with the thought that Sun-Tzu Liao had heard of her injury and now waited at her side. But the man pacing her hospital room, dressed in the uniform of the old Federated Suns, could not have been more different from the Capellan Chancellor if he'd tried. And it would infuriate him to know he might have been taken for Sun-Tzu.

Victor Steiner-Davion must have caught a hint of movement. The flutter of an eyelid, or perhaps she'd twitched a finger. He made it to her side in three quick strides, then bent to look into her face. Isis saw the concern there, as well as a hint of embarrassment. Men were so obvious in that regard. She must look a fright.

"Omi?" she asked, her voice a dull croak. The words scratched her throat, and she had a dry, antiseptic taste in her mouth.

He smiled bleakly and nodded. "She's fine. Waiting for you on the *Alacrity*." He picked up a glass of water from her bedside table, helped her sit up slightly, and held the glass to her lips. "You saved her life."

The water was only lukewarm, but it eased the scratchiness in her throat. "Heard someone fall." She closed her eye. When she opened it again, Victor had turned away. "Who?" she asked.

He didn't answer right away. "Tiaret. She took several needles close to her heart but is healing fast. They took her off the critical list this morning."

This morning? "How long have I been here?" she asked, feeling a touch of strength returning. The right side of her jaw ached, and she still couldn't open her right eye, but she felt more drugged than injured.

Victor looked down at her with concern in his gray eyes. "Four days. You've got a concussion. And your cheekbone was broken in several places." Isis reached up with tentative fingers and explored the swollen side of her face.

"They were thorough and very careful, Isis. You'll be fine. There won't be any scars except for the small scalp cut in your hairline."

No scars. The idea made Isis want to laugh. Not all scars were visible.

"I thought it was me," she said then, wanting to talk in spite of the pain. "When I saw him creep by."

She paused to put some order to her thoughts. "I couldn't sleep, even though I told Omi I was tired. So much going on, and feeling rather useless. You'll never know what it meant to me—coming here, seeing you . . . and Omi."

"You couldn't sleep," Victor said gently.

She nodded. "I went into the office adjoining my room. Sat there in the dark, feeling sorry for myself, I suppose. I heard the first few steps and didn't think anything of it. I was facing the window, and there was just enough light bleeding in from the hall that I saw his reflection as he crept past the open door. A dark ghost, crouched over, pistol in both hands, ready. He looked in—I was sure he saw me and that I was going to die. But he passed by."

She laughed painfully. "It's a good thing when even the assassin fails to notice you, right? All along, I've been waiting for Kali Liao to send her Thugee assassins after me again."

Victor patted her hand, perhaps trying to reassure her. "Kali has been exiled to Highspire for her Black May attacks. She'll be kept there for the rest of her life. You don't have to worry about her."

"Don't I? I know you find it hard to believe that I was happy living on Sian, but I was. The only bad part was that Kali Liao terrified me. I'll never believe she can be contained." She looked up at Victor and read the fear in his eyes as he thought again how close Omi had come to death.

"You can't live your entire life in fear, Isis. As for Sian—" he exhaled noisily and clasped her hand warmly between both of his—"I would never begrudge you any happiness, especially after what you've done for me. I'm sorry I can't help with regard to Sun-Tzu. But if there is ever anything I *can* do for you, you have but to ask. Anything. I mean that."

What Isis wanted, Victor had no power to grant. "You're sending me away, aren't you?" she said.

"With Omi," Victor said gently. "Tukayyid is the safest place in the Inner Sphere right now, and I want you both to get there by the most secure method possible. Captain Gaines is making himself personally responsible for both of your safety."

He released her hand with a smile. "You need to rest. Jerrard Cranston will come to personally escort you to the spaceport. Thank you again, Isis. I'll never forget what you've done." With a final nod, he turned to go.

Despite her injuries, Isis was still the daughter of one of the Inner Sphere's most powerful leaders, and she quickly grasped the situation. Franklin Gaines? And Victor had mentioned the *Alacrity*, hadn't he? The WarShip he'd used to travel to Mogyorod?

"Are you sure that's wise, Victor?" she called out, her voice weak but loud enough to turn him around. "You've spoken out to oppose Katherine, haven't you?"

He nodded.

"Then you're at war, or will be soon enough. Are you certain you should send away your WarShip? Now?"

"The fact that you would ask that, Isis, makes me very glad you'll be with Omi. It's good to have friends I can rely on." He smiled again with real warmth, though there was a faraway look in his eyes. "But where I'm going, ComStar cannot follow."

Then he was gone, or maybe Isis drifted back to sleep. She was never certain which.

Bueller, Robinson
Draconis March
Federated Commonwealth

The *Overlord*-class DropShip sat on a distant ferro-crete pad, towering over the five spheroid *Unions*, the only vessels still waiting to blast free of Robinson. Lined up along the Benjamin Sandoval Memorial Spaceport, they looked almost like a false city skyline of high-rising edifices, especially the *Overlord*, ovoid and some one hundred-thirty meters tall.

Bright flame suddenly roiled and burst under it, scorching the pad and sending out a huge blast of smoke, steam, and dust. The leviathan rose slowly, almost grace-fully. The tremors from its launch could be felt all the way back in the main terminal where Tancred Sandoval watched from a private observation deck. His father found him there just as the *Overlord* completed its roll and, gaining speed, thrust for the heavens. The First Robinson Rangers were on their way to attack the Dra-conis Combine.

Tancred wondered if he'd ever see any of them again.

"Mai radioed me," the Duke said shortly by way of greeting, referring to the commander of the Rangers and their cousin. He watched the *Overlord* until it was no longer visible behind a patch of gray clouds. "She said you'd decided not to field with the Rangers. Even seeing you standing here, Tancred, I can hardly believe it."

"Can't believe that I'm not getting caught up in the hysteria? That I'm showing some caution?" Tancred was in no mood for their usual sparring. He knew the argument that was coming, and he preferred to get it over with quickly.

"Caution, Tancred? Or cowardice?" The duke held up his hands to fend off his son's angry retort. "I am not calling your bravery into question, son, but you know that same question is being asked on board those DropShips every time someone sees your 'Mech's empty berth or passes by your usual cabin. You're undermining their confidence. Is that really what you want to do?"

Two *Unions* lit off their fusion drives at nearly the same time, and Tancred followed their dual launch with his eyes. "My berth isn't empty, Father. Mai promoted a new officer in my place."

"She did what?"

"Mai was being kind when she told you I decided to stay behind. The truth is that I've resigned my commission with the Rangers."

Tancred watched as the shock in his father's face slowly transformed into darkening anger.

"I also urged her to refuse your orders, even though she would likely face charges—if she made it back. Katherine or Victor, whoever wins the throne, will eventually need someone to answer for this unsanctioned attack against House Kurita. Of course, that assumes Theodore Kurita leaves them a throne to be won." He shrugged. "She went anyway."

The duke fairly exploded. "You had no right to do that!"

Tancred felt a hot flush rise all the way to his shaved skull with its dark topknot. "I had every right! You're justifying your assault as a counterattack against Combine aggression, even when Victor's address proves we've got more important domestic problems. He all but accused Katherine of causing Arthur's death."

"Always back to Prince Victor. How did that man ever secure your loyalty over your family and people, Tancred? We are princes, too, don't forget. Or we were, until Alexander Davion abrogated that title except for himself alone. We were princes of the Draconis March, second only to the First Prince on New Avalon. If not for that, you yourself might have been a serious contender for the throne."

"It's the Davion throne," Tancred said resolutely. "And if Victor's right about Katherine, you're playing straight into her hands."

"Then where is his proof?" James Sandoval demanded. He tried to throw up both hands in exasperation, but with one arm in a cast, it became an awkward flapping motion.

"I tell you, Victor's wrong, or just plain bluffing. Or he's been unduly influenced by the Dracs. For all we know, he's bedding Theodore's daughter. He'll see what he wants to see with regard to her family and nation."

Tancred folded his arms across his chest, careful to show no response to his father's probing remark on the degree of Victor's closeness to Omi. "Victor would not bluff. Not about this," he said. "As to the rest . . . I've seen what happens to those who bet against Victor Steiner-Davion. Do you really want to stand on Katherine's side?"

"I'm on no one's side. My concern is the Draconis March, and nothing more." The duke drew a steadying breath and unclenched his fists. "Tancred, son, this isn't too late to correct," he said in a quieter tone. "It's your responsibility to the March and to me. Get your *Nightstar* and hightail it out to one of the *Union*s. I'll radio Mai and let her know you've changed your mind. And you will lead our forces to a great victory in the Combine. That is what you are going to do."

"I won't. I'm sorry, Father, but that is an order I will not obey. And what's more, I'll fight you if I have to."

The Duke Robinson exhaled sharply, obviously unconcerned by his son's threat. "And I thought you were Arthur's friend."

"I was. Despite your orders," Tancred reminded him. "But I'm not going to tarnish Arthur's memory or destroy what he was attempting to do before the bombs went off. If he'd been given a few more minutes, I think this"—he waved an arm at the landing field—"this wouldn't be happening."

"You don't know what he was about to say. It was unsettling, I admit, but his train of thought could have been going anywhere. We'll never know for sure."

"And that's very convenient for you, isn't it?" Tancred snapped, unable to keep the accusatory tone out of his voice. Another DropShip launched with a ground-shaking roar and a long tongue of fusion-powered flame. Tancred followed it skyward with his gaze, his expression hard.

"This is lunacy, Father. And if you can't see it, perhaps we need a Duke who can." He continued watching the DropShip until it, too, disappeared from view, bound for the Combine.

When Tancred looked down again, his father was gone.

Part 2

Dirge

21

Winding down out of the foothills that pressed Port Lawrence against the coastline, the Coventry Province Militia staggered and straggled across the valley toward the city. Battered though it was, the 'Mech battalion was the city's only protection—a mere four companies left of what had once been two proud regiments protected what remained of the militia's armored column. Behind them, the First Coventry Jaegers commanded the heights, raining down a concentrated missile barrage on the militia's rearguard lance.

Blows hammered like giant fists against the broad back of Kommandant Neil Rikkard's *Barghest*, which was hunkered down in a defensive crouch. The cockpit shook violently as missiles caught the side of the 'Mech's forward-thrust head, but the seventy-ton quadruped kept its feet. Four-legged designs were inherently more stable, but the *Barghest*'s obvious newness and heavier weapons made it a high-profile target.

And better him than any of his men, Rikkard had decided. They only had so much left to give. The last time they'd taken such a savage beating, at least it had been at the hands of Clan Jade Falcon, not their own countrymen.

But why was it happening? That was the silent question he'd been asking himself for weeks, and more often since the death of Colonel William Steiger had thrust him into command. Why? The militia might favor Prince Victor, but they had pledged to remain neutral in the defense of Coventry—as any regional militia should, in Rikkard's opinion. But that had not been good enough for Archon Katrina, who had condemned the militia for its association with Frederick Bradford, Duke of Coventry and a staunch supporter of Prince Victor. Katrina desperately wanted to maintain control over Coventry's important 'Mech production facilities, and her orders apparently left no room for neutrality. Or mercy.

One regiment of infantry spread out in garrison posts over Coventry created numerous easy targets for arrest and detention. But they were still alive, Rikkard thought, or so he hoped. The second infantry regiment had been lost in the outback during three weeks of fighting and running: eight hundred men and women dead, wounded, or captured. The militia's remaining soldiers didn't add up to more than three platoons. Two, if Rikkard counted only those who weren't wounded.

Another heavy rain of missiles blasted away armor and pockmarked the ground around him. A pair of azure PPC beams streaked by overhead and into the flank of a trailing *Hermes*. Armor sloughed away and exposed the critical gyroscopic stabilizer, which ruptured and flew apart in a hail of spinning metal.

Rikkard wheeled a second lance back into the teeth of the Jaeger advance, hoping to distract them, but the Jaegers favored a brute-force approach. Despite the *Her-*

mes's obvious incapacitation, the Jaegers continued to work it over with energy cannon and lasers. They stopped only when one cascade of manmade lightning cored into the head, burning through the ferroglass shield into the cockpit.

Cursing his countrymen, Neil Rikkard clenched his teeth and shoved his throttle to its forward limit. Like the mythological creature that was its namesake, the *Barghest* leapt forward at a full run for the Jaeger line. An enemy *Hauptmann*—named for the Alliance workhorse soldiers of that rank—flashed onto his HUD, stepping from behind the cover of a light stand of yellow pine. Rikkard tied his large lasers together and stabbed megajoules of crimson energy at the assault-weight Omni-Mech, scoring molten weals across its chest and legs. They were solid hits, but they barely slowed the massive war machine.

Rikkard's thirst for revenge was slaked for the moment, though, and he spun the *Barghest* with a nimble grace that belied the awkwardness so common to quadrupeds. He raced back for the militia's line under an umbrella of long-range missiles, gaining some measure of safety, if only for a few seconds.

Long enough to regroup the militia for its final stand.

Sitting on the edge of Port Lawrence, the Coventry Military Academy covered more than several square kilometers and divided the city proper from the Cascade Valley. At Duke Bradford's urging, the academy had scavenged from among its own machines and supplies to form a stockpile for the militia. That support, grudgingly accepted at first, had kept Rikkard and his people alive and hopeful against all odds as they fell back toward this final staging ground. Riding herd from behind, the Jaegers seemed perfectly content to allow the militia this maneuver. That worried Neil Rikkard more than anything so far.

A cadet company of light 'Mechs led by a *Wolfhound* came forward, welcoming the battered militia command. Rikkard quickly ordered his people into a line of battle, spreading the light armor out onto the flanks and holding the center with his 'Mech forces.

"Militia command, this is Hauptmann-cadet Guerro," came a voice over Rikkard's commline. "Colonel Steiger?"

"Dead, Guerro. The colonel died three days ago," Rikkard said into the mic mounted in his neurohelmet's face guard. His throat felt blistered by the heat inside his cockpit as he spoke.

"This is Kommandant Rikkard. I've got a lot of wounded here. Have you made arrangements to care for them and ship them out?"

"Putting them into hiding is about the best we're going to manage, Kommandant, sir. Kristen's Krushers hemmed us in to the south, preventing any escape. We threw a reinforced company at the mercenaries to test their resolve, and they sent our people back in pieces. We're out of options, unless you think the Jaegers will give us the day we'd need to force that blockade."

"I think they're going to give us about five minutes," Rikkard said. His heart sank at the mention of the mercenary blockade—another indication that Katrina's supporters wanted to pin the militia here.

Watching, he and the rest of the militia waited as the Jaegers descended from Cascade Heights and ranked themselves in an arrowhead aimed straight at the heart of Port Lawrence. On his heads-up display, he saw two 'Mech battalions with armor support and two squads of the new Lyran *Fenrir* battle armor.

It was no surprise when the *Hauptmann* OmniMech took point; Rikkard had already guessed that the assault 'Mech belonged to the Jaegers' Colonel Walker. He walked the *Barghest* forward, setting himself between the Jaegers and his command while mentally railing at the situation. These were his soldiers—his kids—now. Some had barely graduated from the academy grounds they now defended. They deserved a better fate than this.

The first shots were traded at range, with longer-reaching missile launchers and light autocannon. A brief hail of fifty-millimeter slugs skipped off the *Barghest*'s shoulder. The

Jaegers moved forward slowly, almost hesitantly, now picking at Rikkard's line with extended-range lasers and PPCs. Were they trying to lure his force out of the city once more?

Rikkard sent two lances of Plainsman hovertanks backed with Alacorn heavies into the no-man's land, testing the Jaeger resolve. Concentrated fire blasted one of the lighter vehicles to ruin, but not before the triple-gauss rifles of both heavier tanks punched nickel-ferrous slugs into the enemy formation. An *Enforcer* caught two of those in the chest, caving in the torso cavity and all but rupturing the 'Mech's fusion engine.

Now the Jaegers moved forward with determined stride, the BattleMechs taking point, the MechWarriors seemingly incensed over the rough treatment handed out by a pair of armored vehicles. Not to be discounted, the militia Alacorns swung out to strike the Jaeger flank, thinking to sting them again.

They never made it.

Founts of scorched earth and fire geysered up around the Alacorns. One pillar erupted at the right tread of one of the tanks, flipping it over before dropping it turret-down against the ground. The other Alacorn split open under the hard-hitting strike of three such eruptions, leaving behind a ruined, twisted shell that might once have protected a working machine.

"Artillery! Artillery!" Hauptmann-cadet Guerro had walked his *Wolfhound* out to one side and was now pointing with the stubby barrel that was his right arm. "Ridgeline, east-southeast. Long tom cannon mixed with Arrow IV."

In angry frustration, Rikkard slammed one fist against his thigh, tearing away one of the sensor patches taped to it. He pressed it back on, knowing it made no difference now. The Jaegers had wanted to bunch up his people in a killing zone; trapping them between the mountains and the city made their artillery all the more effective.

"Fire! We have fire on the academy grounds!" It was

a voice Rikkard didn't recognize. One of the cadets. "Damn the Jaegers. They're raining artillery into the academy!"

Rikkard punched up his rear camera on an auxiliary monitor and saw explosions rock one of the large barracks as artillery fire gutted the building. Murdering, Archon-loving bastards! Tears of frustration and anger welled in his eyes, blurring his vision.

He blinked them away. "Coventry Province Militia, forward at a walk, line abreast," he ordered, throttling up his own machine. His cross hairs burned the dark gold of target lock, and his large lasers stabbed out brilliant destruction, cutting into the Jaeger line. A returned gauss slug smashed his forward-right shoulder, raining armor to the ground in shards and splinters. "Hauptmann Guerro, your company has one task. Break through to that ridge and silence the artillery. Permanently."

A good soldier, Guerro was loping his *Wolfhound* forward even before replying, his company in tow. "We'll never make it past the Jaegers," he said.

"They'll have other worries," Rikkard promised. "Militia, forward at a run. Begin concentrated fire at my target, now!" His lasers lashed out again, drawing molten wounds across the *Hauptmann* assault Omni heading the Jaeger arrowhead formation. "We punch through their formation rank by rank," he ordered, knowing they would never make it.

But they would certainly try.

At fifty-four kilometers per hour, the *Barghest* barreled in at the enemy. Not the First Coventry Jaegers—not anymore. Not Alliance. Not even Lyran. The enemy! The *Hauptmann* might have been formidable one on one, but as the last of Rikkard's command turned every weapon against it, the assault Omni went down under blistering fire. Armor splashed across the ground in molten trails as autocannon hammered it with slugs tipped in depleted uranium. A gauss rifle rammed its rail-accelerated projectile into the 'Mech's chest, opening a breach into which five PPCs poured cascading energy. There wasn't enough left of it to recognize as the blasted skeleton finally crumpled with graceless abandon.

Rikkard's lasers lanced the enemy formation again and again with crimson beams, his heat scale shooting into the red as he worked his heat sinks overtime. The distance closed rapidly, but not before the enemy's arrowhead formation had been severely blunted.

Their response took its toll, however. Their concentrated fire did not match the militia's, but Rikkard began to count his own 'Mechs as they disappeared from his HUD. Two . . . five . . . six.

Only a company was left to back him when the *Barghest* leapt between two *Garm*s and finally cut loose with the Disintegrator autocannon he'd held in reserve. Flame leapt several meters past the end of the twelve-centimeter bore, its furious assault taking the leg clean off one *Garm*. He shouldered into an *Axman* that tried to block his path, but the *Barghest*'s momentum knocked the other 'Mech aside before it could bring its lethal hatchet-arm down on him. His lasers cut at the *Awesome* trying to muscle in on his left.

Heat washed over him in dizzying waves, overwhelming his life support, stabbing hot coals down into his lungs and distorting his vision. Alarms wailed for attention, though he concentrated only on meeting the needs of his shutdown override. The enemy surrounded him, coming in at every side. Some of his men fought on out of his sight.

With no need to power forward—no need even to aim with the enemy so thick—Kommandant Neil Rikkard hunched the *Barghest* down on its metal-shod haunches and held on to the trigger.

His weapons fired as fast as they could cycle, running his heat scale past its maximum range while a dozen enemy machines tore at the beast in their midst. Unable to breathe the scorched air, his eyes clenched shut against the furnace that was slowly cooking him, Neil Rikkard's last thoughts were still on his trigger and the override that prevented a heat-induced shutdown. No machine—no warrior—could take this kind of punishment for long. But he counted each second as that much more precious time to hurt the enemy.

It was sixty-two seconds, in fact, before the blackness finally claimed him.

22

The press corps stood by respectfully as security agents escorted Katrina through the Davion Peace Gardens, also known as Peace Park. A tranquil setting of thick grass and towering trees, flowers, and ferns, it stretched for several kilometers along the edge of the palace grounds, the NAIS university, and a stretch of Avalon City itself. A few reporters shifted uneasily, no doubt uncomfortable covering the rebellion here in Peace Park.

Good. Katrina wanted them uncomfortable, wanted them thinking about her brother's call to arms, as compared to her own platform of peace.

Stepping up to the podium, she waited politely as the ladies and gentlemen—the rabid animals—of the press readied themselves. Holocams whirred to life, and a few static shots were taken, though without the aid of any flash. Strobes made her skin appear pasty and sallow, and she never allowed them up close. Natural light was always best, bringing out a healthy color in her cheeks and highlighting the pale red lip gloss she favored for such appearances.

"I will make a brief statement," she said, "and then take those questions pre-approved by my press secretary. I apologize for the brevity of today's session, but I'm afraid my brother has complicated all of our lives tremendously."

Katrina paused for effect, pretending to gather her thoughts. She pulled her hands from the pockets of her knee-length parka and folded them on the podium's velvet-covered top. She had dressed for the invigorating spring coolness in a silver parka, gray scarf, and silver-gray boots. The outfit was chosen to suit the weather, but it was also as far as she could get from any kind of a military look. Her golden hair spilled down across her shoulders, framing her face and softening its lines.

"I know that many of you have only today learned of the unfortunate happenings on Coventry," she began. "Let me assure you that there has been no attempt to undermine the efficacy of the press. Free media has always been a primary concern of mine and will remain so. That said, my military advisors *are* restricting HPG traffic to certain worlds, but only to prevent further loss of life as my brother tries to incite riots and rebellion in what was, not so long ago, a nation at peace.

"Unfortunately, Victor has apparently had agents in place on Coventry for some time. I do not want to say that Duke Frederick Bradford was subverted, for I maintain hope for him yet. But certainly he is misled—misled by a soldier who cannot put away the supposed glories of war. Who thinks to place himself above the Star League, and proves himself far beneath its ideals as he resorts to baseless accusations in his attempts to sow chaos. Amaris himself could not have been so deceitful, or so cruel."

Many in the press corps grimaced at the mention of

Stefan Amaris, the man whose greed for power had brought about the bloody destruction of the first Star League. If she could paint Victor in that light, as ambitious and reckless, his public support would evaporate.

"Coventry, I'm sorry to say, has now paid a heavy price for my brother's thirst for power. I wish it could be otherwise. With luck, and with help, we will see to it that no other worlds have to pay such a price." She sighed, quick and steadying. "I'll take your questions now."

A younger woman, dark, hungry, and intense, was first to be heard. "Highness," she said, "Gloria Cantwell, Avalon Free Press. Wouldn't you say that the recent violence on Solaris VII was a sign that trouble was already brewing in the Commonwealth and Alliance months ago?"

Katrina had been pleased to see that question on the list submitted by Dehaver. It saved her from having to plant it herself. "The riots on Solaris were indicative of nothing except the need for stable, central leadership," she said. "And I believe we still have that across most of the Alliance and Commonwealth. As for the Inner Sphere, there is the resurrected Star League. And perhaps what we need is a First Lord who looks to all of humanity first and his personal concerns last."

The vagueness of that criticism could apply to either Sun-Tzu Liao or Theodore Kurita, and so would play well within both the Capellan and Draconis Marches.

"Mr. Kalawesa," she said to another reporter who had prepared a question she wanted asked, "you're next."

The man half-bowed. "Thank you, Highness. You mentioned Duke Bradford as a possible rebel, but what about Duke Sandoval? We have reports now of five—perhaps six—regiments fighting on Combine soil. Proserpina has fallen to the Robinson Rangers—a Combine prefecture capital! Tell us, do you support his actions?"

Katrina looked troubled. She had to. There was simply no way a peace candidate could support such a blatant campaign of military aggression. But she also realized that James Sandoval was doing an important service by distracting people from Victor's call to war.

"Duke Sandoval has been a trusted and valuable leader within the Commonwealth since before it was the Commonwealth. He is a contemporary of my father, and I am reluctant to condemn his actions outright. I await his personal and detailed report as to why such measures were necessary, much as I still await Coordinator Kurita's report about the annexation of the Lyons Thumb." That reminder of the Thumb's loss would help justify Sandoval's actions as long as she needed.

She nodded to another newsman. "Mr. Hartford?"

"Back to Coventry and the prospect of civil war, Highness. Duke Bradford's collusion with Prince Victor aside, it was the Coventry Province Militia who paid a heavy price. Can you comment?"

That was not quite the question she had approved. Katrina wanted to avoid any mention of a "civil war" or her brother's old title of "First Prince," not the least because she refused to concede to Victor anything close to equal footing with herself.

"The militia, according to all reports tendered by the Coventry Jaegers, went mad and had to be destroyed," she said patiently. "Remote infantry garrisons surrendered easily enough, but the main force fought to the last man. There was no other way. The destruction visited on Port Lawrence during the final battle is very unfortunate, but just another sign of the militia's disregard for lives. The Jaegers are distressed that they failed to turn the militia away from the city. Gun-cam footage will be provided to you later today, showing how the militia formed up a reckless charge after ignoring terms for a peaceful surrender."

"Last question," Dehaver called out, prompting a flood of shouts for the Archon's attention.

She nodded to Caroline DeWhit, one of her favorite interviewers. Caroline, for all that she was born on New Avalon, actually preferred the Alliance and had made no secret of the fact that she intended to apply for a change of citizenship soon. Katrina regarded her as "safe." DeWhit also had the perfect question on which to end the press conference.

"Highness, if you had one thing to say to your brother . . ."

Katrina dropped her gaze, staring mournfully at her hands for a moment. When she looked up again, she could feel the summoned tears welling in her eyes.

She looked out beyond the throng, as though he were standing just within sight. "Victor," she said, "whatever you decide, this will be the moment that matters most. Stop the violence. Let go of your warlike visions. Coventry and Benet III—these are senseless tragedies that need not spread to other worlds.

"It is not too late," she said, knowing full well it was, "to prevent such unnecessary bloodshed."

Fort Dylan, Cassias
Draconis March
Federated Commonwealth (Suns)

Tancred clenched his hands into impotent fists beneath the table as General Zardetto took up the flag.

"This is preposterous, being kept waiting for General Evans," Zardetto was saying. "Leftenant General Dzuiba, I must demand that you interrupt him." Dzuiba was aide to Kev Evans, commander of the Seventeenth Avalon Hussars.

Tancred had chosen his ally most carefully, or so he'd thought. General Acabee Zardetto was commander of the Third Crucis Lancers, also stationed on Cassias. No great friend of Duke James Sandoval and openly loyal to Prince Victor, Zardetto was an important officer whose support Tancred thought might give weight to his arguments.

Except that Cassandra Dzuiba was shielding her commander from hearing those arguments as he busily prepared to launch the Seventeenth Hussars into Combine space. "That is not possible," she said again with a determined air. "The general is in negotiations to acquire JumpShip transport for our support forces."

"That is precisely what we hope to dissuade him from, General Dzuiba." Tancred tried to capture her eyes with his, pitting his will against hers. "This rash course of action will only cause more trouble for the Commonwealth, and for you all. Can't you see that?"

"You think we can't take An Ting? We did back in '39, and then the Dragon wasn't distracted by a two-front war. This time we'll kick the snakes all the way back to Galedon V, maybe."

Tancred's pent-up energy finally got the better of him. He stood abruptly and began to pace the small conference room, feeling the eyes of both commanders on him while he forced himself to calm down. Anger would serve no one here.

"You can't seriously believe this attack will be supported by either Victor or Katherine," he said.

Dzuiba shrugged. "What does that matter? The March Lord—your father—has authorized the operation, which makes it as binding as we need it to be. Katherine . . . Katrina . . . whatever, she'll support us once the Kurita forces are thrown back. She has to. And Victor? We've never counted on his support. Not since he threw in with the Dracs. In fact, if he hadn't robbed us of our JumpShips and DropShips for Operation Bulldog—loaning them to a Combine regiment, no less!—we'd already be on An Ting and looking to drive deeper."

And that effectively summarized Tancred's opposition here. Not Cassandra Dzuiba personally, or the absent General Kev Evans, but the Seventeenth's history. With no strong ties to either ruler and a known hatred for the Draconis Combine, they were willing to take his father's lead and strike at House Kurita for what they saw as decades—centuries—of wrongs.

That made for a daunting foe, except that Tancred still believed that being on the right side had to carry some weight. "If you truly believe that Katherine or my father would support this action, why not wait for them to supply you with proper transports?" he asked.

"And be left behind? Proserpina has fallen, Baron Sandoval. Marduk, too. The Combine's teetering on the edge. If that hasn't been among your family's dreams these last twenty-five years, what has?" She grinned without humor, the MechWarrior in her showing through, hungry for battle. "It's been first among ours, I promise you."

Tancred came over to the table and leaned forward, his hands propped on the wood veneer as he met Cassandra Dzuiba's resolute gaze. "You have responsibilities here."

"And we'll return to them," she promised. "Right after we deal with the Dragon." She looked to General Zardetto, her green eyes dancing with eagerness. "Why not field with us? You have enough transport capability to round out our task force. Take the fight to them for once!"

"And leave Cassias defenseless?" Zardetto asked. "Thank you, no. I have a greater appreciation for our position here, and for our duty to the Commonwealth."

"I suppose I can understand why you'd rather sit in a garrison post," she said in a thinly veiled sneer at Zardetto's position as an armor commander. Indeed, he was among the few non-MechWarriors to hold command of a regimental combat team.

"My job is to protect the Commonwealth," Zardetto said. "Not help tear it apart."

Despite his words, Tancred had spotted the split-second of hunger in Zardetto's eyes. The general was Tharkad-born and firmly behind Victor, there was no denying that, and still the promise of glory against House Kurita tempted him. That was when Tancred admitted to himself that he'd lost the Seventeenth—had lost it before ever setting foot on Cassias.

"We should adjourn," he said, knowing that the arguments between the two officers would only heat up now. "I think we've said everything there is to say."

"Indeed." Leftenant General Dzuiba drew herself up stiffly. "I shall pass along your concerns to General Evans." She nodded to Tancred and, ignoring Zardetto, walked proudly from the room.

"We can stop them," Zardetto said as soon as the door closed behind her. "My Lancers could hold them here."

It was a tempting idea, though ultimately self-defeating. There was already fighting on nearby worlds, and Tancred would need to borrow forces from Zardetto if he was to support Victor's move to dethrone Katherine.

"No," he said. "Let them go. We'll deal with them later.

"If they come back at all."

Deschuttes, Mogyorod
Melissia Theater
Lyran Alliance
12 February 3063

Having exchanged the garrison post's war room for Mogyorod's HPG station, Victor had availed himself of better equipment and an atmosphere more conducive to concentrating on the tasks at hand. Like most ComStar buildings, the station boasted high, vaulted ceilings, large rooms, and a stark, utilitarian feel that did not clutter the mind. A place without distraction.

Precentor Irelon and Demi Shakov of the Prince's Men had again joined Victor and Jerrard Cranston. A few Adepts manned local computer consoles, monitoring the regular activity of the HPG station, but they could be dismissed. Gathered about a large table that projected holographic star charts into the air above it, Victor and the others studied the systems that flashed cautionary amber or danger-filled red—indications of unrest or open fighting. Systems such as Tharkad and Coventry, under Katherine's domination, were colored a chill blue. Those declaring for Victor glowed golden, and neutral worlds were gray.

Victor reached past the gold of Mogyorod, here at the far edge of the Lyran Alliance, toward the amber-flashing system of New Avalon all the way on the other side of the table. "Could we be in any worse position for launching a war?"

"You could be on Coventry," Shakov said, without any of his usual humor. The slaughter of Coventry's militia, despite Katherine's cover story, was no subject for amusement.

Also, Shakov had obviously been put off his stride earlier when Tiaret insisted on sweeping him and Precentor Irelon with a handheld "frisker." Back on duty after two months of enforced rest and recuperation, Tiaret was keeping a wary eye on them all. Raymond Irelon accepted the frisk with stoic indifference, but Shakov had looked insulted.

Normally, Victor would never have subjected them to the indignity, but Jerry had insisted on giving Tiaret final authority over such procedures.

"It's the same man, Victor," he told Victor weeks ago. "The assassin who killed Melissa and Ryan Steiner. He's back."

"Are you sure?" Victor asked.

"Absolutely. We typed his blood against the DNA file. There was plenty to sample from, too."

"You think he's looking for revenge?" Victor's people had once trapped the assassin and used him to avenge themselves on one of the conspirators involved in Melissa's death. They'd planned to execute him afterward, but the assassin had staged a brilliant escape.

Jerry shook his head. "This man's a pure sociopath. Revenge would never enter into his calculations. No, someone set him on Omi. Could be Katherine, trying to hurt you, but these days, I can make a better case for reactionary elements in the Combine or the Draconis

March. And given what we know of how he works, we're damn lucky he missed. This time."

He raised his hands, forestalling Victor's outburst. "She's safe enough now, Victor. But the fact remains that the assassin got too close, and we don't have a body yet. We're upgrading all security around you. With Curaitis still missing in action, Tiaret is the best we've got."

"Missing," Victor said, "but hardly absent. Did you know that Countess Drake has a copy of the new Reginald Starling painting?" Which meant that the scheme to prove Katherine's guilt in Melissa Steiner-Davion's assassination was finally under way. It was their only hope of trapping Katherine red-handed and bringing her down with one quick thrust.

Until that day, however, Victor's only recourse to stopping his sister's bloody reign was military. "So," he said, bringing the discussion back toward his position on Mogyorod. "How do I press forward?"

"The Arc-Royal Defense Cordon," Precentor Irelon said at once. "You trust Morgan Kell, so the sooner you get there, the better. The fighting on Kikuyu is too close for comfort. No telling where they'll strike once the Cavalry's dead. Morgan Kell has a dozen solid regiments under his command, ready to defend you."

Kikuyu, a world not twenty light-years from Mogyorod, flashed red on the holographic map. The Sixth Donegal Guards and the mercenary Storm's Metal Thunder had pounced on the Eighth Deneb Light Cavalry regiment for its refusal to take sides.

"More," Shakov said, "if you count the three Com Guard divisions in the ARDC, plus our 244th."

"I can't count the Com Guard," Victor said flatly. "Jerry?"

Jerry Cranston frowned at the map. "The ARDC is yours the minute you call Morgan. That's been his promise for four years. But he's also guarding a large stretch of our border with the Jade Falcons, and if you weaken that border, the Clans will attack."

"My thoughts exactly. I think we've got to forget New Avalon for now, and concentrate on the Alliance theater. The throne isn't the real objective here, and I'm already fighting an uphill battle resurrecting the Federated Suns as my standard. I have to convince the Lyrans that this is as much their war as mine, and pick up an army as I go. What have you got for me?"

"Blue Hole and Chahar are death traps if you set foot anywhere near them. The Thirty-ninth Avalon Hussars on Newtown Square near the Periphery are for you, but you might need them to hold Adam Steiner on Barcelona. I personally believe your best route is through Winter and Inarcs, where you can secure production facilities. The Seventh Crucis Lancers garrison Winter, and it'd be nice to have such elite troops. The Fifteenth Lyran Regulars on Hood IV might swing to your side, as might the Deneb Light Cavalry, now that Katherine has decided she needs to make an example of them."

Precentor Irelon shook his head, making his long gray ponytail dance around his shoulders. "There's no saving the Light Cavalry. They can last another week, at best. You couldn't get there in time, even if you had the forces."

"Wait, wait, wait." Demi-Precentor Shakov held out one hand, totally confused. "You lost me back around Kikuyu." He glanced sharply from face to face. "Why can't you count on the Com Guard? Seems to me that between the Guard and your command of the Star League Defense Force, Katherine hasn't got a prayer of stopping you."

Victor looked over at Irelon, who stared back with a sour expression. "He hasn't been told."

Which Victor translated to mean that Irelon hadn't wanted to be the one to tell him.

Shakov looked at Victor. "Highness?"

Victor exhaled heavily. "I've stepped aside as Precentor Martial of ComStar," he said, "and as Commanding General of the Star League."

"In Blake's name, Victor! Why would you do that?"

Shakov bolted upright, and Victor held up a hand to forestall Tiaret, who glowered dangerously at the outburst. One look at her and Shakov got himself under control, but only with visible effort.

"To keep from being relieved of command," Jerry Cranston said. "Katherine could have swung Thomas Marik and Sun-Tzu Liao behind a vote to censure Victor, claiming the Star League had no authority over what is so clearly a matter between the Alliance and the Federated Suns. The League could only act if the current legal head of either state made a direct appeal."

"Which is Katherine," Shakov said, nodding. "But the Com Guard? Certainly the Primus would back us."

"Perhaps," Victor said. "Though there is some question as to whether the First Circuit would back the Primus. We analyzed the potential vote, and it came down to Gardner Riis, Precentor Rasalhague. I did not think Sharilar Mori's position should rest on that man. So that's one reason."

"And two?" Shakov's dark eyes were clouded with frustration.

Irelon answered him. "Two is that ComStar, like the Star League, *must* be seen as a neutral party. What Great House would trust us if we sided with Victor against a legally constituted government? Think about Word of Blake and the trouble they've had establishing themselves beyond the Free Worlds League. They so obviously favor Thomas Marik and the League that no one trusts them to be impartial."

"Not to mention that this is, in fact, a matter best solved within the Lyran Alliance and Federated Suns," Victor said. "The mandate has to come from the people, not enforced by an outside agency, or we'll simply tear ourselves apart again. When I leave Mogyorod, the Com Guard stays behind."

Shakov gave a curt nod, clearly displeased. "So just who is our Precentor Martial?"

"Precentor Martial pro-tem," Victor corrected. "I haven't relinquished the position, just set it aside temporarily to preserve ComStar's neutrality." He caught Jerry Cranston's encouraging nod and Irelon's look of disgust. "I tapped Precentor Tharkad—Gavin Dow."

The shocked silence lasted all of two seconds. "Dow! Victor . . . Highness . . . Gavin Dow is a dangerous man. Even here at the back end of Lyran space, we've learned to be wary of our own Precentor Tharkad." Shakov looked for help to Irelon, whose expression was even more sour than before. "Whatever made you choose him?"

"Because he's the one person I'm certain will surrender the position once this war is over," Victor said.

"I still say you should give it back to Anastasius Focht," Irelon said, which was the same argument he'd given Victor two days before. "Focht wears the job well, and is as honorable a man as I've ever met."

"True," Victor agreed. After getting to know Focht over the past few years, there weren't many men Victor trusted more to do the right thing. "But Anastasius is en route to Capellan space to help negotiate a cease-fire between the Confederation and St. Ives. Dow will handle the job well enough. He doesn't want to be Precentor Martial, though he'll milk it for quite a few concessions."

Irelon looked far from convinced. "I don't trust that man."

"I trust him to look after himself," Victor said. "I can rely on his motivated self-interest, which makes him largely predictable."

"Besides which," Jerry Cranston put in, "by turning the post over to Precentor Tharkad, one of Katherine's direct representatives to ComStar, she can hardly claim that Victor is abusing his power."

"Not so long as Dow is willing to abuse it in her name," Irelon said, pulling out a missive from within his robes. He handed it to Victor. "Did you predict this?"

"To Precentor Irelon, commander, Com Guard 244th Division," Victor read aloud. "You are hereby ordered to sever any and all ties to Victor Steiner-Davion, his associates, and military forces. He is denied access to

Com Guard assets and facilities until further notice, except in the normal course of business, as might be approved for any customer. Signed Precentor Martial pro-tem Gavin Dow." He smiled thinly at Jerry. "Yes, we expected this, though not quite so soon. When did you get this, Raymond?"

"Off the record? Yesterday. Why?"

Jerry grimaced. "Because Word of Blake's *Divine Will* left the Mogyorod system this morning. They knew Victor was no longer worth shadowing." He shook his head. "Doesn't help, though. The leak could be anywhere between Tharkad and here."

"A Blakist leak? On Mogyorod?" Shakov asked. Irelon nodded, and Shakov sat back, disturbed. He sketched a casual salute to Tiaret, now in full accord with her stringent security precautions.

Victor was careful not to smile at the man's sudden change of heart. But then, ComStar had learned the hard way not to underestimate the tenacity of the Word of Blake fanatics.

"On the record," he asked, "when does this order go into effect?"

Precentor Irelon shifted uneasily. He clasped his hands behind his back and stared into the holographic array of colored stars. "Frankly, Highness, it takes effect when you want it to, or when you leave Mogyorod. Until that time, this station and the garrison post are yours."

Victor exhaled a sharp, decisive breath. "Thank you, Raymond. I'll hold you to that, but not for too much longer. As near as Jerry and I can figure, the first wave is set to go. Correct?"

"Katherine preempted us on a few worlds, locking down those first units who answered your call," Jerry hedged, "but we've got another dozen or better awaiting orders." Then, after a pause, "I'm less than happy about the response we're getting out of the Draconis March. Arthur's death has the entire place turned upside down. We've lost several units I was certain would come over to you, including the mercenary Urakhai Eighth Striker.

They're hitting the Combine on Al Na'ir, along with the Twelfth Deneb."

"We'll see about that," Victor said. "I'll send out a recall with our first orders, though who can tell when it will reach them? But my question stands, Jerry. We're set to go?"

"Yes, Victor. As ready as we're going to get." A sly smile. "More so, actually, than you ever imagined."

"How do you mean?"

"Well, when you told me to put out a call to the troops, I did exactly that. All the troops. Not only Federated Commonwealth and Lyran Alliance units, but to any command that fought for you in Operation Bulldog or Task Force Serpent. And they're responding. On top of the regular regiments who are declaring for you, we have single warriors, lances, and companies from all across the Inner Sphere making their way toward you from every Great House and even two Periphery nations."

"You're kidding," Victor said, knowing Jerry would never joke about something of this magnitude. He felt a swell of pride that the men and women who fought under him would respond so positively, even after two years, and after returning to their former nations and lives. "What will that give us?"

"When they're all assembled? An extra regiment or two, fully supported. And motivated. The messages all say the same thing, pretty much. That if you're calling for an end to Katherine's tyranny, that's good enough for them. Most are also wondering why you took so damn long to make up your mind."

Victor nodded. "Never mind that the necessity was forced on us, right? Start organizing them into a foreign legion as they trickle in. Keep them separate from the regular armies. I'll rely on them when necessary, but this is still a fight that must be won by the regular citizens of the Commonwealth and the Alliance."

"It will be done, Victor," Jerry promised. "We just need a direction."

Victor nodded and looked around at Tiaret, Precentor Irelon, and Rudolf Shakov. Both Com Guard men exuded confidence, but how much was for the plan and how much for Victor himself, he couldn't say. Tiaret remained characteristically stolid.

"Then it's Newtown Square," he said finally. "In and out before Adam Steiner gets wind of it on Barcelona. If he wants a piece of me after that, he'll have to run me down on the way to Winter. We need those production facilities, and I intend to get them."

He leaned over to type rapidly on a keypad. As he did so one small, gold-tinted star suddenly doubled in size over the table, nearly eclipsing the frost-blue system sitting slightly coreward. Two more worlds quickly swelled to match it, both of them neutral gray.

"Newtown Square to Hood IV to Winter. Those are my plans for this first wave." Victor folded his arms across his chest.

"We depart in two weeks."

=== 24 ===

"Yalos!" Tancred said into his helmet mic. "General Yalos, where are those reinforcements?" His *Nightstar* rocked back as a second and third gauss slug slammed into its right side. The last impact cracked the physical shielding around the 'Mech's fusion engine, instantly spiking its heat levels. Armor shards rained over the marshy ground of Mayetta's Tuskange Depression, sparkling like some kind of heavy morning dew.

The only answer to his call was static crackling loudly in the tight confines of his neurohelmet. A wave of heat washed through the cockpit, radiating up from the decking and dumping through the air circulation system. Tancred gasped for breath. The cooling vest kept down his core body temperature, but sweat still ran freely from his brow and down his bare arms and legs.

"Damn," he said under his breath, low enough to keep the voice-activated microphone from picking up his words.

He threw the *Nightstar* into a backward walk, twisting right to protect its injured side. Wrenching the stick to his left, he floated his laser-painted cross hairs across a line of enemy machines before dropping them on the wide-shouldered outline of a 9K-variant *Victor*. Giving back far better than he got, Tancred punched two rail-driven slugs into the *Victor*, then flayed more armor off one leg with his extended-range particle cannon.

Staggered but still on its feet, the *Victor* lit off jump jets and rocketed into the cover of a thick stand of conifers. Two lances of fast hovercraft pursued it despite Tancred's order to let it go.

Only one lance came back.

Although the battalion of MechWarriors borrowed from the Third Crucis Lancers responded well to Tancred's orders, the armor regiment General Zardetto had also lent him were too used to being top dogs on the field. The Bremond DMM played on that tendency, drawing large chunks of his forces away to be massacred. That was impressive for a green militia unit taking their first stab at a planetary assault, but unfortunate that Tancred planned to destroy them if he could. Why couldn't they have declared for Victor?

Instead, it had been the Mayetta DMM, the local March Militia's regimental combat team, under the command of the Yalos family, that had come over to Victor's side.

Considered fair-weather supporters of Katherine, the Yalos clan saw the way the wind was blowing when several nearby worlds pledged support for Victor. As visions of barony danced through their heads, they radically and quite publicly shifted allegiance. Duke Sandoval had not technically declared the militia rebels, but he had withdrawn his support, and that had been enough to persuade the DMMs from Bremond and Milligan to stage an immediate assault. Kirk Yalos called on Tancred for help, in return pledging his son's RCT to Victor's cause.

Should they survive.

Jason Yalos should have mopped up the Milligan DMM's advance force hours ago and rejoined Tancred to head off the Bremond militia. The battle plan was simple—destroy the Milligan air support, and the entire unit would fold—so simple that even a "social" general like Jason couldn't screw it up.

Swinging the remains of his armor regiment to the east, Tancred managed to threaten the Bremond left flank and drive them westward into the fringes of a mine-field laid out by his sapper company. One entire recon lance perished in a stunning cascade of explosions. The majority pulled up short, re-forming with amazing speed.

As the Bremond DMM wheeled back from the almost-sprung trap, Tancred gambled. Ordering Major Lowry to hit the main body at her own discretion, he led his assault company forward and split the DMM's lines.

"I need air support at grid eleven-bravo!" he called over his command frequency, cycling his weapons as fast as possible and running up quite a bill in spent armor and ammunition.

"Copy, Baron Sandoval. We're breaking for the ground. Orders?"

"Strafe the rear lines." Tancred's tongue felt thick and sluggish from dehydration, and he swallowed in an attempt to coax strength back into his voice. "Pin down their infantry and make those 'Mechs think about cover."

He also called up two companies of heavy tanks that speared through the Bremond eastern flank. Losing only two vehicles, they joined up with his command, effectively isolating a quarter of the enemy force just as a full squadron of *Lucifer* aerospace fighters broke free of the air battle being waged overhead to pound the Bremond rear with missile barrages.

Here was where the Crucis Lancers performed far and above the DMM, coordinating disparate forces and reaping advantage from the militia's sudden disarray. Tancred pulled his assault company around, turning its back on the main body of the confused militia and pounding forward into the quartered force while the demi-company left to his own reconnaissance unit stung them from the rear. A battalion of Lancer armor fell on the DMM from the east. He couldn't have asked for a better envelopment. Lowry's second company and more armor pressed the main body of the Bremond regiment, preventing them from pushing forward to catch Tancred with their hammer to the quartered-force's anvil. It bought him seconds only, but that might be enough to severely hurt the DMM.

Walking forward at an easy thirty kilometers per hour, pacing his assault company, Tancred caught a Bremond *Enforcer* struggling between flanking Lancer Bulldogs. With a large laser and twin four-packs each, the armored vehicles refused to give ground and together outgunned the *Enforcer*. With Tancred's ninety-five tons behind them, the *Enforcer* went down without returning much more damage than a blown tread on one Bulldog.

As Tancred became caught up next in a brutal slugging match with a well-armored *Highlander*, his HUD was so cluttered with enemy unit icons that he was unaware of the danger until his missile alarms rang out and he glimpsed the gray contrails of incoming missiles through his forward shield. Two Pegasus scout vehicles were making a break through his assault company toward safety beyond, drilling him with two dozen short-range missiles that pocked and cratered his armor from head to foot. One rang off the side of his 'Mech's head, tossing him around in his harness like a rag doll. A second caught his forward shield, scarring and cracking the ferroglass but failing to do much more.

Tancred somehow held on to consciousness, checking his wireframe damage schematic with a practiced eye. Seeing a damaged arm actuator and two ruptured heat sinks, he counted himself lucky. Miraculously, of some dozen impacts, no missile had exploited the ruined hole in his BattleMech's right side.

Swearing off the *Highlander* for a moment, Tancred dropped his arms and donated one gauss slug each to the speeding Pegasuses. One clipped a fender and skipped off, lost in the battle beyond. The other punched through a turret on the second vehicle, crushing both launchers but catching them empty, in between reloads. Tancred was holding back his PPC, hoping to bring down his heat levels. In frustration, he kicked out with one metal-shod foot as the two fast hovercraft sped past his position.

His kick caught the damaged vehicle under the skirt, rocking it up on its left side as the air cushion spilled from beneath it. The vehicle came back down hard, digging its forward right fender into the soft ground and starting an end-over-end tumble that slowly picked apart the once-graceful hovercraft. It erupted into a fireball while still tumbling, the explosion throwing it into a new series of convoluted flips and spins.

Leftenant Brett Mathews's *Devastator* caught the second vehicle before it cleared the trap, but the exodus had begun, and there was no checking a battalion's worth of Bremond DMM war machines intent on breaking through Tancred's thinly stretched lines. Jump jet-equipped 'Mechs took to the air while hovercraft pushed their throttles to speeds that no BattleMech could match. Others straggled forward as best they could, preferring to kick aside Lancer tanks then face the assault company bearing down on them from the west. Tancred tightened his grip on the *Nightstar*'s control sticks and swore fluently. With just two more companies of BattleMechs, he might have kept his trap closed. Where the hell was Jason Yalos?

"Commander! Baron Sand—"

If Rianna's shout of warning was ever completed, Tancred never knew. His proximity alarm screamed at him a split-second behind the *Highlander* that fell out of the sky with jet-scorched feet. He heard the crunching protest of shattered armor as the *Nightstar* was shoved roughly down and backward.

Death From Above, called DFA in MechWarrior parlance, was known to pilots of ninety-ton *Highlanders* as a "Highlander burial." The idea remained the same. Jump up for maximum height on streaming plasma, then cut out the jump jets and fall straight down on top of another 'Mech or vehicle. The jumping 'Mech had leg actuators to absorb some of the blow, while the less fortunate target usually collapsed under the staggering weight.

Tancred was lucky that neither wide-splayed foot had come down on the *Nightstar*'s head, as that certainly would have killed him. But he wasn't spared the rude shock as ninety-five tons of upright metal met earth in a bone-jarring impact. His teeth slammed together, grinding chips between them, and his spine lit up with pain as his head slammed back hard inside his neurohelmet.

He didn't quite lose consciousness, but swam groggily through a haze of flashing lights and alarms to find his controls. The main stick he located with one flailing hand, though the *Nightstar*'s throttle eluded him. No matter. Through his forward shield, the *Highlander* loomed large and deadly, ignoring intense fire poured on by Tancred's lancemates, swinging a gauss rifle toward his cockpit. He toggled for the left-hand gauss rifle on his only functioning arm. The *Highlander* got off its shot first, but its aim had been spoiled by rough handling from Leftenant Mathews's *Devastator*. The rail-accelerated slug took the *Nightstar* in its right arm, jamming the nickel-ferrous ball of metal into his shoulder and blasting apart the joint to sever the limb.

His enemy would get no more chances, Tancred vowed.

Extending his left arm, he stroked the trigger and sent a gauss slug directly into the *Highlander*'s gyro casing. A meter lower and the high-velocity mass would have passed cleanly between the 'Mech's legs. Catching it in the crotch, though, spelled disaster for the Bremond BattleMech as metal armor slammed into the gyroscope, tearing apart the stabilizer in a catastrophic failure. The

Highlander tipped backward and then seemed to balance itself on its heels a moment as the cockpit's escape panels blew away and the MechWarrior ejected. Having lost its brains as well as its balance, the *Highlander* crashed backward, with nothing left to catch it but the same un- yielding ground Tancred had already met.

"That's gotta hurt!" Major Lowry crowed over the open frequency. "At least, I hope it did. You still with us, Baron?"

Swallowing blood, Tancred checked his teeth by feel and found them all still there. He blinked his way back to steady vision, found his throttle, and worked his *Nightstar* back to its feet.

"Shaken and sore, but still here, Major." He checked his HUD and saw that the DMM had fallen back to regroup after nearly losing a good quarter of their total force. Not bad, Tancred allowed, bloodying the DMM with a force nearly half its size—one-third if counting 'Mech strength alone. Not bad at all.

But it could also have been a lot better.

"Pack it in, Major. Pick up who you can. Let's drag this *Highlander* back, too, as well as any other 'Mechs worth salvaging."

"We're not taking another go at them?" Lowry asked, obviously not wanting to retreat.

True, the Third Lancers had taken a far worse toll on the Bremond DMM than vice versa, but just barely. And Tancred was still aware of the disparity in raw strength. It left no room for mistakes. With General Yalos's ab- sence, the prudent course was to withdraw and see where matters stood.

"I'll take a draw today," he said. "We've hurt them, and they've got to be thinking we're more prepared than we really are. Let's use that and pull some good salvage from the field. Remember, the Bremond and Milligan DMM are a long way from their supply lines. We can afford to take our time. They can't.

"And this war is not going to be won quickly, I'm afraid."

25

Who said the Dracs don't have a sense of humor? thought Colonel Gerald DuBois, taking his *Dragon Fire* through Al Nai'ir's Sherwood Forest at the head of the Fighting Urakhai.

Spread around him in a haphazard formation, his striker battalion traded sporadic fire with remnants of the Twenty-fourth Dieron's command company. As he led his force through the maze of standing rock formations, box canyons, steam vents, and erupting geysers, he laughed humorlessly. This "forest" contained not one actual tree, not one bit of vegetation taking root in the poisonous ground.

It was really very funny.

His mouth set in a hard, grim line, DuBois fired his large laser and managed to slice into the side of a fleeing

Daikyu, a 'Mech he was certain belonged to *Tai-sa* Bunt-ari Akihito. He'd intended to follow up with his gauss rifle, but lost his targeting lock instead. Again. Risking the shot anyway, he sent a high-velocity mass on its way and cursed as the silvery blur careened off a blackened rock face.

The *Daikyu* ducked around the rocky outcropping.

It had been like that all day, his cross hairs flashing intermittent red more often than the strong golden hue of sensor lock. The Dieron Regulars knew what they were about, leading DuBois's unit into this nightmare landscape. The mineral-heavy water venting up through the rocks created frozen cascades of dark, glittering material against the otherwise pale orange stone. Not perfectly formed stalagmites like those DuBois had seen in the caves last week, but flattened, malformed crusts that sheathed the rock face and played merry hell with his sensors. With all the scalding vents and geysers, thermal imaging wasn't any more reliable. When General Holsted had fallen to the Twenty-fourth last week, DuBois had vowed to chase *Tai-sa* Akihito through hell. It seemed that the enemy commander had taken him up on it.

"Colonel . . . Bois . . ." A faint voice crackled and hissed through the speakers in his neurohelmet. It sounded like Captain Harris, who'd been left back at the base the Fighting Urakhai had captured from the Dracs. ". . . a priority-one message . . . Prince Victor."

"Hold off," DuBois ordered, not certain if his transmission had even made it out of the forest. "We're still on the hunt."

They wouldn't be much longer, though. Already reduced to nine machines and separated from the bulk of their regiment, the Twenty-fourth's command unit couldn't afford this running battle in which DuBois had to continue cycling fresh 'Mechs to the front. They had to find a place to make their final stand, to fight the samurai way, choosing their death ground and striking back in one glorious, honor-redeeming charge.

It came around the next corner, while DuBois an-

chored a line of six BattleMechs as he swung his forward
machines into a blind draw filled with Dracs. The HUD
was so much garbage, and understandably so. Gleaming
black deposits sheathed this bowl-shaped canyon almost
completely. A few dirty-orange streaks showed through,
but not many. Steam vents misted the air, and at least
four geysers belched up erratic plumes of the mineral-
salted water. One of the Urakhai 'Mechs, a narrow-
footed *Falcon Hawk*, missed a step in the treacherous
terrain and went down hard, pinning its right arm beneath the *Hawk*'s thirty-five tons and ruining its primary weapon.

It was luckier than the others, as it turned out.

Laser fire speared out from the massed samurai in a
scything attack that cut hard into the Urakhai machines,
quickly followed by pounding gauss slugs and a storm of
autocannon fire. Missiles arced up and over, raining
heavily on DuBois and his warriors. A small flight peppered the head of his *Dragon Fire*, splitting a seam in the
armor plates just back of one ferroglass shield. Shrapnel
pinged through the cockpit, one piece skipping off the
side of his protective neurohelmet and another nicking
his shoulder, drawing blood. The sulfurous stench of
Sherwood Forest seeped in quickly, forcing DuBois to
take short, shallow breaths.

Two more machines went down under the concentrated fire and lay unmoving, while the *Falcon Hawk* was
at least able to pick itself up. Then four more Urakhai
BattleMechs made the draw, adding their firepower to
a savage counterattack. Not relying on sensors, DuBois
targeted by eye, choosing a squat *Komodo*. Designed as
an intercept machine against armored infantry, the forty-
five-tonner packed ten medium-class lasers that could
still deliver a lot of hurt against BattleMechs.

DuBois's large laser stabbed too high, but his gauss
slug cracked the *Komodo*'s engine shielding, and one of
his medium pulse lasers stabbed a flurry of emerald darts
in behind it. A spray of flechette ammunition from his
eighty-millimeter did the rest, worrying the wound even

deeper. The *Komodo*'s fusion engine bled free of its energy shields, belching golden fire out of the ruptured cavity to engulf the narrow, forward-thrust head. Then the fusion reactor let go in a final, ground-shaking explosion that toppled two other Drac machines, hurling pieces of the *Komodo* across the canyon and smashing a chunk of its gyro into the *Dragon Fire*'s chest.

Another three Urakhai 'Mechs made the draw, and those in front moved forward to press the Twenty-fourth Dieron. DuBois paid careful attention to each treacherous step, trading fire with a *Panther* and keeping an eye out for the *Daikyu*. The *Panther* attempted to charge forward, slipped, and sprawled at the *Dragon Fire*'s feet. DuBois put it out of its misery with a well-placed gauss slug to the back of its head.

"COLONEL DUBOIS!"

DuBois had cranked up the gain on his comm system inside Sherwood Forest. Now, suddenly, he had Captain Harris screaming in his ear without distortion, the mineral-rimmed canyon acting like some kind of reception dish. His ears rang, and he slid the gain back down as a full company of the mercenary Urakhai pressed forward to mop up the surviving Dieron Regulars.

"Harris, we're clear. Hunt's over. Counting four, six . . . seven more Dracs. Damn! *Tai-sa* Akihito and his exec must have slipped away while his men bought them time."

"Sorry to hear that, sir. I have . . . Maybe I should report this on your return."

DuBois knew what his officer was offering him. Something important about Prince Victor had come through, but Harris was willing to sit on it until Akihito and his exec were run to ground. That would leave the Twenty-fourth helpless in the face of the combined might of the Urakhai and the Twelfth Deneb.

"Am I going to like this, Harris?"

"No, Colonel. Not one bit."

"Better give it to me then," DuBois ordered, steeling himself for news of Victor's capture or death. With the

Prince too far away to support directly, General Holsted had opted to take out their vengeance for Arthur on House Kurita instead. Had they decided wrong?

They had, but not in the way DuBois feared. As an auxiliary monitor winked to life, displaying the video transmission sent by Harris, the prince looked healthy enough as he glowered from his side of the camera.

"General Holsted," he said abruptly. "I am displeased, to say the very least, that you have ignored my call for aid and instead launched your own private war against the Combine." Victor exhaled sharply between clenched teeth. "I am blood-boiling furious, to put it simply.

"Are you fealty-bound mercenaries or bandits, General? If I had wanted an attack on House Kurita, I would have ordered it. What we are about is removing my sister from the throne to keep her abuse of power from claiming more innocent lives. You are not acting in the best interests of the Federated Suns; you're carrying out a vendetta. This is not the service I expect from a unit such as the Fighting Urakhai. Waco's Rangers, perhaps. And we know what happened to them." Victor allowed a slight pause for DuBois to consider that.

"Abandonment of several posts, including yours, has left the Terran Corridor vulnerable. I do not need this added concern. And so, General, may I respectfully request that you collect your men, your 'Mechs, and your military bearing, and get your asses back into this war." The message disconnected abruptly, with no farewell.

Some request. Colonel DuBois's face burned with embarrassment. Victor Steiner-Davion certainly knew how to cut to the quick. And, more to the point, he'd been correct to do so. A domestic enemy took precedence over a foreign one any day, but while General Holsted had been in command, DuBois had swallowed his doubts.

"What are your orders, Colonel?" Harris asked, sounding very uncertain. No doubt the message had hit him hard as well.

DuBois summoned his command voice, wanting to reinstall confidence in his subordinate. "Start packing it up, Captain. That was no invitation; that was an order from the First Prince. Inform the Twelfth Deneb and invite them to return with us." He scrunched up his face in brief distaste. "I guess this buys Buntari Akihito his life, for now. Hell."

This was a very abrupt end to what had looked to be a stunning assault. Gerald DuBois recognized the need to abandon this campaign, but he didn't have to be happy about it. "Harris, make certain we leave the Urakhai standard flying over that base. Let the Dracs know this isn't over. Then get salvage crews out to Sherwood Forest and arrange DropShip pickup at once.

"Let's get home and find out what Prince Victor needs."

Plains of Culd,
Newtown Square
Melissia Theater
Lyran Alliance

What Victor needed more than anything else was time. Time to fall back and regroup. Time to pull the Thirty-ninth Avalon Hussars together as a coordinated Regimental Combat Team that had some hope of throwing back the Fourteenth Donegal Guards. He watched the lowering sun carefully, counting the minutes to sundown. Too many. The Donegal Guards would make at least one more hard assault this day.

Throttling into a run, Victor edged his *Daishi* Omni-Mech up over fifty kilometers per hour in his search for a good, defensible position on the Plains of Culd. Long-range laser fire and the occasional PPC continued to snipe at him, but Adam Steiner's command company was wary of closing with Victor's assault unit just yet. As in the days and weeks gone by, both men were seeking a tactical advantage, but so far, neither commander had made a major mistake. At least, not since Victor had realized too late that the Avalon Hussars were spread over the entire planet of Newtown Square and had failed to concentrate his forces in time.

That had been three weeks ago.

A distant relative and onetime supporter of the Federated Commonwealth, Adam Steiner had ended up in Katherine's camp after receiving "proof" of Victor's compliance in Melissa Steiner-Davion's death. Proof handed to him by Katherine, of course. An invitation to visit Victor on Mogyorod before the civil war, had come back with the message, "Only with an RCT behind me." The pain of Melissa's death ran deep in Adam, helping him buy into Katherine's machinations.

He and his entire RCT must have been in-system waiting for Victor to arrive; they had hit the planet not ten hours later in one of the Fourteenth's trademark "dawn assaults." It was the same strategic brilliance Adam had shown behind Jade Falcon lines during the Clan invasion. Thrown off-balance, Victor had been forced to lead two battalions of 'Mechs and armor in a quick retreat from Newtown Square's capital, surrendering his motley DropShip fleet but keeping the civil war alive by preserving his own life.

Damn his cousin anyway for setting such an effective trap. Adam had used his RCT to pin the outlying Hussars in place while hunting down Victor. The running battle pushed Victor out onto the Plains of Culd, unable to do much more than stay ahead of the advancing Fourteenth. Making rendezvous with an armor battalion at a small training outpost the week before, the Hussars had held it long enough to fix up their machines and restock mobile field base vehicles. Victor took that opportunity to change his OmniMech's configuration, swapping out his normal lasers and assault autocannon for PPCs, an LB-X heavy autocannon, and a brace of four ultra-class thirty-millimeter cannon. The thirties made quite a difference on the open plains, with less severe ammo-consumption rates and longer reach.

A difference being shown to Victor now, as light autocannon fire chewed into his lower left leg, worrying it like a dog its favorite bone. He replied with two searing bolts from his particle cannon that drove back a *Kraken*, one of the Clan designs Adam had captured from the Jade Falcons. All along his flank, the Donegal Guards were edging forward, trading shots with the Hussars.

"Jerry," Victor called, "Adam's feeling brave over here. Where are you?"

"Spread to hell and gone, Victor." Transmission didn't rob Jerrard Cranston's voice of its frustration. "Bella and I are still trying to rendezvous with that recon company the Guards pushed north of here. We're in contact with them but have no visual sighting yet."

"Tell me you've found something."

"I've found a lot of nothing is what I've found. How far do these plains stretch, anyway?"

"Sea to shining sea," Victor said. "Or close enough." The Plains of Culd extended over some two-thirds of Newtown Square's primary continent. It was a savanna, actually, with pale sword grass and good soil; the wonder was that more agricultural concerns hadn't moved in to take advantage of the long growing season. "I'd settle for some scrub trees or a couple of low hills right now."

"Good," General Bragg, who was leading the battalion Jerry had joined, broke in. "Because that's all you're likely to find for another hundred kilometers. We've held maneuvers . . . hold one!"

As the transmission abruptly cut off, Victor reached out with his light autocannon, which all by itself matched about half the *Kraken*'s firepower. He chipped away at the hundred-ton behemoth, trying to open a breach, and then whipped a high-amperage energy bolt across its narrow torso as another PPC found its mark. The *Kraken* turned away, and Adam Steiner's *Thunder Hawk* stalked up in its place. Knowing what kind of destructive power its three gauss rifles could throw at him, Victor edged his *Daishi* out of Adam's immediate reach and called back Bravo lance, which had worked its way too far from the protection of the rest of the company.

"Jerry, what is it?" he finally asked after a silence that stretched too long.

"Sorry, Victor. We had another run by the Second Somerset Wing. We're still sorting out the damage, but it looks like we lost an *Enforcer*, at the very least. And they were banking in your direction, so expect them in about five minutes."

The *Thunder Hawk* reclaimed Victor's attention when the first gauss slug slammed into his right arm, wrenching it back at the shoulder joint and smashing a full ton of armor into impotent splinters. Another dug into the soft ground, kicking up a spray of black earth that pattered against his forward ferroglass shield. The third rail-driven mass flashed by overhead in a silvery blur that missed his 'Mech's head by less than two meters.

Swallowing dryly at that glimpse of death, Victor dug in and wrenched his controls to drop the *Daishi*'s targeting reticle over Adam's *Thunder Hawk*. The cross hairs burning a welcome gold, he tied everything at his command into a single salvo and cut loose. PPCs flashed out their manmade lightning, blasting away armor into tiny shards and splashes of molten fire. His thirty-millimeter autocannon pockmarked the *Hawk*'s chest and legs, and one lucky brace of slugs rang off the assault machine's head. That would give Adam something to think about as he fell back again, though not far. Never far.

"I'll have bigger problems in five minutes than some Donegal sky jockeys," Victor said through his teeth. "The way the Guards are acting, I'd say they've got reinforcements moving in fast. From our flank, most likely, trying to lock us into a pincer. They're gearing up for a new charge."

And then, above and behind the Donegal line, the dimming sky suddenly lit up with three new stars—too bright to be anything but the drive flares of descending DropShips. And falling on hard burns, Victor thought as he watched the tongues of white flame elongate faster than they should, braking hard enough to generate quite a few extra Gs.

This wasn't what he'd expected, and Victor felt his hopes rise a notch.

"DropShips!" one of his warriors called out in warning. "Two . . . three . . . burning in hard on the Donegal line."

Jerry Cranston wasted no time. "Cut and run, Victor. Leftenant Parques? Escort the Prince out of there. We're reversing toward you, but it'll be thirty minutes at least."

"No," Victor said. "Disregard, Parques. Pull in and everyone regroup, because here they come." The *Kraken* led a hard charge on Victor's position. Adam Steiner was only meters behind it as his people committed to what looked like an act of desperation rather than strength.

"Retrograde maneuver," Victor ordered, pulling the *Daishi* around and throttling into a backward walk that made it more difficult for the Donegal Guards to close, keeping his weapons pointed in their direction. Two gauss slugs slammed home into his chest and left leg, and Victor used his own sense of balance to assist the gyroscopic stabilizer.

"Don't worry, Jerry," he said. "We can hold out for the DropShips. Two minutes, people! We need to buy two minutes to get them on the ground."

"How can you be certain they're friendly, Victor?" asked General Bragg.

Victor gave a short laugh. "Well, we might as well assume they're on our side, because if they're Adam's backups and not ours, we're as good as dead anyway."

"I'd hate to hear that, Highness." The new voice rang with forced cheer. "Or we would have come all this way for nothing."

Even through the distortion of transmission, Victor recognized the voice. He could imagine the man talking through clenched teeth, bearing up under several gravities as the DropShips continued their hard plunge toward Newtown Square.

"I don't believe it," Jerry said. "Tell me that's who I think it is."

Victor grinned, even as he whipped particle beams across the advancing *Kraken*, exploiting earlier damage.

"Welcome to Newtown Square, Demi Shakov," he answered as his PPCs touched off one of the ammo bins stored in the *Kraken*'s left chest. "You'd be more welcome if you were dropping on the right side of the battle. We're the unit on the western side, about to be trampled."

A violent eruption of flame and metal burst through the *Kraken*'s side, sending the machine staggering to one knee. Thanks to its cellular ammunition storage, most of the blast channeled through blowout vents and left the machine in fighting condition.

Victor left it for someone else to finish off and turned his attention to the advancing *Thunder Hawk*. As he did, a gauss slug ricocheted off his shoulder, carrying away another ton of armor protection with it.

"Sorry," Shakov said. "We assumed you would be on the winning side. Our pilots are making the adjustment now."

Realizing that the balance of power on Newtown Square was rapidly shifting out of his favor, Adam Steiner seemed intent on forcing one last head-to-head match. His *Thunder Hawk* led the charge, weathering a storm of firepower from Victor's assault company. The 'Mech's three rail guns continued to spend ammunition as fast as they could cycle. Two more gauss slugs took the *Thunder Hawk* in the chest, shattering the last of its armor there and crushing two heat sinks. Another caught the right leg over the hip joint, locking the leg straight out.

Victor added his autocannon to the fusillade and cheered along with his unit as the *Thunder Hawk* finally stumbled and crashed to the ground under withering firepower. It moved at once, though, trying to regain its feet or at least prop up on one arm to continue firing.

"Where's Precentor Irelon?" Victor asked, waiting for his PPCs to clear for another salvo.

"Right where he should have been from the start," came Raymond Irelon's deep, steady voice. "Bringing the Prince's Men to the Prince's aid."

"Gavin Dow won't be happy with this," Jerry Cranston said.

"I could care less." Victor's light autocannon chipped at the downed *Hawk*, trying to cut the arm from underneath it as Adam attempted to bring his gauss rifles back into the battle. Victor held into long pulls, raining hot metal on the prone machine, determined to put his cousin down and end this fight. Thirty seconds—sixty at most—and it would be all over.

At that moment, he felt invincible. Until one last gauss slug from Adam Steiner's *Thunder Hawk* slammed into the *Daishi*'s shoulder, ricocheting up to its head. The slug burst through the cockpit with a thunderclap of shattered armor and a storm of high-velocity metal.

And then Victor felt nothing at all.

26

Iome, Mayetta
Draconis March
Federated Commonwealth
1 May 3063

Tancred massaged the back of his neck with one hand as he studied the tactical map transparency Jason Yalos had laid over the lighted table in their Mayetta bunker. It was allowing them to analyze the latest movements by the Bremond and Milligan Militia RCTS.

His joints were weary, and every muscle felt taut and bruised, the ache extending down through his shoulders and upper back. Both hands felt arthritic from days on the stick, and his thighs burned from working the *Nightstar*'s pedals. Too many hours in the cockpit. Not enough rest.

"I think they're finally realizing that a two-front war isn't working," Yalos said, scrubbing at the red stubble of his freshly cut hair. Acne-scarred and jaundiced, Yalos looked even less like a general than he did a noble.

Though only twenty-seven, he had enough conceit for them both. "We're holding."

Tancred nodded more out of reflex than actual agreement. Even with Yalos falling for textbook traps and delaying tactics, any war of attrition stacked the deck favorably toward the defenders. "They're massing for a combined assault, and I think they'll use this pass to come at us." Tancred stabbed at the map. "So we mine stretches of Hogan Valley, draw them in, and bottleneck the exit with 'Mechs backed by armor. We place infantry and heavy armor on the Valley ridge, with artillery to close the door behind them."

Jason Yalos brought his hands together with a loud clap. "And then we destroy them."

"And then we hold them as long as we can," Tancred corrected. "You don't destroy two RCTs in a single battle unless both are stupid enough to stand in one spot and get massacred. They'll push through eventually, but this will buy us maybe another week. Less, if they swing their armor around through a smaller pass to flank us."

Yalos frowned. "Then what?"

A new voice, soft yet sharp, surprised both men from behind. "You should plan one victory at a time, Jason." Jessica Sandoval-Groell came forward on the arm of her granddaughter. "Even Dorann here knows that much."

"Countess Sandoval," Yalos said, recovering quickly. He half-bowed over one arm. "The March Lord did not inform my father, or the local baron, that he was sending additional support. But it's very welcome."

Jessica smiled thinly, her lips pressed together. "No support. Just one old woman." Her tone was most regal, despite her humble words. "I've come to see Tancred."

"And while they're talking, General," Dorann Sandoval asked, "is there someone who can give me a closer look at the *Cestus* out front? It's a design I've never seen before."

Shocked to see members of his family here on Mayetta, Tancred found his feet quickly. "That *Cestus* happens to be Jason's BattleMech, Dor."

"How fortunate," Dorann said innocently, leaving her grandmother's side and slipping a hand inside Yalos's arm. He practically strutted from the Bunker, obviously thinking about potential ties with the Sandoval family. Was there no end to his ambition?

"A shame Dorann has no military ability," Jessica said, watching them go. "She does have her charms, though."

Tancred drew himself up, as on guard now as any time he'd faced his father. His aunt properly deferred to her brother on matters of state, but he knew her mind was as sharp as anyone's. "What are you doing here, Aunt Jess?"

"Don't worry, Tancred. It's not about your father. He's fine, and the March has taken four important worlds in Combine space. Your concern is commendable, though. No, the reason I'm here is to look after family affairs."

"What's that supposed to mean?" Tancred asked. He'd been expecting her to deliver his father's latest offer or ultimatum.

"It means that it's time you stopped thinking like Victor Davion and began thinking like a Sandoval again."

There it was. Back to Tancred's choice of supporting Victor over Katherine. His face got hot as his temper rose. "What's so wrong with emulating Victor?"

"For starters, you don't have the Com Guard behind you, ready to catch you when you stumble."

"That's very unfair," he said, but it was true that Victor's expeditionary force to Newtown Square had been saved by Com Guard's 244th Division. Tancred had yet to hear from Victor himself, and meanwhile Katherine was reaping good press about ComStar's failure to control their own unit.

Recognizing that she had struck a nerve, Jessica allowed a trace of good humor into her smile. "Oh, I think not. But it wasn't the insult you're taking it for, Tancred. Victor's strength—one of his primary strengths, anyway—has always been his friendships. You can judge a man by the company he keeps, and a leader by his supporters. I think Victor is doing very well." The countess glanced back at the door by which Dorann had led Jason Yalos from the room. "You, on the other hand, are not."

"The Yalos family controls the Mayetta RCT, and they've declared for Victor. This is where the fight is."

"And is this a fight that can be won?"

"Yes," Tancred said, lowering his voice, though no one else was nearby. "With my help, and with the Third Crucis Lancers, not even Jason Yalos can lose this battle."

"Spoken like a Davion." Jessica Sandoval clucked disapprovingly. "Ready to fight the good fight. And why? Because it's there. Or, rather, here."

"You're not trying to tell me I shouldn't be involved in Victor's battle, are you? I've already gone through this with my father."

"And you're just as stubborn as he is, so I don't expect to change your mind. I might even agree with you. But you still aren't thinking like a Sandoval. I ask you to consider what difference it will make whether Mayetta supports Katherine or Victor."

Tancred opened his mouth to speak and then snapped it shut again. A glib response would not win him any points with his aunt. The Sandovals put great stock in deliberation and preparation. "I did have a plan," he finally said, very cautiously. His aunt had just agreed with his decision to endorse Victor, but was that personal sympathy or an offer of support? "A series of steps that would take me toward what Victor truly needs."

"Robinson," she said, a touch of exasperation in her voice. "Tancred, if you think I don't know what you're about, and that your father hasn't also thought of this, you are in worse shape than I thought. Victor needs the Draconis March. It will be the first battlefield when he reaches the Federated Commonwealth."

"All right," he said. "Robinson. But I can't challenge Father without some kind of mandate, and Victor can't give it to me. He can't afford to alienate my father and push him completely into Katherine's camp. And are you ready to stand up to our March Lord? Publicly?" He saw his aunt's guilty start and knew her answer as well as his own. "So I need a groundswell of support first."

"And you think the Yalos family will get you there?"

"They're a start, along with the pledge of the Third Crucis Lancers on Cassias. Okay, I'll admit I was going about this Victor's way, planning some kind of grassroots movement." He hedged, chewing his lower lip, knowing what his aunt would think of the alternative.

"There's another way," he said finally, before she had a chance to sell him on her own scheme. It was as certain as a Lyran with a business proposal that Countess Jessica Sandoval-Groell hadn't come all this way without a political agenda.

"Yes," she said, "there is. Go after the Rangers. Bring them home. I think you can win the regiment away from Mai Fortuna, and if the Rangers are with you, the people of Robinson will follow. If James tries to fight you then, and I don't believe he will, I will stand with you publicly. And he'll lose. Either way you'll have Robinson, and the March capital will be safe if and when the Combine brings this war back to us."

Her moderate leanings notwithstanding, his aunt still had a Sandoval's natural distrust of the Draconis Combine. "Any retaliation by House Kurita is Father's problem," Tancred said. "He created the situation. He'll have to deal with it. You fight one enemy at a time, and right now that's Katherine."

"You're not listening. Your"—she obviously did not want to use the word 'enemy'—"your first target has to be Robinson."

"But the keys to Robinson, at this moment, are the Kilbourne and Milligan PDZs. Those farming worlds are being hard-pressed to make up the supply shortages Katherine blatantly engineered. It's Robinson's worst vulnerability."

His aunt looked stunned almost past speech. "Tancred! You would try to starve out Robinson? Victor won't thank you for such tactics. Neither will your father, and neither will I!"

"I won't have to," he said easily. "Katherine will do it. She'll choke off the supply line at Woodbine, and I'll open it up again. Once she demonstrates Robinson's current reliance on the Woodbine Operations Area, I won't have to be so blatant."

That gave his aunt pause. "What makes you so certain that Katherine will take Woodbine?"

"Because you have me thinking like a Sandoval, remember? I'll make it irresistible. And as capital of the Woodbine Operations Area, it gives me a political platform. If I get Duke Rein and his family behind me, I'll be in position to knock Father's strongest support out from under him." A large void opened inside Tancred even as he put the thought into words.

"It might work. Perhaps." Jessica frowned. "Except there are no Katherine loyalist units on Woodbine."

"Don't worry about that." Tancred smiled without humor. "There will be by the time I get there."

27

Forbidden to overexert himself, Victor suffered the indignity of being pushed into the 39th Avalon Hussars' command post in a wheelchair. His entire right side was heavily taped, but every bump still sparked fresh pain in his ribs. Jerry Cranston took over for the orderly at the front door. On Victor's insistence, he left the ungainly collarbone brace with the orderly, then quickly wheeled Victor to the control center, where several dozen warriors and technicians stopped work to applaud and cheer the returned prince.

Victor felt like throwing up.

The ride over from Market's city hospital had been exhausting, leaving him drained and his head throbbing. Post-concussion syndrome, the doctors called it, predicting everything from nausea to blackouts to head-splitting migraines. The dull pain of his fractured collarbone paled in comparison. He began to regret not giving himself another few days to rest, but he knew that each lost day might mean more lost lives.

Victor stood shakily. Most of those present cheered again and then reluctantly returned to work as he waved aside their applause. That left him facing the core of his command staff. He returned General Bella Bragg's salute, and then carefully embraced Precentor Irelon and Demi-Precentor Shakov.

"I can't tell you how grateful I am," he said, noticing that both men had torn the ComStar insignia from their caps.

"Highness, you just did," Shakov said, stroking his dark goatee and smiling. He stepped back and bumped into Tiaret. He turned to her with a nod of apology, and the two began a whispered conversation while Victor gratefully settled back into his wheelchair.

"Has Gavin Dow tracked you here yet?" he asked Precentor Irelon.

"Two days ago. He relieved me of command, and Demi-Precentor Hullinger was promoted in my place, with orders to take me into custody and return to Mogyorod at once."

"How did you respond?"

"Respond? I was relieved of duty, Highness. It wasn't my place. I turned command over to Hullinger, who refused the orders and remanded authority to Shakov. Then command passed through Demi-Precentors Akhlaq, Chaps, and so on. When we finally ran out of senior officers, each warrior was given a choice. Three men eventually returned to Mogyorod with two DropShips and one of our JumpShips. I expect they will make the proper reports."

Bella Bragg frowned but looked at Irelon as if seeing him in a new light. "Precentor Martial Dow will demand back all his ships and equipment. What then?"

Irelon tugged thoughtfully at his ponytail, considering. Victor drifted for a moment, then snapped immediately back to awareness as he saw two guards escort the man he'd been waiting for into the command center. He locked gazes with the prisoner, still listening to Irelon but mentally steeling himself for the coming confrontation.

"Respectfully," Irelon was saying, "we will decline any such order. To the point of defending ourselves against any attempts to enforce it. There is no going back to ComStar. We know that, and we accept it. Dow is welcome to whatever equipment is left once we've ended Katherine's rule." He shrugged. "I'm more concerned with acquiring more transport, actually. Your forces, General Bragg, have one JumpShip left since the Clan wars. Together, we can only move slightly more than half our forces."

"That shouldn't be a problem," Victor said, loud enough for the prisoner and his escorts to overhear. He stood once again, trying not to show his weakness. "There's more than enough transport available in-system, isn't there, Adam?"

Due to his rank and relationship to Victor, Adam Steiner had not been shackled. But both Tiaret and Demi Shakov edged protectively closer to Victor.

Adam glared at his cousin with something less than hate but more than rivalry. "If you mean the vessels belonging to my Donegal Guards, I suppose you're right, Victor. Why not? Taking things that don't belong to you is quickly becoming a habit of yours."

Victor glanced at Jerry Cranston, who nodded slightly. "I know Jerry has filled you in on what we know and suspect, Adam. You can't seriously believe that Katherine should be left on the throne."

"Proof, Victor. Where's the proof? Cranston told me you weren't behind the assassination of Melissa, but that's just his word. The most he can pin on Katrina is that she might have known something about the death of Galen Cox."

Victor cast a sharp, sidelong glance at his friend, who flicked his blue eyes back and forth once in negative response. He had not revealed his real identity to Adam, but he had obviously shown him what little damning proof they had on Katherine.

"Yet you believe Katherine," Victor said, stressing her real name, "when she accuses me of murdering my own mother."

"Katrina has documents that show how the assassin was paid. A land-sale scam that was ultimately backed by the Federated Commonwealth. Information is ammunition, Victor. Your state paid for Melissa's death, and you were in the best position to arrange that."

"Did Katherine mention that it was a corporation tied to her that brokered the deal?"

Adam faltered. "No. Cranston showed me your evidence, and I admit there could be a connection. Although any corporation might have been duped into the role if the scheme was set up beforehand. And"—he regained some momentum—"she said you admitted to hiring an assassin to kill our cousin, Ryan Steiner."

Tossed out so boldly, before everyone in the room, the accusation caught Victor completely unprepared. The weeks of hospital care, today's stress, and Adam's accusations—all sapped what little strength he'd been able to muster. Victor all but collapsed into his wheelchair, staring dumbly at Adam.

"Then it's true!" Adam surged forward, not in violence but angry all the same. Tiaret stopped him with one large hand against his chest. "You don't need to admit it, Victor," he said. "I see it written in your eyes."

"You have no idea what you're talking about, Adam. And even if you did, you can't judge it personally." Victor heard the weariness in his own voice and checked to see who could overhear them. Fortunately, Adam's initial accusation hadn't traveled beyond the small group gathered around Victor. It was more than he would have wanted to know the truth, but he owed them all some kind of explanation now that it was out.

"The average man doesn't have to make life-and-death decisions, and should never have to," he began. "Corporate executives—well, they hire and fire ordinary people, and in doing so, they control other lives. In the military, warriors shoot on our orders, but what about nonmilitary engagements? You're a commander, Adam. Have you ever had to cashier a man, slap him with a bad conduct discharge and maybe jail time that would follow him for the rest of his life?"

Adam nodded curtly. "Of course, when it was warranted. There was a sergeant caught dealing . . ." He trailed off, noticing several other nods around him and suddenly glimpsing where Victor's line of thought was leading.

"Multiply that a thousandfold, Adam, and you might have the smallest idea of why Ryan Steiner had to die. And I'll tell you this: he died more by his own hand than mine. Or, more to the point, by the hand of the assassin Ryan hired to kill my mother, but who I caught and turned against him in retribution. An eye for an eye."

Adam had cooled visibly but not enough to give up the fight. "Proof, Victor. Where is it?"

Victor sighed heavily. "I still have people working on getting it. When I get it, you'll have all the ammunition you want." He paused and let his implied message sink home. "But I can't leave Katherine on the throne while I'm waiting."

"So, now you'll loot my Donegal Guards, hijack our transports, and leave us jailed here on Newtown Square. That's your plan, isn't it?"

"I'll confiscate what I need from your unit and local supplies to refit, yes. But I'll leave you about half your transport capability. Not enough to send sufficient forces after me, but enough to get half your people back to Barcelona."

Victor read the doubt in Adam's eyes and knew he'd won at least a partial reprieve from his headstrong cousin. "The last thing I want is to leave the Alliance vulnerable to attack by the Clans, Adam. So, you're welcome to take whatever is left in the local supply depots. It means you'll be a few months refitting your RCT, but you can rebuild close to full strength. Can I trust you to watch the border here? Newtown Square and Mogyorod will also need some kind of garrison."

Adam Steiner's expression shut down, and his voice was cold when he spoke. "You can trust me to do as I see fit to safeguard the Alliance, Victor. That's the best promise you're going to get from me.

"For now."

28

"**Y**ou were wrong," Katrina said, glaring at Richard Dehaver, defying him to contradict her. She had tracked Dehaver here after reading his latest report, and found him in the company of Simon Gallagher, Marshal of the Crucis March and her "Champion." This room, "the Fox's Den," had once been her father's war room on New Avalon, and its advanced computer systems and halotables served her equally as well.

Despite the need for Dehaver's staff to monitor the important battle being fought only two hundred kilometers east of Avalon City, Katrina dismissed them. The door had barely slid shut behind the last man before she began tearing into Dehaver.

He stood mute for several long seconds and then nodded. "Yes, Highness, I was wrong. I truly did not believe the Seventh Crucis Lancers would go over to Victor so easily."

"Not a shot fired. Not even an argument." Katrina had secretly held out hopes that the elite Seventh Lancers would declare for her and put an end to her brother the minute he arrived on Winter. "They formed up a parade review for him, Richard!"

Damn Adam Steiner, anyway, for failing to kill Victor. That had also been in the report, along with a summation of Victor's injuries. It was as close as her brother had come to death since taking a katana through the chest on Luthien, though not close enough for her. Like the title character in the *Immortal Warrior* holovid series, Victor kept going and going and going. But not forever—not if she had any say in the matter. She also damned the assassin for failing to kill Omi Kurita. Had Omi died as she was supposed to, Victor wouldn't have had the heart to fight her.

"What happened?" she wanted to know, including Simon Gallagher in her accusing glance. "What did you two miss?"

"In retrospect, a number of things," Dehaver said. "Victor's success on Newtown Square. His proximity to Winter versus your distant location. Our failure to capitalize on Arthur's death—for which I hold myself accountable," he added quickly. "And, forgive me, Archon, but also your orders to attack neutral commands as an example to others."

Katrina's temper flared at the implied criticism. "You will not put this failure on me, Richard." Neutrality was a coward's way of supporting rebellion. It could not be tolerated.

"Nor am I attempting to, Highness. Ultimately, though, we think the Lancers turned to Victor because Leftenant-General Jasper Zibler, the Seventh's commanding officer, lost his nephew in the recent fighting on Kathil. He was killed by forces outspokenly loyal to you."

Gallagher adjusted his square-lensed glasses. "Also,

the Lancers have always been fanatically loyal to the Federated Suns, which your brother resurrected to justify his actions."

Katrina noted and approved the way her advisors continued to avoid referring to the events in terms of civil war, even after seven months. As long as Katrina refused formal recognition of Victor's grievances, it granted her field commanders greater latitude to treat opposing forces as traitors and rebels rather than as honest military units. "Where will my brother strike next?" she said, her anger cooling slightly.

"We're getting a solid idea of his strategy now," Dehaver said, moving to a computer terminal and pulling up a two-dimensional star chart of the Lyran Alliance. "He picked up the Avalon Hussars on Newtown Square. On Hood IV, he tried to swing the Fifteenth Lyran Regulars and failed. On Winter, he added the Seventh Lancers."

Newtown Square shifted blue for Katrina, the result of Victor's leaving Adam Steiner behind to safeguard it, but Winter shone the danger-filled red of open rebellion.

"Victor didn't have enough transport to take the Lancers along with him. They're being sent to Inarcs to secure the production facilities there, while Victor reportedly continues on toward New Capetown and its training academy. He is gathering men and materiel. I believe that will remain his pattern."

"Then Coventry is next," Katrina said, eyeing that important industrial world so close to New Capetown—a world she currently held only by force of arms. Until, that is, Duke Bradford could be ferreted out and executed for treason.

Gallagher shrugged. "We're not certain about 'next,' but it is certainly on his short list." He saw Katrina's dark look and hedged. "You may want to contact Nondi Steiner on Tharkad. She may have new data on that."

"And nothing out of Arc-Royal?" she asked Dehaver, though still with a glare fixed on Gallagher.

"It's quiet," Dehaver said. "Morgan Kell seems to be

making no overt moves to support Victor at this time, except to offer safe haven for any unit declaring for your brother. Remnants of the Argyle Lancers retreated in that direction."

"And speaking of retreats"—Katrina's voice dropped into frosted tones—"where is my promised victory over the First Davion Guard?"

Caught off guard, Gallagher stammered briefly before regaining his composure. He took his glasses off and polished them vigorously. "It . . . ah . . . The fight has not gone as well as we . . . ah . . . would like. However, the Guard has not forced its way any closer to Avalon City. They are stalemated, and we will soon roll them back."

"You have three regiments on New Avalon at your command," Katrina reminded him, each word laced with acid. "The First Guard should not be alive to fight at all. I told you to take them into custody or destroy them the moment Victor made his call for support. Instead, you let them smash through the Third Robinson Rangers and achieve the safety of Camelot Province."

"We have them contained," Gallagher said again.

"I don't want them contained. I want them destroyed!" Katrina would not suffer challenges on the Commonwealth's throne world. Here she would—she must—reign supreme. To do otherwise invited Victor and his supporters to fight all the harder. Couldn't Gallagher see that?

Then again, he probably could not. Simon Gallagher's best claim to command was his skill at organization and logistics. Katrina almost regretted naming him to the position of Field Marshal and Director of the Crucis March Regional Command. And her Champion, she reminded herself, studying the hatchet-faced man. But Gallagher was as loyal as he was weak-willed, and that made him easy to control. As the "Prince's Champion," he could be used to bypass Jackson Davion, a distant relative who served as Katrina's Marshal of the Commonwealth armies. Another important benefit.

"Take whatever you need and get it done, Simon. We

only have to maintain ourselves here until I can summon extra support from my Alliance." In the Alliance, Katrina was stronger, which was why she needed a physical presence on New Avalon. "But we must hold the capital absolute and keep a strong presence in the Draconis and Capellan Marches."

"Yes, well . . ." Dehaver shifted uneasily and rubbed at the side of his freckled nose. "We do have new developments there." He paused, and Katrina guessed that the news was not good. "Tancred Sandoval has fled Mayetta and talked half of the militia into following him."

"Perfect," Katrina said. "The two DMMs on Mayetta can't fail to take the planet now." Then she recalled his hesitation to speak. "Where is Tancred going, Richard?"

"Woodbine," Dehaver said, naming the capital world of the local Operations Area. "He has already issued a statement declaring Woodbine's neutrality in an effort to keep the food supply lines to Robinson open and uninterrupted. It doesn't help," he added, "that the Rein family is likely to get behind him on this. They have long-standing ties to the Sandovals and want no part in the fighting. I would let this one go, Highness."

"Let it go?" Katrina flexed her fingers as if they were claws to gouge out Dehaver's dark eyes. "Tancred Sandoval may be one of the most dangerous men in the Commonwealth. I'm not about to allow him to challenge me over the principal world of the Woodbine Operations Area. Who can get to Woodbine quickly?"

"The Third Lyran Regulars are sitting on Pitkin," Dehaver said. "Though I believe Marshal Jackson Davion planned to use them to hold down the First Ceti Hussars, who declared emphatically for your brother."

Katrina looked to Gallagher. "Handle it," she ordered. "I want the Third on Woodbine before Tancred gets there." As usual, action was the tonic for any feelings of uncertainty. "I'll handle the Reins once we have military control of the system."

She studied the star chart of her Alliance that Dehaver

had left up. The system of Donegal, in the shadow of Tharkad, called something to memory.

"Isn't there a new WarShip undergoing trials between Donegal and Tharkad?" she asked.

Dehaver nodded. "The *Angela Franks*. She is set to enter service in three months."

"No longer. It will now be known as the *Arthur Steiner-Davion*, renamed in honor of my poor brother. Press it into service immediately and assign it to safeguard Coventry."

Dehaver and Gallagher exchanged glances. "Spacers consider it bad luck to change the name of an already-christened vessel, Highness," Dehaver said. "Certainly, the WarShip can accomplish the same thing as the *Angela—*"

"But it can't," Katrina interrupted, keeping her voice silky-smooth. Coventry seemed to brighten on the screen even as she watched, its importance revealed in added phosphorescence. "Victor will have a hard time fighting a ship that bears Arthur's name. And we'll see to it that he has to. Oh, Victor may talk those bigots on New Capetown into taking his side, but then he'll go to Coventry. He won't have a choice.

"And when he gets there," Katrina said, "he'll die."

29

Darrant River, Woodbine
Draconis March
Federated Commonwealth
13 September 3063

The two 'Mech battalions squared off across the Darrant River, which ran a meandering course along the northern and western borders of the Rein family's extensive ducal estates. The manmade lightning of particle cannon and the gem-tinted lances of lasers reflected dully in the slow-moving river. Shallow but wide, its gray waters occasionally geysered into the sky after a misplaced artillery round. Autocannon fire tore into both armor and the riverbank, and missiles arced up and over on their gray contrails to chip away at the positions so quickly dug in by Tancred Sandoval's support infantry.

Several kilometers beyond the river, the grand, blue-stone mansions of the Rein estate covered the side of a snow-swept hill. It was an improbable jail, but a jail nonetheless. There, the Third Lyran held just about every member of the Woodbine nobility in "protective custody"—those few who were not collaborating by choice or under duress. They consisted of seven landed nobles, another dozen honorary or military-awarded titles, and their extended families. It was the largest case of house arrest Tancred had ever heard of and, as his first military action on Woodbine, he meant to break it.

If he could.

A swarm of missiles stung at his *Nightstar*, pitting and gouging its thick armor. He checked his line of sight for a clear path and then punched back a single gauss slug that smashed into the chest of a Lyran *Stealth*. The assault 'Mech's PPC swung down toward the Darrant, challenging one of the hovercraft the Third was using to control the river. The cascade of blue-white energy cut the air just behind a speeding *Plainsman*, shattering into a dozen smaller electrical arcs that whipsawed briefly over the water. The *Plainsman*'s short-range missiles hammered back. One explosive warhead detonated against the *Nightstar*'s head, leaving a high-pitched ringing in Tancred's ears. Shaking off the stunning effect, he walked his BattleMech farther south toward the hotly contested trestle bridge.

If Tancred held any advantage, it was in his combined-forces approach: infantry, some armor, and a dual flight of aerospace fighters that routinely dove from the snow-heavy gray skies to strafe the opposite shore. The rest of his forces, scraped together from the Third Crucis Lancers and Mayetta's DMM, were staging a diversionary raid against the spaceport to keep the Third Lyran from reinforcing their position here.

The Third had its strengths: faster machines and heavy hovercraft support. They maintained a flexible defensive line, always shifting, ready to reinforce any unstable position. Given time, Tancred knew he could beat their defense. But time would cost both sides more men and equipment and might allow the Third to bring in a new flight of VTOLs to evacuate their prisoners. Their first attempt had come in too high and met a fiery death under the guns of Tancred's fighter cover. They wouldn't make that mistake again.

The question now was whether to force them into a new and more costly mistake.

The trestle bridge rose up from the roadway a half-kilometer back from the river, limiting access on both sides. Tancred had set two lances of heavy armor to secure his end and to work on forcing a way across. It was the best route for MechWarriors, who were always leery of making easy targets of themselves by getting their 'Mechs down in the water. It was also the only path possible for his ground-bound armor. The Third knew this and had set their own lance of heavy 'Mechs at their end of the bridge. The only reason they hadn't blown it yet was that the bridge offered them their best chance for a counterattack. Blow it they would, though, if they lost control of the bridge. Tancred didn't doubt that for a minute.

A burning LRM carrier currently clogged the trestle, and a pair of Tancred's Brutus assault tanks now rolled forward to bully the wreckage over the side of the bridge and into the water.

"BAT One and Two, press forward," he called to the bridge assault teams, consisting now of seven battered heavy tanks. "Double column, Brutus tanks leading."

Knowing he'd just issued a certain sentence of death to the lead tanks, Tancred brought his *Nightstar* right up to the water's edge to give them supporting fire. He fired a pair of gauss slugs, which passed over the shoulders of an enemy *Centurion* that managed to drill him in the chest with its autocannon. A *Firestarter* OmniMech and a *Cestus* crowded in to join Tancred, the *Firestarter* concentrating more on the Lyran hovercraft that slalomed in between the bridge supports, fanning up sheets of the icy water and proving nimble enough to evade the Omni's lasers. The *Cestus* cored into a *Quickdraw* with both large lasers, and the enemy 'Mech's armor ran down onto the bridge in molten streams.

Tancred waded forward until the river streamed

around the *Nightstar*'s ankles, not enough to confine him
but enough to tempt the Third Lyran to advance as well.
The shore-running machines stayed out of his reach, but
two of the 'Mechs defending the bridge advanced as their
combined fire drilled into a Brutus tank and pumped
megajoules of energy into its ammunition magazine. Missiles erupted in a cascading wash of fire, bursting through
the side of the vehicle and sending it tumbling end over
end across the bridge and into the river.

"BAT One, stall!" Tancred ordered quickly, thinking
to spring a new trap. "Hold position. BAT Two, fall
back. Pull the defenders forward."

The lead Brutus would take a savage beating, but Tancred hoped it could ride out the damage. "Lancer Flights,
line up for a river run."

Not for the first time, Tancred thanked Woodbine's
reversed seasons and the perpetually overcast skies that
allowed him to move aerospace assets around without
detection from the ground. He licked sweat from his
upper lip and throttled forward another half-dozen steps
to put himself knee-deep in the river.

On the bridge, the LRM carriers began to fall back,
while three remaining Brutus assault vehicles made their
stand. Pairing large lasers with a solid missile array, the
tanks concentrated fire on the wounded *Quickdraw* and
pounded the sixty-ton 'Mech to its knees. Then the lead
Brutus erupted in a fireball that took off its turret and
roiled a plume of oily smoke skyward as the rearward
pair of heavy Lyran 'Mechs stomped forward to press
the tanks back. Ten meters out over the water. Twenty.

That was all Tancred had been waiting for.

"BAT One, fall back," he ordered, his voice echoing
loudly in the tight confines of his neurohelmet. "BAT
Two, lay out Thunders. Walk that bridge from as far as
you can reach to the midway mark. Lancer Flights, begin
your run."

As the last two Brutus tanks retreated from the fighting, the LRM carriers each spewed three score missiles
skyward in short, sharp arcs. But it was not the usual

payload. Thunder LRMs delivered a minefield, and in a matter of seconds, the three carriers had the Lyrans so locked in that they risked destruction moving either forward or back along the trestle. So they didn't. As the *Quickdraw* regained its footing, the heavy lance poured new fire on the assault tanks and claimed another *Brutus*.

But not before the LRM carriers combined their fire with Tancred's *Nightstar* and the *Cestus* to crack the chest of an *Orion*. The fusion engine burst free of its containment in a blossom of golden fire, lashing out with violent energies as the BattleMech quite literally came apart at the seams. The ruined husk slammed into the back of the Lyran *Centurion*, knocking it forward into the minefield. The scattered devices erupted, shredding armor from the *Centurion*'s legs.

It might still have jumped free of the trap, with the other two 'Mechs risking a fall into the water, if not for the aerospace fighters that now streaked down to pummel the 'Mechs on the bridge without mercy. As they did so, Tancred turned his PPC against the trestle supports, joined again by the *Cestus* and *Firestarter*, while the remaining tanks lent their own support atop the bridge. In those few seconds of hellish destruction, the *Centurion* went down for good, decapitated by a pair of fightercraft autocannon. Then the trestle began to sway and buckle, tilting into the river as the supports finally crumpled under the abuse. Like falling dominoes, each stretch of the trestle collapsed into the waters of the Darrant.

Two enemy hovercraft, still thinking the river their own private skating rink, were lost under the bridge when huge slabs of ferrocrete collapsed over them, driving them underwater to a wet, cold death. Another lance of the fast assault craft were trapped on the downstream side, unable to skate back through the wreckage. Tancred throttled forward, fording the river only a moment behind the *Firestarter* and the *Cestus* and two DMM *Grasshopper*s, all of which lit off jump jets to sail across the water.

There had been no need to order the maneuver. The other MechWarriors had instinctively grasped the opportunity. Tancred had only to follow up with supporting commands.

"Pull south, all pull south," he ordered, wading free of the Darrant's embrace. "We are holding a beachhead near the bridge. Converge!"

The Third Regulars began to react now, but it was too slow, too late. Tancred's *Nightstar* anchored a solid position, protecting the eastern bank of the river as two more assault 'Mechs waded over, followed by a pair of jumping mediums. There would be no pushing them back now, especially as the heavy tanks discovered they could bulldoze their way across the river on the broken spine of the trestle. This battle was over. The Lyrans had to know that.

And even if they didn't, Tancred did.

Port St. Johns, New Capetown
Coventry Province
Lyran Alliance

Victor considered it a tactical victory, persuading the pro-Archon administrator of the Royal New Capetown Military Academy to open the doors and allow him to address the academy instructors and student body. Granted, the concession was won under duress of the threat implied by Victor's two combat regiments and a newly arrived WarShip. Crewed by Davion loyalists pledging for their exiled Prince, the Avalon-class *Melissa Davion* had spent the better part of six months finding Victor after going AWOL from its post over Kittery. Victor was not above using them as a trump card.

Jerry Cranston had explained to Victor that John Harrison, the Academy Commander, was pro-Lyran, not necessarily pro-Katherine, and that the training battalion's Kommandant, Alfred Vaughn, was decidedly cold toward both him and his sister. That was a window of opportunity Victor hoped to exploit.

"This is not a war of conquest," he explained to the assembled crowd, summoning his most reasonable tone. "This is not a war of pride or prejudice. This is a civil war, thrust upon us against our choosing, but necessary to decide how we shall be governed. With fairness and equality, guided by justice, or with the heavy and bloody hand of a power-seeking despot who subverts justice as it suits her own needs."

Nothing. No reaction. The room that had stood respectfully for him as he entered was now swinging against him. The audience filled the small auditorium all the way to the upper doors, creating a sea of intense glares staring back at him. If this was neutrality, Victor needed to talk with Jerry about the other neutral units they hoped to convert. A few in the audience looked scandalized. Other faces looked so pale that Victor thought they might be in shock at seeing him on their stage.

Some even looked ready to pull a needler or other hand weapon and shoot him on the spot. Despite the armored vest worn under his uniform, he was starting to think he'd prefer the protection of an infantry platoon instead of the small cadre who stood behind him in a line of solidarity. The cadre consisted of the top three officers from both the Avalon Hussars and the Prince's Men, who fanned out to either side of Tiaret.

"These men and women," he continued, half-turning to gesture to his officers, "have already pledged their support to this cause. Not to glorify my position or install themselves as leaders, but in the cause of justice. And in the end, that is what we are seeking. Justice."

Victor spied Jerry Cranston hovering at the edge of the stage, hidden behind folds of the heavy, black velvet curtain. He must have just arrived from an errand at the ComStar compound. Jerry was peering through the space between curtain and wall, his face showing the same confusion over the audience's lack of reaction that Victor was having to work so hard not to show. Victor quickly looked back at the crowd to keep from creating a long pause that might somehow convey uncertainty or weakness.

"We have come here to New Capetown in the hope— the desire—that you might join us in this endeavor. That you would rise to the challenge set before us all, students and veterans alike, and champion a just cause."

Despite the lackluster reception, Victor's voice rose toward the crescendo of his speech, still trying to move his audience. "This is such a time that will try the souls of men and women, to test whether their spirits are strong or lacking, to measure our worth against a scale that not many are privileged to know. We have come here," he said in conclusion, "hoping to name you as friends, as allies, and as patriots."

What should have been a strong ending, followed by cheers and a new commitment to oppose Katherine's unjust rule, fell on deaf ears. Victor didn't understand it, unless the people of New Capetown were so naturally taciturn that it would take a few tons of explosives to liven them up. He managed one short, sharp nod, claiming a victory he didn't feel, and then left the stage, trailed by his line of officers.

"What the hell happened out there?" he asked Jerry the moment they were all clear of the stage.

Jerry looked worried. "Let's get you out of here first. Our vehicles are waiting out back." He nodded toward the emergency exit being held open by two infantry from the Prince's Men.

"Not quite the reception we hoped for," Victor said as the armored sedan passed through the academy gates on its way back to the spaceport. Tiaret took up most of the rearward-facing jump seat across from them, with Precentor Irelon squeezed in next to her.

"Stupid," Cranston said, shaking his head. He mixed Victor a light drink from the bar. "How could I have been so stupid? I should have been there, Victor. I saw it the minute I walked in."

"You were needed at the ComStar compound to clear the latest messages," Victor said. "You warned me that you might run late. The speech was well-crafted, and I thought my delivery was spot-on."

"It wasn't the delivery, Victor. Think about it—who did you have standing behind you?" Jerry leaned forward. "Who did you have anchoring your officer corps?"

"Tiaret?" Victor glanced over at his dark-skinned bodyguard, who frowned, also confused. "What does Tiaret have to do with it?"

"Victor, you've spent so much time with her that it's blinded you. It blinded me. Can't you see what she is?" Cranston shook his head again. "It's obvious, isn't it? She's Clan."

That was true. You couldn't get more obviously Clan than an Elemental, their impressive size and strength genetically tailored to fight in Clan battle armor. "New Capetown has always been a bit elitist," Victor admitted. "But—"

"But over the past seven years that pride has been focused outward, against the Clans. Harrison and Vaughn were outspokenly critical of you when the Star League chose the Smoke Jaguars to destroy rather than the Jade Falcons. And so who do we have up there as one of your supporters? A Clan Elemental. If you had brought her into the auditorium in chains, driven before you with a neurowhip, they would have cheered themselves hoarse." Jerry sounded as disgusted with himself for not seeing the problem as he was with New Capetown for creating it.

Tiaret nodded, partially understanding. "If we explain to them that you took me as bondsman after your military victory on Huntress, it would help matters, quiaff?"

Victor shook his head. "Neg, Tiaret. It wouldn't. Prejudice runs deeper than we can counter with a simple explanation. Bigots hate without a sense of logic or reason." He sipped at his drink, a weak whiskey and soda. "Think about how the Clans—your Clan—often viewed the Inner Sphere. Weak. Without honor. Unworthy of anything but contempt."

A light dawned in Tiaret's eyes. "Aff. This I understand. But you taught me otherwise. Can you not teach them?"

"No offense, Tiaret, but it took the Star League's annihilation of your Clan to change many of those attitudes. And even if I thought that were an option, I have neither the time nor the resources to waste on it." Victor shook his head. "We could have used the manpower boost from New Capetown, but now I think we're better off without such narrow-minded warriors."

"Not that we don't have enough of those anyway," Raymond Irelon reminded him. "The two lances that came in from Kingston's Legionnaires are still feuding with that First Regular Hussars company out of the League. And the battalion we've created from Combine warriors wants nothing to do with either of them."

Victor dismissed the problems inherent in his "foreign legion" regiment with a careless wave. "Nationalism I can handle, so long as they are all committed when it comes time to fight Katherine. And they will be." He took another pull at his drink, enjoying the Glengarry Reserve's smoky flavor, and then handed it over to Cranston. He had to keep his head.

"Our next target will keep us all busy," he promised.

"Then it's on to Coventry?" Irelon asked. "You're not concerned with the rumors that Katherine has moved a WarShip into the area? This LAS *Arthur Steiner-Davion*?"

"It concerns me, yes. But I can't let the threat of a WarShip shut me down. Coventry is the most important planet marked for our second wave, not the least for its factories. I also need the support of Duke Bradford. We must have that world, and I intend to take it."

October fifteenth, Victor promised himself silently. Just over four weeks to prepare and make the jump to Coventry.

"And don't forget," he reminded them, "now that the *Melissa Davion* has arrived, we've got our own WarShip support. If Katherine wants to play at symbolism, that's fine with me.

"I have our mother fighting by my side."

30

Cruising through Coventry's umbra, the rechristened Lyran Alliance WarShip *Arthur Steiner-Davion* prowled the deep. Two hundred thirty-five thousand metric tons of lethal intent, it was poised for the kill. Biding its time. And cursed, Admiral Jurgen Haas told himself, adjusting the ball cap that covered his bald head. Never forget cursed.

By Haas's reckoning and his own intelligence sources, they had seven days before the rebel task force arrived. He was going to need every single second of that time to beat the jinx laid on the *Arthur* when it was renamed from the *Angela Franks*. Battle drills, damage-control rehearsals, general-purpose time for familiarization—anything to help his crew get over their superstition about piloting a vessel with two conflicting souls.

One week.

Then, ready or not, they would be under orders to kill the FCS *Melissa Davion*, and Prince Victor along with her.

"Contact," Sensors called. A young staff sergeant named Andrayev, he was thin, gangly and with a voice that screeched like fingernails on slate. But the kid was as good as Haas had ever seen at reading the complex instruments that were the vessel's eyes and ears. "IR signature, designate contact Romeo-seven." Infrared signatures warned of the imminent arrival of other jump-capable vessels, from merchants to WarShips. The warning set everyone on edge, wondering if this contact heralded Victor Steiner-Davion, and battle. "Very faint."

Station-keeping drives provided a one-third standard gravity environment, enough for Haas to glide across his bridge without the need for magnetic soles.

"Doesn't matter how faint it is," he said, moving quickly to his command chair. He strapped himself in and clipped his mug of tea into a holder. "We're expecting hostiles. Battle stations!"

A gong rang seven times over the ship's 1MC channel, echoing along the steel corridors and shocking sleeping crewmen out of their racks. A twenty-year veteran, Haas could easily imagine the dropped cards and abandoned meals as the off-duty men struggled into their uniforms and rushed to their stations while all of the vessel's air-tight doors slammed shut. It was a drill run many times in the life of any spacedog and one always taken seriously, especially on a WarShip.

"Secondary contacts!" Sergeant Andrayev called out, his shrill voice excited and nervous. "Romeo-eight, nine . . . and ten! All infrared signatures consistent with arriving vessels. Bearings are mixed but fall in the same general location. Median two-five-two by negative zero-one-eight. Range . . ." He trailed off, double-checking. "Median range is roughly one hundred seventy klicks."

One hundred seventy kilometers. Combat range! And coming in at an unconventional jump point deep within the system's gravity well—the kind known as a "pirate" point for its use by raiders wanting to surprise their victims. Haas felt the first sharp thrill of danger and clenched his hands into fists.

"Helm, come about at point-five Gs. I want some momentum behind us. Weapons, stand ready. What's their ETA if they're coming in from New Capetown?" he asked his navigation officer.

"If they managed it in one jump," Lieutenant Sarah Gespers informed him, "less than two minutes. From the closest system to Coventry, which would be Tertia-R12, as little as twenty seconds."

Kommodore Tarn Earhart, the ship's executive officer, gained the bridge just in time to hear the estimation. "Merchant shipping?" he asked, assuming it was another false alarm.

Haas glanced over at him. "Not unless these merchants are bringing in a fleet, and at a pirate point less than two hundred klicks off our position. I think we've got them, Tarn."

No need to say that "them" was the rebel Prince Victor, his renegade Com Guard division, the Thirty-ninth Avalon Hussars, and, reportedly, a motley assortment of foreign troops. Haas would blast them into component atoms. Or he would try, at any rate. The Fox-class corvette was no standup match for an Avalon-class cruiser like the *Melissa*, but Haas also commanded three Overlord DropShips refitted as "ship-killers." Bristling with naval-grade missiles, the Overlords doubled his effective firepower. He would release them the moment Sensors identified enemy ships.

Sixty seconds. Ninety. Two minutes.

Helm began a gentle curve around the reported entry vector, keeping a broadside angle against that location while trying not to skate in too close. The emergence wave of an incoming JumpShip could damage other vessels as far away as two thousand meters. Haas didn't want to give the jinx anything to bite on.

Two minutes thirty seconds.

"Sensors, what the hell is going on? Recalculate."

Andrayev shook his head. "I did. We're now at contact plus two-forty. At a maximum jump distance of thirty light-years, that kind of IR signature might be consistent with an Avalon-class cruiser but not any JumpShip except a Monolith or a fully loaded Star Lord."

The young officer was right. The DropShip capacity of any jump-capable vessel was directly related to the displacement field generated by its Kearny-Fuchida drives. At full capacity, a JumpShip could be matched against a simple curve of distance traveled versus time in transit. The only inexplicable disparity was that the subjective time of a jump seemed instantaneous, while infrared signatures gave a warning twice as long as the actual jump procedure. In an example every first-year spacer knew, an Invader-class JumpShip making a maximum hyperspace jump would seem to take only a few seconds to someone on board the ship. In actuality, roughly forty-five seconds passed between disappearing from one jump point to reappearing at another. But the IR signature showed up ninety seconds before arrival— or forty-five seconds before the JumpShip ever engaged its KF drive.

"We've passed contact-plus-three minutes," Kommodore Earhart announced, his steady eye on the chronometer. "That is the theoretical maximum for an Avalon-class cruiser."

"IR signature is reading high in the band," Andrayev announced, his shrill voice sounding worried. "They're almost here."

"Screens!" Haas ordered sharply. "Show me that space." The main screen filled with a few thousand tiny points of light separated by infinite black, an uninterrupted starscape.

Four minutes.

"Thirty seconds until we hit the IR ceiling for a loaded Monolith," Staff Sergeant Andrayev announced. "You know," he added hesitantly, "I've studied the signatures and readings of HPG transmissions. The way they fade in is very similar to the faint reading on our initial contact. And HPGs can reach fifty light-years. What if the NAIS has improved K-F drives to that theoretical maximum?"

Navigator Gespers shook her head doubtfully. "So they jumped from New Capetown back out to Sargasso before coming to Coventry? Just to give us warning?"

Haas felt sweat beading under the rim of his cap. "Well, someone had better explain this," he growled. "Because we just passed the four-thirty mark." He clutched the arms of his chair. "Andrayev. What would be your best guess if the wizards on New Avalon had somehow managed to make fifty-light-year jumps possible without ever telling us?"

"Seven and one-half minutes lead time on the IR sig," Andrayev answered immediately.

Haas grunted and nodded. "Order all stations to double-check their areas. Weapons, prepare for full broadside. Engineering to ready the engines for one hundred-twenty percent of full thrust. DropShips disconnect now! I want us ready, people. Make it happen."

The chronometer's digital numbers counted down with incredible slowness, each second drawing out as the crew waited. Haas allowed himself one sip of his tea, wincing as the hot liquid burned his tongue. That only made him think again that this was a cursed ship and that he was captain of a doomed vessel.

"Seven-thirty," he finally said. "This can't be! Sensors, what's the IR reading?"

"It edged out of band two minutes ago Admiral," Andrayev said helplessly. "I can't tell you what's happening. I've run two diagnostics, and everything checks out."

"Run a third!"

But Haas knew the third check would turn up no discrepancies. This was something else. Something he'd never considered or prepared for.

"What ship can generate an IR signature in excess of eight minutes?" he asked his exec quietly.

Tarn Earhart frowned. "There's only one kind of Clan

WarShip I know of that can do it. Do you think the Wolves on Arc-Royal might be in on this? We'd have heard something if they were on the move."

"I want you down at Central Control," Haas told Earhart quietly. "Get them plotting emergency-jump procedures from the nearest pirate points, and keep another set of calculations running for our current location—and damn the gravity."

Earhart's eyebrows crept up into his dark hairline. "We're going to risk that?" He wiped sweat from his upper lip. "What if this is simply some kind of trick by Victor?"

"You don't believe that any more than I do," Haas said, keeping his face set in a tight mask to conceal his own nervousness. "Whatever shows up—*if* something shows up—we'll take a bite out of it. The *Angela Franks* will go down swinging."

His exec glanced around to see if anyone else had heard the slip. "You do mean the *Arthur Davion*, right, Admiral?"

Haas nodded but continued to stare straight ahead, his eyes riveted to the main screen. "Arthur, Angela, Victor, Katrina," he said, then shrugged.

"Whatever you call it, something's coming for us all."

Molson's Wash, Woodbine
Draconis March
Federated Commonwealth (Suns)

"So, my father is coming. What does that mean to me?"

Tancred had sensed the nervous energy in the field command trailer the instant he walked through the door. He was preparing himself for a confrontation even before Duke Ferdinand Rein stood up from the swivel-back chair Tancred usually occupied. It was an ambush.

Duke Rein never took to the field, but he had brought

in Tancred's top officers for this visit to Tancred in the field. Present were Battalion Major Darrin Hespers of the Third Crucis Lancers and Baroness Monique Rein, Ferdinand's niece and a fine MechWarrior. Also with him were several representatives of the Mayetta DMM and the newly arrived First Crucis Lancers.

"It should mean *something* to you," Ferdinand said in his deep, sonorous voice. "Duke James Sandoval is our March Lord."

If Tancred hadn't spent the past thirty-six hours in the field, sleeping in his 'Mech between fighting two rear-guard battles, maybe he would have been more receptive to this discussion. Tired, dehydrated, his skin scaly with dried sweat and his muscles aching from enemy weapons pounding against his *Nightstar*'s armor, he was in no mood for a debate. He rubbed at the spasm that gripped the back of his neck and pinned Rein with an angry glare.

"A March Lord who turned his back on you to go chasing after the Dracs while Katherine rode roughshod over your hereditary fief," he said sharply. "Need I remind you that you were her guest not long ago? Woodbine is still nominally under the command of her military governor, in fact."

"Something James Sandoval has pledged to correct. If given a choice, I would prefer to recover my world through negotiation."

"And I'm saying you won't be able to." Tancred folded his bare arms over the padded chest of his cooling vest. "You lost that right when Katherine threw the Third Lyran Regulars at you. The same way she did on Kentares. Duke Eric Dresari could certainly give you some sound advice on this matter, Ferdinand, if he were still alive."

Tancred saw Rein wince and knew he'd hit a vulnerable spot. The nobility often believed itself inviolate, but the heavy-handed tactics Katherine's forces had employed on Kentares put that conviction to the lie.

"We saw the same thing on Mayetta," said Captain

Paulos Vencen of the Mayetta DMM. Vencen was Jason Yalos's hand-picked officer to liaise between Tancred and the DMM contingent. The man was so obviously ambitious that Tancred secretly believed that he had to be somehow related to the Yalos family. In planning sessions, he too often spoke up just for the sake of hearing his own voice.

"Admittedly, our stance was slightly firmer against Katrina's tyranny," he said, "but how could any just-minded soldier do otherwise? The Yalos family stands squarely behind Prince Victor and Tancred Sandoval." Vencen gave Tancred a self-righteous nod, ignoring or completely missing the sneers directed at him by some of the others.

Tancred wished Vencen would stop trying to help him.

"Duke Rein does make a good point," Major Hespers said. "General Zardetto rallied to your call for Prince Victor, but that was partly because your father seemed to be ignoring the crisis. Now that the duke has finally noticed the problem, wouldn't it be better to work with him, Lord, in hopes of bringing him over to our side?"

Except that Tancred knew that his father would not come over. Not while Katherine held a dagger to the belly of his shipping lanes through the Draconis March. Then he berated himself silently for thinking like Victor again, trying to win the minds of his troops rather than playing on their loyalties to achieve his ends. Think like a Sandoval, he ordered himself. He should not be debating with men and women already committed to his command.

"Major Hespers," he said, rounding on the man with all the authority he could muster. "General Zardetto placed you under my direct command. Has that order been countermanded?"

Hespers hesitated slightly and then shook his head.

"And is this military action being run as a democracy?" His tone was even harsher this time.

Hespers stiffened. "No," he said.

Tancred nodded. "Then return to your duties, Major

Hespers. I have a very tired battalion straggling in, and we need to out send another one at once if we're going to force Treckle Pass by week's end. You will lead that command, and the First Crucis Lancers will relieve you in two days."

Hespers drew himself up formally and gave Tancred a salute straight out of the military rulebook. With a glance, he drew a Lancer subofficer along with him as he left.

Tancred waited until Hespers was gone and then said, "Everyone else not directly related to Duke Rein, dismissed!"

For a moment, Tancred thought even Monique Rein would abandon her uncle, but familial ties still counted for more than military orders on many worlds and among many noble lines. She stayed, though she didn't hide the hesitation in her eyes.

"Much better," Tancred pronounced, looking around the empty trailer and moving to a thermal chest to get a drink. His first swallow of a lime-flavored Sports-Aid washed away the sour taste of dehydration. He stood facing the map of Woodbine's northern continent that hung on one wall of the trailer.

With a glance, he traced the red arrow that tracked his movements from the Rein Estates toward Gastogne, the actual capital of Woodbine. So close now. If he could juggle the disparate forces coming together under his command for another month, he would have it. Gastogne, Woodbine, the Operations Area—everything in one fell swoop.

"You still have something you wish to say to me, Duke Rein?" he asked after a moment.

Rein chuckled dryly and retook his seat. "You handled that very well, Baron. Better than I would have expected. Not that it matters. We both know that this boils down to you and me. You control the military on Woodbine, at least until your father arrives. I expect that many of your warriors are walking a fine line and will default to the strongest political power—which is the March Lord.

In the meantime, I still control Woodbine's unoccupied territory. You will hardly be able to maintain, much less press forward, without my direct support and mandate." His voice hardened. "Which means I have something to say about what you do and where you fight."

Praise your opponent, then gnaw away at his supports before the final attack. Tancred easily saw through the trick of debate.

"That's true," he agreed, though not quite in the way Duke Rein imagined, "I'd hate to spend forces securing local cities. But I will. Make no mistake, Duke Rein. I will have the support I need to prosecute this battle one way or another." He could see the man's rage building, and decided to hack away at his confidence. "The problem is that you're relying too heavily on my father's promise to come to Woodbine."

"He'll be here in four weeks," Monique said, obviously privy to some message.

"My father *could* be here in four weeks," Tancred allowed, "the breakdown in transportation caused by this civil war notwithstanding. Except that he has no reason to come here at present. Though he nominally supports Katherine, he'll come only if it looks like we'll take this world back for Victor. And we will. And then, finally, he will. And then you'll have a very important decision to make."

"Are you certain you're not letting your personal feelings color your arguments, Tancred?" Duke Rein kept his voice calm and reasonable, trying to underscore the fact that Tancred had let some of his anger seep through.

"I'm telling you," Tancred promised, ignoring the comment, "that in two weeks or less you will receive my father's first message telling you he's been delayed. Then what, Ferdinand?"

"One delay would not constitute proof of malicious intent," the Duke said cautiously.

"Malice or Katherine's interference, the result will be the same. A week later you'll receive a second delay. Then a third. If and when we take Rhinehold, which is the last stepping stone to Gastogne, *then* you will hear that he's left Robinson."

Ferdinand Rein rubbed the side of his face with one flat palm. "You sound very sure of yourself," he said.

Tancred caught what sounded like a touch of deference in his tone. The Duke was too skilled to let it show inadvertently; he had used it for a reason. "What if you are wrong?"

"I'm not," he said, knowing he'd just bought himself two weeks. At the least. "And if I am, Monique is your witness before the other officers. She is welcome to try and take command from me at that time."

Ferdinand nodded slowly and stood. "I will consider your argument," he promised. A deep nod, respectful if not deferential, and the two nobles left as easily as if they'd won the debate.

And Ferdinand Rein would consider, Tancred knew. He'd consider for at least two weeks—which was their unspoken arrangement. It protected the duke from the consequences of making a formal deal and it gave him room to maneuver in case Tancred was right.

"I'm right," Tancred said softly, sitting in the chair Rein had so recently vacated. "I've got no other choice but to be right."

James Sandoval would delay on his own accord or Katherine's or Tancred's. Aunt Jessica would arrange for it on her brother's behalf. Tancred would send her a message immediately. A problem in local military materiel production, threats of unsecured transportation, the need to make a public address—since when had his father passed up a chance to endear himself to Robinson's public? There were numerous ways to prevent the Duke of Robinson from leaving his capital.

One way or another, Tancred would prove himself right. "I'm sorry, Father," he whispered to the empty trailer, "but I can't afford to allow you to come here.

"Not yet."

31

The Dales, Coventry
Coventry Province
Lyran Alliance
21 October 3063

Alarms wailed for Victor's attention, and a new swarm of long-range missiles stung at his *Daishi*, chipping away at the OmniMech's valuable armor. Light autocannon fire hammered his lower legs, making the whole machine tremble as if suffering from palsy. Victor left the minor hitch in his stride to his neurohelmet and the massive gyroscopic stabilizers that worked together to keep his one-hundred-ton machine upright and moving forward. He was firing his lasers at Colonel Jason Walker's First Coventry Jaegers command, but his attention was on co-ordinating the maneuvers of his various forces now battling for Coventry.

Half a kilometer distant, the canary-yellow Jaeger machines stood out against the verdant Dales, their 'Mechs and armor piling together in uncertain islands as they hit the deep stands of tall aspens flanking the nearby Rid-seine River. A new run by Victor's aerospace fighters roared across the overcast skies, picking away at the Jaeger line, a torment they had borne ever since losing air superiority the day Victor arrived. Earlier, if one wanted to consider the mysterious death of the WarShip *Arthur Davion*. Right now, he didn't.

Victor also knew that the Jaeger scouts would be reporting contact at the river's edge as his Outland Legion began to trade heavy fire with them across the Ridseine's sluggish waters.

Pressed from the south by Bragg's Thirty-ninth Avalon Hussars and from the north by elements of Victor's 244th, Katherine's loyalists were faced with only one open direction. East, toward the seaboard. But like any well-trained military command, they resisted being herded.

Swinging his lighter armor back to the rear, Victor wheeled them toward the river's edge. That left only an assault armor company and some infantry backing the equivalent of a single 'Mech battalion. If the Jaegers opted to make a final charge, he'd lure them in this direction. With any luck, though, they'd choose the temporary escape being offered them.

"Skirt the river and press the Jaeger scouts," Victor ordered Adept Brighton, the Com Guard warrior who commanded the armor from a very rare, Star League-vintage *Kanga*. "Don't get yourself flanked. We only want to discourage them from fording the river."

A double-click of acknowledgment was the adept's only reply. Then, his jump-capable hovercraft bounced up on thrusters to rise up and come down in the lead position of the forming column. Every tank under sixty tons made a beeline for the Ridseine.

"Cloudburst, this is Swift Wind," General Bella Bragg's throaty voice said in Victor's ear. "We're still pressing up from the south, slowing under their rear-guard fire as ordered. We can hammer through at any time," she said, as if Victor needed reminding.

Victor ignored his general for the moment. Topping one of the low, rolling hills for which the Dales were known, he worked his stick to bring his targeting cross hairs over one of the enemy 'Mechs—a *Hauptmann*.

Emerald lances speared out, one from each arm, and took the *Hauptmann* in an already-wounded flank. Armor sloughed away under the focused energies, large pieces of burning composite splattering over the ground and the 'Mech's feet.

"Negative, General," he finally replied. "Keep the pressure on but don't break up the advance. And keep your Third Battalion hanging back on strong safety." Victor throttled into a run, moving the *Daishi* to support a medium-weight unit taking harder fire from the Jaeger armor detachment. "If the Jaegers force an opening through your lines, then they're right back into the Richland Valley. We just spent three days pushing them out of those cities. They get back in there, I expect their first order of business will be to finish wrecking the factories."

As his sister was learning while trying to bring the First Davion Guards to bay on New Avalon, there was no single battle that would win this war. Not until he personally got to New Avalon. Until then, it would be a slow-fought battle of attrition. Controlling important facilities, such as the ones here on Coventry, would make all the difference. As it was, this world's largest production lines would already be down for weeks, if not months, due to sabotage by the retreating Jaegers.

"Then let's swing our lines out a bit farther and box the Jaegers. What are they going to do against two of our regiments?"

"Completely decimate one of them," Victor answered, cycling his lasers and this time cutting an arm off the luckless *Hauptmann*. A new stream of autocannon fire ripped into the side of his 'Mech's armored head, and Victor winced involuntarily. Memories of Newtown Square were still fresh in his mind. He knew that unless a commander has overwhelming force, he should always leave the enemy a path of retreat. If soldiers were given an alternative to death, they did not have to fight as if their survival depended on it.

"You may not have that option, Prince Victor," said Duke Bradford, who had come out of hiding with Victor's arrival and was now leading Victor's strategic reserves several kilometers behind the 244th. "Your sister has convinced the Jaegers that you will show no mercy for the earlier destruction of the Coventry militia." From the hostility rampant in his voice, Duke Bradford no doubt agreed with Katherine on this point.

"All the more reason to demonstrate mercy," Victor answered calmly. "The Jaegers have lost their mercenary support and much of their logistics capability. They'll start thinking about surrender soon." Victor broke off the conversation as Colonel Walker chose that moment to drive a probing force back into the teeth of the Com Guard division.

Two *Blitzkriegs* loped out from the Jaeger line. They were flanked by a *Night Hawk* and a *Commando* while a lance of light hovercraft provided armor support. The bulk of the Jaeger command shook itself out into a wedge, aiming into the heart of the Prince's Men. Victor sent a Level II unit to meet the probe and called in his air support. "Duke Bradford, bring the reserves up to reinforce the Com Guard position, and make a showy arrival." He wanted to convince Walker that he did not really want a piece of the Guard. At least, not today.

But Jason Walker had other ideas. Not only did he want a piece, but a very specific piece at that. With the hovercraft spearing forward to harass Victor's Level II unit and slowing down any assistance, the four Jaeger 'Mechs suddenly shifted course and threw themselves at Victor's *Daishi*.

From as far out as half a kilometer, the *Night Hawk* stabbed at the Omni with its lasers. The *Blitzkriegs*, showing off the incredible speed for which they were famous, sprinted forward at better than one hundred kilometers per hour to bring their devastating ultra-class autocannons into range. With a twelve-centimeter bore and cooling fins to promote rapid fire, the *Blitzkrieg*s were 'Mech-killers. The overhead weapons spat out long tongues of flame, and slugs tipped with depleted uranium walked over the *Daishi* in furious lines. They cut deeply into the *Daishi*'s right arm, severing it at the elbow joint and leaving a broken stump swinging from the shoulder. Another salvo ripped through armor and myomer musculature to smash the left leg's foot actuator, hobbling the mighty OmniMech.

A dangerous gamble, spending these medium and light machines against Victor's position, and one that almost paid off as Victor fought for control of his 'Mech. Recovering the balance of a one-hundred-ton machine was no easy task. Throttling into a backward walk stole some of the autocannon fire's force, and he managed to compensate for a slight sideways lean by throwing his left arm out wide to counterbalance. Not pretty, but effective.

Many other designs caught with one arm lying on the ground and the other swung out of alignment would be left stranded in the open with no hope of defense. But Victor had ordered his technicians to restore the *Daishi* to its original configuration for Coventry, and it now mounted a blistering array of pulse lasers in its torso as well as an autocannon of similar bore and design to the *Blitzkrieg*s. A flurry of hot metal spat out, catching the lead *Blitzkrieg* across the chest and tearing through armor and titanium skeletal supports. Emerald energy pulses probed in behind the hard-hitting slugs, cutting away reactor shielding to open a lethal wound directly over the BattleMech's fusion heart.

All this before the Com Guard 'Mechs backing Victor's position cut loose with their own hellish firepower.

Two *Raijin* added a particle projection cannon each to the *Blitzkrieg*'s misfortune, blasting away armor from the legs. A *Lancelot*, not to be outdone, followed Victor's damage through the chest of the enemy machine and skewered the fusion reactor with one well-placed laser that cored through the 'Mech. The *Blitzkrieg* toppled forward, plowing headfirst into the soft ground and kicking up a spray of black earth. The ground shook under the assault, and a split second later golden fire exploded from the chest cavity and mushroomed a column of fire, smoke, and plasma into the air over the fallen machine.

That was enough for the Coventry Jaegers, who had seen their bid fall short of Victor's asking price. The remaining *Blitzkrieg* sprinted back for the safety of the Jaeger line, with the *Night Hawk* and the three remaining hovercraft speeding after it. The *Commando* never made it, though, caught in midturn by a gauss slug that snapped the left leg clean off, flipping the severed limb into the air as the twenty-five-ton machine fell gracelessly to earth.

"They're pulling back," General Bragg shouted over the commline, the volume-dampening circuitry cutting back to save Victor's hearing. "I hope that was Walker's *Hauptmann* we saw drifting up into the clouds."

"Not so lucky," Victor said, deadpan, staring through his ferroglass shield as the named *Hauptmann* struck a path eastward. Another 'Mech of the same design, the one Victor had wounded earlier, took up a rearguard position with another seven assault 'Mechs. They promised a hard rearguard action against anyone looking to take advantage of the retreat. "But they're pulling east. Which means we'll have them trapped against the ocean now." And *that* meant Victor's forces could herd them up and down the coastline, nipping off pieces here and there, until Walker finally surrendered.

"We pursue, yes?" Bradford asked as his relief forces began to appear on the rear edge of Victor's heads-up display.

Victor counted his losses for the day. "We let them run," he said. "Let them wonder, and worry, while we rest and refit."

"But we could end this now," Bradford said. "After what they did to the CMM, to the military academy, and Port Lawrence, we're going to let them get away?"

Watching as the First Coventry Jaegers lost themselves down in a shallow valley, Victor spotted General Bragg's

Hussars as they crested a distant hill in pursuit of the rearguard force. It was her regiment, a Com Guard division, and two battalions of the Outland Legion against a wounded combined-arms regiment. A tough battle, perhaps, but one with only a single outcome.

Victor shook his head again. "They're not going anywhere."

32

With sweat pouring off his brow and alarms constantly blaring as enemy machines popped from around the corners of redstone buildings to snipe at his column, Tancred Sandoval leveled the *Nightstar*'s arms at a retreating *JaegerMech* and used his gauss rifles to break both of its stumpy legs. The barrel-chested 'Mech went down hard, striking sparks from the ferrocrete-paved street, but it could not be counted out of the fight yet. It crabbed around, obviously hoping to bring one of its autocannons back into the fight. Tancred blistered its back and side with every energy weapon at his disposal, his PPC cutting at the gyroscope housing while his lasers concentrated on the *Jaeger*'s supporting arm.

Then the *JaegerMech* sprawled forward and made no attempt to regain its feet. Either the machine or the

MechWarrior inside had apparently decided to simply give up a lost cause. A Centipede scout car wheeled toward the cockpit, ready to take the 'Mech pilot prisoner, while a single *Firestarter* fell out of formation to cover the retrieval. The better part of Tancred's battalion filed by without giving the fallen warrior a second glance, intent on working their way free of the confining streets. Tancred took a brief moment to check that his damaged engine's shielding breach had not worsened, then partially purged the stifling, sweat-heavy air that was baking him in the *Nightstar*'s cockpit. It was all he had time for.

Two Kestrel VTOLs, having already dumped their infantry load several blocks back to secure Rhinehold's industrial sector, sped past, one off either shoulder of the *Nightstar*. They skated between the last two buildings, banking out low and furious over the open ground beyond. Their tactical data streamed back to the 'Mechs following them to confirm what three days of intelligence-gathering and today's spotty radio traffic had already suggested: the siege of Rhinehold, Woodbine's largest industrial center, had become the battle for Woodbine itself.

Caught in a pincer between Tancred Sandoval's ad hoc regiment and what was left of the First Crucis Lancers, the city had seemed certain to fall. But that was before the Third Lyran Regulars, Katherine's supporters, began pouring their whole strength into holding it. It was an interesting call that they abandoned the capital of Gastogne for a proxy fight over Rhinehold. Tancred knew that he had relatives of Duke Rein, the ones collaborating with the enemy, to thank; the nobles had finally realized that the deciding battle would be fought in one city or the other and were looking to preserve Gastogne from such abuse.

Light elements of the First Crucis Lancers and the Mayetta DMM were now battering the heavy-armor force, determined to safeguard the local spaceport. In actuality, they were simply pinning the armor in place to prevent the tanks from rejoining their parent command.

The same orders held for the company of 'Mechs Tancred had split off earlier to delay the long Lyran infantry column, which could force a costly door-to-door battle to clear the city. That was a battle Tancred had no intention of fighting.

This—the conflict raging before him as he cleared the final buildings—was what he'd come here for.

At the heart of Rhinehold was a kilometer-wide industrial park, dividing the city into two sections connected only by thin commercial centers around the outside. It included a manmade lake set among grassy banks that put much-needed space between the heavy industrial sections and the administrative and residential areas of the city. Now the lightly wooded grounds also served as a much-needed arena for BattleMechs and armor to move freely without having to walk through buildings to get at one another. Not that some nearby buildings weren't already burning or demolished from stray weapon fire— the always tragic result of urban warfare—but with luck, the workers would have vacated the premises hours or days before.

Two battalions of the Third Lyran Regulars defended the kilometer-wide park, tearing into a mixed assortment of armor and BattleMechs from the First Crucis Lancers. The First had jumped the gun, and they were now paying for their early arrival with lives and equipment as they struggled to hold out in the chaotic firefight. The azure streams of PPC fire spread out in a latticework of manmade lightning that seemed to jump from 'Mech to 'Mech and occasionally from 'Mech to ground. Autocannon slugs chewed up armor and infantry while the tread of heavier machines did just as much damage to the once-pristine turf.

Laser fire flashed out in colorful strobes, stabbing into opposing machines like the lances of high-tech knights jousting for the favors of Woodbine. One spread of laser pulses missed their intended target and splashed armor off the right side of Tancred's *Nightstar*. Tancred returned the courtesy with interest in the form of two gauss slugs—and throttled into a fifty kilometer-per-hour run that would put his 'Mech into the thick of the fighting.

"Form two battle lines," he ordered, careful to pace the *Dragon Fire* piloted by Monique Rein. She had just as big a stake in this battle as Tancred, and he would need her support later. Combat did not preclude him from "thinking like a Sandoval." As the battalion swung out into two lines, one hidden behind the other, both he and Monique dropped their cross hairs over Lyran machines and began to fire as fast as their weapons would cycle.

A pair of Lyran *Maelstrom*s led the counterattack over one of the two bridges, fronting an armor-supported company that wheeled through a thick line of maple. Across the lake, a full battalion of mixed armor and 'Mechs peeled away from the reeling First Lancers to meet this new threat. With reactor damage dumping waste heat into the *Nightstar*, it took all of two salvoes to spike the heat in Tancred's cockpit into the yellow, bordering on the red zone. He gasped for breath as a new wash of burnt air slammed over him, but managed to croak out, "Captain Vencen, bluff the *Maelstrom*s. Everyone else, forward to the lake."

The Mayetta DMM commander, leading his jump-capable lance, touched off his *Grasshopper*'s jump jets and sailed his seventy-ton machine up and over the heads of the two lead BattleMechs. A combined weight of one hundred-sixty tons followed him, his lance cutting off not only the *Maelstrom*s from the bulk of their company but a *Challenger* XMBT as well. The *Maelstrom*s and the *Challenger*, with an enemy lance threatening their weaker rear armor, attempted to curl back in on the jumping lance.

Knowing what kind of damage Vencen might face from the battle tank and heavier machines, Tancred pivoted on one broad foot and turned his assault lance away from the main drive.

"All yours, Monique," he said. "Good hunting."

"Don't take too long," she called back, her voice

barely audible over the frantic chatter as the battle communications began to bleed into one another.

"Long" was a relative term in battle, where combat could rage unchecked for hours, and then, in a matter of minutes, a whole battalion be lost. Lives and machines often hung on a balance of seconds, on who fired first or who made the more damaging mistake. This time, it would be the Lyrans.

Turning away from Tancred's main drive, trying more to preserve themselves than to carry out any coordinated plan, the two *Maelstrom*s and the Challenger-X battle tank opened themselves to a murderous rearward assault. While Paulos Vencen delayed the bulk of the attacking Lyran company, Tancred led his assault lance into the fray. He toggled for gauss rifles and lasers, using the heavy, rail-propelled slugs to crack open the battle tank's protective shell. His pulse lasers spat out a fury of emerald darts, playing over and through the tank's ruined rear end, seeking critical equipment but not finding it. This time.

As one of the *Maelstrom*s fell to the combined fire of Tancred's lancemates, the Challenger attempted to turn out to protect its vulnerable back end. But not fast enough. Relying on a BattleMech's inherent superior handling, Tancred managed to keep an angle on the rear of the tank and cored through it with his ready PPC. The argent stream blasted through the last scraps of armor, filling the body of the armored vehicle with hellish energies that split open an ammunition bin and touched off the ordnance inside. The turret assembly came off with a cork-popping eruption that flipped the assembly side over side like some improbable bottle top. Fire belched from the top and ruined back end as the Challenger burned itself into a charred, impotent husk.

Captain Vencen was down one *Enforcer*, and his own *Grasshopper* wasn't looking too good when Tancred's *Nightstar* and a *Victor* finally reinforced the Mayetta lance. The Lyran drive slowed, hesitated, and stalled in the face of such a hard-hitting attack force. The decision of whether to press forward or retreat to the safety of their own lines was taken from them when a heavy armor lance from the First Crucis Lancers secured the far side of the bridge they had used to cross.

Even the *Maelstrom*'s fall to a lucky PPC shot coring through the ferroglass shield to incinerate the assault 'Mech's cockpit was little cause for celebration. In the next moment, Tancred and his *Victor* lancemate teamed up to savage a Lyran *Bushwacker*. A Mayetta *Quickdraw* gave up one arm in an intense firefight between itself and two Plainsmen hovercraft but recouped the loss when a heavy kick crushed the skirting on one of the vehicles, grounding it. Captain Vencen then defied the odds with his large laser, carving through a weak spot in an *Orion*'s chest to turn its gyroscope into several tons of metal slag.

Though the loss of their one remaining assault machine merely evened the odds, it was still enough for the Lyrans. The armored vehicles cut away first, the few hovercraft jumping down the bank to skim across the lake and rejoin the main force. High-speed tracked vehicles throttled for the safety of the industrial sector, barely leading the seven remaining BattleMechs of the Third Regulars. Then it became six remaining 'Mechs, as Vencen's three-man lance stumbled and limped after the fleeing command to bring down an already-wounded *Blackjack*. Then five.

Tancred let them go, Lyrans and Mayetta DMM both, leading the two machines left to his own assault lance over the bridge. Farther down, Monique Rein waded her *Dragon Fire* out of the water and up the northern bank. Two lances of ground-bound machines had also braved the sluggish trek across the narrow lake, with every jump-capable 'Mech preceding them across to secure a beachhead. A company of longer-reaching designs still held the other side of the lake, presumably on Rein's orders, and now began to cross one lance at a time.

The Third Lyran Regulars were fast running out of room to maneuver, pressed on two enveloping sides by the First Crucis Lancers and Monique Rein leading Tancred's rump battalion of mixed forces. It strung the Lyrans out into a ragged line, uncertain of which direction to face or what BattleMech to concentrate fire against. Their tactics fast degenerated into one-on-one sparring matches as they waited to be destroyed.

Tancred obligingly destroyed them.

"Borrowing" the lance of heavy armor that the First Crucis had advanced to guard the bridge, Tancred slotted his newest makeshift command into the gap left between the collapsing "V" and ran the gauntlet at full throttle. Crossfire between the Crucis Lancers and Monique's forces filled the battle zone with intense fire, some of which splashed collateral damage against the *Nightstar* and the machines following. Meanwhile, Tancred's armor-supported lance tore along the line of enemy machines, which had no idea there was a devil loose among them until it was too late.

An enemy *Barghest* was the next 'Mech to fall before Tancred's flanking attack, oily smoke pouring from several gaping rents in the chest cavity. The *Victor* and two of the Typhoon assault vehicles added to its dismay, stripping it of any last armor protection and rupturing the engine shielding. Dampening fields dropped into place in time to save the machine from a catastrophic failure, but the feral design had lost its teeth, and it dropped from the battle.

Tancred, riding his heat curve carefully, wary of the engine damage he'd already suffered, bypassed the next few enemy 'Mechs until he came upon a mostly intact *Gunslinger* that held the center of the field. It would be as good a place as any to end his drive; the battle was quickly winding down. His next salvo emptied his fourth gauss ammunition bin but also struck deep into the *Gunslinger* as the rail-accelerated nickel-ferrous slugs smashed one of the enemy machine's gauss rifles into a twisted mess of metal and mechanism.

The machine stumbled but amazingly kept to its feet, swinging around to face Tancred's approaching *Nightstar*. Then Tancred noted the three gold bands on the chest

of the other assault machine. Leftenant General Jessica
Carson, the Third's commander, had also survived to this
final battle. She gave Tancred all of two seconds to appreciate that fact, and then blistering counterfire from
the *Gunslinger*'s four medium-class lasers splashed the
Nightstar's armor to molten rivulets from head to toe.
One reddish stream of burning armor composite carved
a channel across the ferroglass shield. Then a gauss slug
smashed the last of his right flank armor into shards,
opening up a dangerous breach in the defenses that protected his fusion reactor.

"Sandoval, you're in everyone's way," Monique Rein
said, finally realizing that he had taken the higher road
over the bridge. "Back out, Tancred. This is all but
over."

"Can't do that," he said, summoning a strong voice.
"You stuck with me these last few weeks. Now I'm in
to the end." *One way or the other,* he finished silently,
squaring off against Carson's *Gunslinger*.

One of the *Nightstar*'s next two gauss slugs missed
wide, furrowing the soft ground several dozen meters
beyond, but the other caught the *Gunslinger* in its left
knee. The damaged leg wrenched back in the hip joint,
locking the limb. With a frozen hip and damaged actuator, the assault machine could do no more than hobble
about the field. That, and deliver another damaging
salvo, which ravaged Tancred's armor and ruptured two
heat sinks.

For a second, Tancred hoped that Jessica Carson had
missed his vulnerable reactor. Then the heat leeched up
through the decking and dumped through his air circulation system as the thermal scale leapt deep into the red.
His vision swimming from the intense heat, Tancred
slapped at the override barely in time to avert a
shutdown.

"Not yet," he promised, though not quite loud enough
to trip his voice-activated mic. "Not so easily." Tancred
twisted his control sticks to the right, turning away from
the *Gunslinger* as he throttled down into a walk. It cost

him another salvo of lasers, which peppered his left side and back, but prevented further reactor damage.

Then, twisting to the left, Tancred reached back with one gauss rifle and pulse laser. The emerald darts stung at the *Gunslinger*, weakening the armor over its left chest, followed by the high-velocity mass of the gauss slug. Imparting most of its force directly into the chest cavity, the heavy slug bent and smashed aside supports and punched a hole directly into the side of the large VOX extra-light fusion reactor. Golden fire bled through, widening the breach. Dampening fields came down, trying to contain the damage. They failed.

Carson managed to punch out on her ejection chair, chased into the air by a gout of plasma-fed fire erupting up through the cockpit. The explosion struck Tancred's *Nightstar* full in the back, shoving it forward. Arcing his head back into his command couch, he fed enough positive equilibrium into his gyroscope to compensate. He held to his feet, if barely, and slowly walked his *Nightstar* in a tight circle that came back to stand over the *Gunslinger*'s ruined corpse.

As if that final explosion signaled the end to the fighting on Woodbine, BattleMechs all across the field began to grind to a halt as the Third Lyran powered down in surrender. Not that there weren't a few last-second salvos, tempers trying to even the score, but not enough to keep the melee going.

Tancred turned toward Monique Rein's *Dragon Fire* as it limped up next to him. Staring through the ferroglass shields into her cockpit, he bowed an exaggerated nod so that she could see it.

"Now it's over," he said, for the benefit of the troops under his command. Her sketchy salute signaled that she didn't believe one word of it.

In fact, the battle for Woodbine wasn't over. Not even remotely.

33

Port Nichols, Coventry
Coventry Province
Lyran Alliance
12 December 3063

Trotting out from beneath the Cyrano VTOL's spinning blades, Victor Steiner-Davion met up with Jerry Cranston and Tiaret's security team at the edge of the Hannah's Ridge battlefield. The ground no longer smoldered in areas where lasers had set small grassfires, but thin wisps of smoke still rose above the charred remains of what had been thick brush, a wooded windbreak, and functioning BattleMechs.

Jerry welcomed Victor with an outstretched hand. The look of dull pain in his normally bright blue eyes told Victor that his friend was beginning to feel the full weight of this civil war.

Or maybe it was just this last battle, in which Jerry had played his part as Victor's man inside the Thirty-ninth Avalon Hussars. A light breeze off the nearby coastal range brought the acrid scent of heat-scorched myomer. He grimaced, swallowing against the oily taste coating the back of his throat, and looked over the battlefield with an experienced eye, imagining the Coventry Jaegers' final run.

"You set an assault company up on the ridge," Victor said, remembering Jerry's report and eyeing the low scarp. "Mobile elements at the edge of the hills there, and armor clogging up the lanes." Looking south, he could just make out the valley mouth from which the Jaegers had poured up onto this short plain.

"The first 'Mech fell just inside the valley," Jerry said. "Artillery got lucky. Then the Jaegers just seemed to break, losing all cohesion as they rushed us. Bragg lost two armor lances at the first windbreak, and then the Lyrans plowed into and through the trees. But it slowed them, making their lead machines easy targets for Hammer Company. Missiles rained down so thick you could hardly see the enemy at times."

And in a staggered line from that first windbreak to the base of the ridge, Jaeger 'Mechs lay in final repose. "They didn't stop and deal with the missile boats?"

"No, they simply drove forward, hard and furious. We began taking sniping shots on the ridge, and then full salvos as the Jaegers moved closer. General Bragg went down with a ruined gyro—she's shaken, but alive. My *Devastator* has seen better days, too. Jason Walker's *Hauptmann* fell right over there." He pointed to the smoking husk that had once been among the strongest assault 'Mechs fielded by the Jaegers, now reduced to about seventy-odd tons of scrap.

Victor closed his eyes and shook his head. The futility of the scene weighed heavily on him. "What a waste of fine men." He looked over at a knot of infantry, the armed guards penning in a smaller group of warriors. "Prisoners?"

"Not as many as there should be," Cranston said, leading Victor over to the remnants of the Coventry Jaegers. "They were fighting with their safety systems disengaged.

No ejections. No heat-induced shutdowns. Two of their machines simply erupted under preventable reactor overloads."

If Coventry was any indication of the opposition he faced, it would be a very long road to New Avalon. Victor blew out an exasperated sigh. He had secretly hoped that the better warriors would renounce Katherine as a political despot. But did he really expect them to do it on his word alone? He shook himself mentally, bracing his resolve. He would get such defections and converts as Katherine continued to show her true nature.

But it would be costly, every time.

Six men and women remained under guard from a final stand of more than twenty, counting Jaeger armor.

"We sent another eight wounded to Port Nichols already," Jerry said.

"Which was the only way you could make the port," Victor said, loud enough for the prisoners to hear. "Colonel Walker had to know that. Damn it, why didn't he turn away? I left him an out."

"Dead now or dead tomorrow," a bedraggled captain in a torn cooling vest answered, glaring daggers at Victor. "What kind of choice is that?"

"I let Jason Walker know several times that I would accept a peaceful surrender," Victor replied calmly. "There would have been no dishonor, not with the odds so heavily against you."

The man kicked at the ground, sullen and silent. No one else, though, seemed ready to step forward, so finally he said, "The militia . . ."

"The Coventry Province Militia is dead!" Victor snapped, not quite shouting at the man. Still, Tiaret moved forward protectively while Jerry Cranston laid a cautionary hand on Victor's arm. Victor shook him off without looking away from the Jaeger captain. "My sister ordered their deaths, and you executed them. Nothing is going to bring them back, but your surrender might have prevented more good men from dying." He calmed himself, folding his arms over his chest. "I have your surrender now, don't I? Does that help the militia?"

Naked fury gleamed in the other man's eyes, but he held his tongue. For a moment, Victor thought he might have reached the man—hoped that he had, since any acceptance would be a sign of Katherine's weakening grip. The captain stared at the ground for a moment and then brought his head back up and spat full into Victor's face.

Though farther back, Tiaret was the first to put herself between Victor and the cheering survivors of the Coventry Jaegers. Jerry pulled Victor back several paces before Victor shook him off. He felt the warm spittle tracing a slow path down the side of his cheek but refused to wipe it away. He matched gazes with the defiant captain, soaking up his hatred as if he might drain away the poison from the man. "A very long road," Victor whispered.

Then he wiped his face clean and turned back toward the Cyrano. There was nothing more he could accomplish here. Jerry would see to the salvage and prisoners, Bragg would report on her warriors, and Duke Bradford would reclaim his fief and hold it in Victor's name. Victor's priorities now involved their next step on that road to New Avalon.

He still had a war to fight, and win.

Gastogne
Woodbine
Draconis March, Federated Commonwealth (Suns)

Tancred stood as his father entered the room, the Duke escorted by Marquessa Isabelle Rein, who had traveled with him from Robinson. The bulk of Isabelle's local relations were also present for this reception of their March Lord, standing at Tancred's signal. James Sandoval did not miss this obvious sign of support for his son, and their gazes locked in a silent contest of wills.

Tancred noted that his father all but ignored the assembled leaders of Woodbine, obviously considering the Reins' loyalty as a given.

That was a mistake that would be clear to him very soon.

"Duke Sandoval," Ferdinand Rein said formally, breaking the uncomfortable silence. "Welcome to Woodbine. I believe you know most of my relations here, and I thank you for returning my sister safely through the Draconis March. I'm not certain if you have met Major Hespers of the Third Crucis Lancers, or Marshal Mordecai Rand-Davion of the First." Major Hespers bowed uncertainly. Mordecai Rand-Davion nodded as might an equal. "Of course," Ferdinand continued, "you do know the Liberator of Woodbine."

He awarded Tancred the mostly empty title the two had agreed upon—a show of support that could be easily abandoned if Tancred did not hold out against his father.

As expected, the Duke Sandoval scoffed. "Liberator? Is that what we call resistance to our lawful ruler? As promised, I have brought Katrina's declaration that you are completely cleared of all baseless charges of treason and reinvested as sovereign ruler of Woodbine and the Woodbine Operations Area." He looked to Isabelle Rein, Ferdinand's young sister, who held up a verigraphed missive and nodded.

Duke Rein accepted the noteputer from his niece and pressed his thumb against the reader, which performed a DNA check and opened the file for his perusal. "Dated two months ago," he noted, and then eyed Tancred, "but officially sent to you on the first of December, after the fall of Rhinehold."

"ComStar is a bit unreliable at the moment. As you might expect."

"I was under the impression," Tancred said, finally entering the conversation, "that the Archon-Princess recently applauded ComStar for maintaining solid communications despite a few notable defections in their ranks."

"A necessary salve to ComStar's fragile ego," his father said, his voice tightening. "Privately, it seems there is a kind of passive resistance being implemented among local HPG networks." His eyes narrowed. "But speaking of defections, Tancred, I am wondering about your presence here on Woodbine. As I recall, you resigned from your military command."

"No, I resigned from *your* military command. This command, and this world, supports Victor Steiner-Davion."

If his father had been expecting such a blunt declaration of independence, he hid it well behind a look of feigned surprise. "Does it now? And you, Duke Rein—you concur with this?"

Ferdinand Rein weighed the noteputer in one hand, as if divining its worth, and stared questioningly at the Marquessa Isabelle. She obviously supported the Duke of Robinson, and it was hard for Tancred to tell which was more pained with the other's position.

"Perhaps I do," he finally admitted. "You are late in arriving, Duke Sandoval. We expected you much earlier."

"Affairs on Robinson kept me in check."

Tancred nodded to Mordecai Rand-Davion, a distant cousin to Victor who had never traded on his family connections—not until Tancred had pressured him to corroborate what he suspected. "You mean Katherine Steiner-Davion kept you in check," he said now in a soft but strong voice. "I have it directly from Jackson Davion, Marshal of the Armies, that you were ordered to first quell disturbances on Dahar, Bennet, and Allerton."

"Likely because Katherine hoped that her Third Lyran Regulars could hold Woodbine," Tancred said, "and prevent any need for negotiation."

James Sandoval stiffened at the implication that he might intentionally abandon or even neglect one of his subject worlds. Tancred felt brief pity for his father, knowing that the great Duke of Robinson and Lord of the Draconis March could never, not in his entire rule, have felt so beleaguered as now.

"As important as Woodbine might be, Ferdinand, I must attend to the needs of the entire March," the Duke said now. "Surely you see that."

"I do, James." The shift to the less formal address worried Tancred slightly. But after a brief pause, Ferdinand Rein chose sides. "But to me," he said, "there is no world more important than Woodbine. Surely you can understand that. Not even New Avalon—no matter who holds the throne."

Tancred was watching Isabelle Rein closely, knowing that she might undo everything he had worked for with Ferdinand Rein. "Perhaps, my brother, not everyone in the family feels as you do," she said. There were a few nods, the cohesion built on victory at Rhinehold now showing a few gaps in the presence of the March Lord.

Fortunately, Ferdinand Rein was not a man to reverse his course, once chosen. Sadly, he said, "Perhaps not, Isabelle. That is a choice everyone will certainly make for themselves." With that, he rose to his feet and left the room without even a courteous salute to his March Lord. Monique Rein was first to follow, tossing a salute back to Tancred for his victory. More than half the assembled nobles and officers also filed out, leaving Tancred alone in a room with the Duke Robinson's few supporters.

"The fourth tier leading to victory is direction," Tancred said softly, "and it points toward New Avalon, not into the Combine." He had watched his father's face the entire time, seeing the lances of pain and anger that showed in his eyes with each defection. Once all but deified throughout the Draconis March, his fall from grace came hard to James Sandoval. And that it came by the hand of his own son ate at both of them—Tancred as much as his father.

But today was not the time for empathy or reconciliation. Today was about choosing sides, and his father would never endorse Victor. His pride and too many decades of distrust stood in the way. "If you think I'll simply give up Woodbine—or any world—so easily, you've made a drastic mistake," he told his son. "The Draconis March is still mine, and I'll hold it against any challenge."

"I expected nothing less," Tancred said before he turned for the door. "Go home to Robinson, Father."

"Do not think to order me, boy." James Sandoval caught Tancred by the arm, holding him in a vise-like grip. His anger and humiliation stood out clearly on his flushed face. "We're going to discuss this matter."

"Agreed," Tancred promised darkly, twisting his arm free and turning again for the door. "I will be there soon enough."

Epilogue

Ronde Tableau, New Avalon
Crucis March, Federated Commonwealth
20 December 3063

Armstrong One's rotor blades beat the air overhead, blurring the azure sky into a grayer tone as the luxury-converted *Nightshade* banked over New Avalon's Ronde Tableau. In Katrina's insulated compartment, she barely felt the throbbing pulse of the engine. She leaned to her left, gazing down through a large, copper-tinted window at the painted desert and its new scenery of widespread destruction. A gift, coming just in time for the holiday season.

It had been a year—twelve full months since her brother's declaration of war. At times she hardly believed it, having thought to put a quick end to this rebellion. Twelve months of fighting on a hundred different worlds. Thousands of men and women dead or wounded. Several dozen regiments decimated.

"But New Avalon is mine," Katrina whispered to herself, counting the dozens of BattleMech corpses that littered the desert below.

The Tableau had been a national park ever since the world's founding. The struggling First Davion Guard had thought to seek sanctuary there, hoping that the pursuing Rangers would not track them so far or, if they did, would decide to wait them out. The Rangers had waited, all right, but only long enough to summon up the Tenth Deneb Light Cavalry and the local Crucis March Militia RCT.

By all reports, the Cavalry had located and pinned down the Guards, which let the Rangers and CMM to move in on flanking positions. With the final battle pitching three regiments—however battered by heavy losses from the long campaign to bring down the guards—there could only be one outcome. Victory. Katrina's father had proved that military axiom during the Fourth Succession War, and her brother Victor had certainly capitalized on such odds on Coventry. Now it was Katrina's turn, and her prize was so much more important than Capellan worlds or production facilities.

The executive VTOL pulled up short and hovered over a vast stretch of petrified dunes stained in layers of ochre, sienna, and rust. Laser fire and heavy artillery bombardment had permanently scarred the once-pristine landscape. Looking on as salvage crews worked to remove severed limbs and blackened husks, Katrina made a mental note to endow a hefty sum for the restoration of the area. Mere scraps were all that remained of those machines that had once been mighty avatars of war.

Traitors every one, she mentally branded the destroyed Guard regiment. Their colors would be retired and the unit stricken from the rolls of the AFFC. Any surviving officers would stand quick and decisive court-martials, though there wouldn't be many. Her orders, filtered through Simon Gallagher, of course, had been specific on that point. Katrina might publicly endorse the more tolerant policies of Marshal Jackson Davion these days, but here on New Avalon there would be—could be—no mercy. This was her world, worth more than any other save Tharkad. She would give up neither to her brother, and Victor's forces had to be made very aware of that.

And with the two capital worlds firmly under her control, her brother's ill-advised civil war was doomed. Katrina could wait him out, strangling his armies in a war of attrition if necessary. But she doubted it would come to that. Eventually, the Lyran Alliance would rally to her and drive Victor into the Federated Commonwealth. Then, with the majority of both interstellar states behind her, she would crush him with overwhelming force.

That was just the way it would happen. As it had here on New Avalon.

Katrina thumbed the intercom that connected her private compartment to the cockpit up front.

"Back to the palace," she ordered, sparing one last, long glance for the battlefield below and smiling with sour humor.

It was beginning to look a lot like Christmas to her now.

He awoke to darkness and disorientation, his mind swimming with hazy images of crumbling walls and smoke-filled hallways, with the memory of pain and weakness and fear.

He must have died, his mind kept telling him. But if so, why could he still think? He decided by a subtle pressure that he could blink his eyes, yet no light ever reached them. Was this damnation, to be smothered in everlasting black? It felt as if his muscles responded and made his arms and legs move, but there was never any sense of touch or true motion. It was like swimming in velvet, restrained by an unseen force, and that sense of helplessness chipped away at the edges of his mind.

Where was he? He wanted to ask out loud, tried to, hoping to attract attention or simply be comforted by his own voice, but no sound reached his ears.

An everlasting nothingness consumed him, dragging by

in minutes or hours. Possibly even days, as the line between sleep and waking blurred hopelessly without any
reference points. He went through bouts of thrashing
rage and then terror, finally settling into a kind of numb
existence that worried away at his sanity.

"Soon."

The whisper echoed dully in his mind, and he saw a
faint halo of light far in the distance. Like a far-off beam
in the woods seen by a lost traveler, it both scared and
thrilled him. Who was out there? What was out there?
The voice—would it come back? He tried to kick and
shout for help, but those efforts quickly exhausted him.

He had imagined it. That was the only explanation.
But then it came again. A faint flash of light, just enough
to tease his eyes and make him long for more, and that
calm, chilling voice.

"Soon, Arthur."

About the Author

Loren L. Coleman first began writing fiction in high school, but it was during his enlistment in the U.S. Navy that he began to work seriously at the craft. In the past seven years, he has published (at the time of this printing) ten novels, a great deal of shorter fiction work, and written for several computer games. *Patriots and Tyrants* is his seventh BattleTech® novel, and his first in taking over the main storyline of the BattleTech® universe. He is also the author of *Into the Maelstrom*, the first novel of the Vor™ series, and *Rogue Flyer*, set in the fascinating universe of Crimson Skies™.

Though he has lived in many parts of the country, Loren currently resides in Washington State. His family includes his wife, Heather Joy, two sons, Talon LaRon and Conner Rhys Monroe, and a young daughter, Alexia Joy. The household also includes three Siamese cats—Chaos, Rumor and Ranger—who are generous enough to share their domain with their human pets.

Don't miss out on any of the deep-space adventure
of the Bestselling **BATTLETECH**® Series.